White Warrior

He saw two large Indian bucks standing before
his lodge. The bigger one was spoiling for a
fight.

He knew that the angrier he could make this
buck, the better his chances were, so he leaned
suddenly forward and spit squarely into the
heavy face. The buck gasped in surprise, then
lunged forward swiftly.

He swung his right fist against the Indian's unguarded jaw with every ounce of strength he
possessed. The buck's moccasins flew into the
air, and his head hit the ground with a thump.
The wide open and crossed eyes told him that
this buck's nap was far from over, so he advanced upon the other one.

"Do you also wish to die?"

DEAD MAN'S CACHE

M. PAUL WHITE

AVON
PUBLISHERS OF BARD, CAMELOT, DISCUS AND FLARE BOOKS

DEAD MAN'S CACHE is an original publication of Avon
Books. This work has never before appeared in book form.

AVON BOOKS
A division of
The Hearst Corporation
1790 Broadway
New York, New York 10019

First Avon Printing, January, 1984

Chapter 1

In the southeast corner of the Canadian province of British Columbia there were two identical peaks. The snow caps of these two great peaks were locked with a gigantic glacier, which appeared to extend completely around both mountains and fill the vast valley between them all the way to timberline level. This great glacier sloped steeply to the south, and miles below, at its base, was a verdant meadow of grassland, which was totally devoid of trees. This meadow, when viewed from a distance, seemed to completely circle the lower edge of the glacier, and it was dotted by many large patches of blazing wild flowers.

Below this seemingly endless sea of grass were two brisk mountain streams, one flowing east and the other west. They converged at a point almost due south of the peaks, and the stream they formed cut through the heavily timbered ridge that outlined the southern boundary of the valley. This ridge, or low circular mountain, supported upon its northern slope a tremendous forest of varied mountain timber, and the only break in it was where the stream cut through in a narrow gorge near its center. The northern slopes of this ridge were gentle, but its southern sides were very sheer. In fact, they were almost a continuous series of rock slides and precipitous cliffs. At the point where the stream cut through the ridge was a high waterfall, and from there the stream wound lazily through a large, fertile valley of giant trees, flowery swamps, and grassy meadows, and went on to form a tributary of the Flathead River.

On the northern side of this particular geographical spot, some ancient upheaval had apparently caused the strata to sink, leaving a sheer wall of broken stone and ice. Since the sunlight never fell directly upon it, this fault was so slippery and dangerous that even the surefooted mountain sheep shunned it. These conditions left this peak region completely isolated in a vast sea of mountains.

The Indian name for this place was White Bosom Bare, and to anyone who viewed it from any place south of it where both peaks were visible, it was easy to see why it was so named. For, from this position, it resembled very closely the bared bosom of a reclining giantess. This picture was much more pronounced during the summer months. For then the two streams, which followed the curve of the rugged mountain that formed the southern boundary of it, were more distinguishable, and above them the flower-dotted meadow gave more color to the scene. Also, the distant range, which was visible between the two peaks, bore the dim outline of a prone face when viewed from such a position. These phenomenal details, which appeared to be so carefully placed, caused the entire picture to border upon the uncanny. Very few white men had ever viewed this scene, but there were a few trappers and prospectors who had ventured into this hostile country far enough to have become acquainted with it. These men, being unfamiliar with the Salish tongue, had immediately dubbed it "The Witch's Tits." However, these men were so few and usually so uncommunicative that it can reasonably be said that this place was unknown to the white man.

There was an Indian legend connected with this place that was exceedingly strange, and made doubly so by the threads of truth that were woven into it. This legend had been told by many Indians of high repute who had wandered into white settlements, and also by trappers who were acquainted with Indians from this particular location, Indians whom they knew to be both truthful and trustworthy. These Indians were of the Flathead tribe, a tribe that was known to be a branch of the Nez Percé, who were by far the most progressive tribe of western Indians. It was the Flathead tribe under whose territorial boundaries this isolated valley lay.

It was the Flathead who were responsible for the name and also the strange legends concerning this particular location. It was they who pronounced the valley sacred, and it was also they who maintained what little force was necessary to discourage any attempts by their own tribesmen or outsiders to surmount the barriers with which nature had surrounded this picturesque spot.

The substance of this legend was that in the beginning, the Great Spirit had foreseen the necessity of maintaining a breeding ground for the animals that were the Indians' means of survival. And for this purpose he had chosen the high valley of White Bosom Bare and had protected it in this manner.

On the northern slopes of the insurmountable U-shaped mountain that formed its southern border, he established a wide forest of varied species of shrubs and trees. At his command, this forest would send up a terrible wailing sound that was far more soul searching than the death chant of a thousand squaws. He placed inside this valley two small streams, flowing in opposite directions, whose functions were to drain away the rain and melting snow

3

and also to provide a home for beaver, mink, marten, water rats, and various species of fish and other aquatic life. Beyond these streams he placed all of the things necessary to maintain his vast and varied herds of animals. First was a chain of shallow swamps where the wapiti and the moose fed leisurely and at peace. Next was a vast meadow of rich grass that supplied the needs of all, especially during the severe winter. In this grass the deer hid their fawns, and the wild sheep, the goat, and the wapiti could feed and hold communion at will. The small rodent flourished there, and fox, mink, marten, lynx, and eagle were never hungry. He also saw fit to place the great wolf, the grizzly bear, and the cougar in this valley, chiefly to assist the moose bull, the male wapiti, and their vicious mates in guarding against trespassers or unsolicited visitors.

Above this great meadow, he placed a wide expanse of frozen snow, which cooled the valley in summer and kept it well watered. At his command, this great body of snow would sing the weirdest song ever heard by human ear. The vibrating notes of this song would slowly rise to fill the entire valley, and oftentimes it left the listener with ringing ears and dancing eyesight for many minutes after it had subsided.

To the Indians the wailing forest constituted a warning against trespassers; the singing snows were the lamentation of the Great Spirit for the souls of those who disregarded his warning; and the vicious beasts were placed there for enforcement.

Because the Great Spirit knew of man's tendency to become doubtful and forgetful, he arranged to always have among mankind one person whose integrity was above question. This man's duty was to act as his messenger. He also knew that in every generation there would be a few men whose curiosity, bravery, and ambition would place in them the longing to walk where others feared to tread. For this reason he placed in a secret location a stone ladder. From among these few men, he chose a messenger, only one messenger in each generation, and the secret of the ladder was handed down by this messenger to his successor.

Because this messenger had to be one who excelled in strength, speed, and bravery as well as being of a high moral standard, he was chosen by a series of eliminations. For this purpose, an obstacle course had long ago been chosen, and the rules of the contest were made known only to the participants, who swore to an oath of secrecy. Although the chieftain of a tribe had great power, in this contest he had no voice whatsoever. There could be only one winner, and he had to win with enough margin to erase all doubt of his superior ability. Because of the severity of the oath, the details of this contest were never revealed. Thus, the messenger and the chieftain of the Flathead tribe alone knew the secret of the stone ladder, and only the messenger knew where it led.

Chapter 2

On a winding tributary of the Flathead River and near the center of a beautiful valley was a small Indian village. This valley, which was bound on the north by a great horseshoe-shaped mountain and on the other sides by a broken mountain range, was beautiful. Game was plentiful and the vegetation, lush. The village was composed of sturdy lodges that marked it as a permanent installation.

Into this village one day came a lone white man, with a great shaggy dog close by his side. The man was tall and broad of shoulder, and held his head in the same proud manner as did the inhabitants of the village. In fact, to one who was not a close observer, he could have easily been mistaken for a husky Flathead brave, but his dark auburn hair, his steel-gray eyes, and his slighty heavy shoulders spoke plainly of a different race. Upon his face was the flush of youth, but his stalwart frame, his firm, purposeful stride, and his steady eyes strongly suggested experience. The dog was also large and strong looking, but in her eyes was a gleam of hatred, and as she glanced sharply about her, her lips often quivered, exposing long, sharp fangs.

On a small knoll near the banks of the stream was a sizeable lodge, which was surrounded on three sides by a score or more of smaller lodges. This lodge was adorned with a set of gigantic moose antlers that were made fast to a post driven into the ground close beside its door, and on a neatly folded elkskin in front of it sat a rather large Indian. Even to one who was only slightly familiar with the Flathead costume, it was easily discernible that this Indian held some degree of rank. His name was Wa-neb-i-te, and he was the chief of this particular village.

The man with the dog kept his head high, and his steps did not waver as he approached this particular lodge. To a casual observer, it would have appeared that the man was familiar with his surroundings and knew where he was going. However, although he had been in the vicinity of this village for several days, this was the first time he had chosen to enter it.

The Indian did not raise his eyes from the task of balancing an arrow, even when the white man halted before him. The man crouched and slid the palm of his hand down the back of the dog, then gave her a meaningful look. When he had regained his posture, he said, "I am Enir Halverson, and I would speak with the great Wa-neb-i-te, chief among the Flathead."

The Indian eyed him sharply, and the expression in his eyes told the white man two things. First, his arrival was no surprise, and second, flattery would get him nowhere. This man was both alert and intelligent, and Enir Halverson felt a growing respect for him.

Presently the Indian rose, and stretching his body in an effort to gaze levelly into the eyes of the visitor, he said, "Let Enir Halverson speak."

"I am a lone traveler," began Enir, "and I wish to stay in your village and to hunt in your forest."

The Indian let his eyes travel curiously over Enir's tall, broad frame. He glanced at the extremely short bow, which was strung Indian-style, over his left shoulder. His eyes met the unwavering stare of the

7

large dog, then came to rest upon Enir's right hand, which held a gold sovereign between its thumb and forefinger. Enir extended his hand, saying, "Would Chief Wa-neb-i-te accept this gift, which signifies my willingness to abide by the Flathead law?"

The Indian extended his hand in turn, saying in a loud voice, which was intended for other ears besides Enir's, "You are welcome, Enir Halverson. In my village are many empty lodges. Choose one and be at home."

Enir bowed low from the waist and said, "Enir Halverson thanks Chief Wa-neb-i-te for this favor," then, turning on his heel, he walked proudly from the village.

Chapter 3

Enir Halverson was born in Liverpool, England, and, being the son of a Norwegian immigrant, it is very likely that there was a strain of Viking blood in his veins. Being reared upon the waterfront not only contributed to his physical development, it also awoke within him at an early age the spirit of adventure. He left school at the age of fifteen and immediately signed on with a freighter for an extended voyage that included a visit to America.

Tradition dictated that regardless of a man's former training and experience, his first appearance upon the high seas as a sailor should be as an apprentice seaman. For this reason, the menial duties, the rough hazing of the crew, and the restrictions imposed upon him not only obliterated the adventurous pictures that Enir had carried aboard in his mind, but they also aroused within him a feeling of resentment. Consequently, when the ship reached Saint John, New Brunswick, Enir was well primed to listen to the strange tales brought in by drifters from the interior of this new country. He decided to jump ship and seek his fortune in this vast wilderness.

Enir worked for a while in Ottawa, then moved to Winnipeg, where he hired out to a freight company. He worked his way to Regina, which at that time was considered a border town. During his stay at Regina, Enir listened to still wilder tales of the rugged, unexplored country to the west. This decided him to venture farther into it and, if possible, to realize his secret dream of emerging upon the Pacific coast. So he struck out alone and eventually wandered into a trading post, which was later to develop into the city of Calgary. It was here at the trading post that he made the acquaintance of an old prospector who was known only as Stripe. This prospector had lost his partner the summer before, and his loneliness prompted him to cultivate the companionship of the young adventurer. Enir enjoyed the company of this blunt and gruff old character, so, when Stripe suggested that Enir go into partnership with him on a prospecting venture, he quickly accepted.

The season for prospecting was just about over, but old Stripe had time to accomplish a few things during their short trip into the hills. He taught Enir how to work a gold pan, how to recognize color, and how to identify certain types of gold-bearing quartz. He also taught him how to foresee and prevent danger. He showed him the devastating results of landslides and avalanches and alerted him to the danger of traversing a slide area. But the main thing Stripe accomplished during their short excursion was to instill in the mind of his young partner a soul-gripping lust for gold.

They went into winter quarters at a northwestern mounted police station that was located where Willow Creek joined the Oldman River. There was also a tiny trading post here, and Zeb, the old factor, was a close friend of Stripe's. Stripe liked this place because it had plenty of wood and water and was close to the territory that, he had long been convinced, held rich gold deposits. He also enjoyed the company of the old factor and the small group of mounted police who remained on duty during the winter.

During the long winter months, Stripe entertained Enir with hair-raising tales of his experi-

10

ences. He also taught him much Indian lore and how to speak the Salish tongue, which was the Flathead's language. He coached him in the use of Indian sign language, which was the common means of communication throughout the western provinces as well as the northwestern territories of the United States.

Among the many other things that old Stripe taught Enir were how to feather an arrow, use his bow, and assemble his pack. Enir was quick to recognize the importance of learning these lessons well, so he listened closely and worked diligently. His determination to reach a state of proficiency before spring and his uncanny perceptiveness caused a gleam of pride to appear in the eyes of his grizzled instructor.

However, in the narrow confinement of their one-room stone and sod shanty, Enir found it extremely difficult to become proficient with the bow. He had noticed that each of the policemen possessed a side arm and a rifle and that ammunition seemed to be plentiful. So one day he broached the subject with Stripe by asking why he did not place the bow with these superior weapons. Stripe eyed him in silence for a full minute, then said, "Sit down, and I'll tell you a few things about Indians."

When Enir had complied, Stripe cleared his throat and began, "As you know, the Indian and the white man are at war. The whites are winning this war for one and only one reason. They possess the gun, or what the Indians call the thunderstick. If you took all of the thundersticks away from the white man, he would not last a season. It is not the white man so much as it is the thunderstick that the Indian hates. Of course, he hates the white man for taking what he considers an unfair advantage over him by using it, but he hates the thunderstick because it is instrumental in depleting the great herds of buffalo, wapiti, and other game upon which he depends for his livelihood.

"A bow-and-arrow prospector has little to fear among the Indians so long as he does not meddle in their affairs, but should they catch you sneaking around where you have no business or attempting to take something they consider theirs, they will be quick to eliminate you. If you attend to your own business and leave theirs alone, you will have no trouble with them. If you are in possession of a thunderstick, unless you are well known to them, you are considered an enemy. Should you happen to meet with a group of braves on the warpath, you would be in danger, of course, regardless of what kind of weapon you carried, but that is the reason I have taught you how to listen to the birds and watch their actions. The safest thing to do when you are in Indian country is to stay as far away from the thunderstick as you can. The bow is the Indian's weapon as well as his method of obtaining food. He believes that the noise of the thunderstick will frighten away the game, therefore he considers it only a weapon of slaughter. When he sees a group of whites slaughtering a herd of buffalo with thundersticks, it fills him with disgust and hatred. He considers the buffalo his property the same as we do our cattle, with one exception: If the white man or his family is hungry, he is welcome to take what he needs. No white man is that generous. No, you just forget about the thunderstick and learn to use that bow. Zeb has plenty of arrows, so get outside every time you can, and practice shooting it until you get the hang of it. The Indians both understand and appreciate the bow, and any white man who is adept in its use is both admired and respected."

Enir glanced down at the short bow he held in his

12

hand. He had been eyeing it critically during Stripe's rather long lecture.

"If our bows are so important, then why don't we get us some better ones? Why don't we have bows like I see some of the Indians carrying?"

Stripe scratched his head a moment, then replied, "Do you remember the day you started to jump over that stream and your bow caught on a limb, and you sat down in that cold water? If our bows were a foot or so longer, we would be like a couple of yoked steers. These bows will shoot plenty hard if you will just rear back on them."

Enir's training continued. During the clear, cold days, while Stripe played chess with the factor, he would prowl the brushy banks of the Oldman River and Willow Creek searching for grouse and rabbits. For a while he spent a lot of his time searching for lost arrows, but gradually his aim improved until he was finally able to bring in enough fresh meat to cut their jerky bill in half.

At last the days began to become noticeably longer, and a few dark spots began to appear upon the vast expanse of snow that surrounded the tiny outpost. Enir paced the floor of the cavelike shanty, pausing frequently to glance out the single small window, which was merely a piece of glass sealed into the crude masonry of the wall. He had noticed a slight change in his elderly partner during the last few days. He had also noticed that Stripe had begun to visit the government building, which was something he had never done before. He was well acquainted with all of the police officers at the post, and he could think of no reason for Stripe's sudden interest. Maybe old Doc has improved his game and beaten Stripe a couple of games of chess, he told himself. For Stripe was the undisputed champion chess player there at the post, and Enir knew how it hurt him to lose. He recalled the time Stripe had challenged Zeb and Doc at the same time, and how after they beat him he had sulked the rest of the evening.

One day when Stripe returned from the government building, he found Enir standing on the south side of the shanty gazing off toward the distant mountains. He knew that Enir was longing for the time when they could resume their search, for he had spoken often of following up the lead they had been forced to postpone until spring. As Stripe brushed past Enir and entered the cabin, he said nothing, but there was a look of deep sadness in his eyes.

"Come inside son," he said as he eased himself down onto the foot of his bunk. Enir responded eagerly because he thought that Stripe had gathered some news. Any news, rumor or suspicion, would be welcome to break the monotony. The old prospector noted his eagerness but did not smile.

"Sit down over there," he said. "This will take a little while."

He must have got in on something big, thought Enir. He sat down on one of the rawhide stools in front of the fireplace, crossed his legs, and eyed Stripe expectantly.

Stripe gazed down at the scuffed toes of his moccasins for a moment, then said, "I hardly know how to tell you this, son, but I won't be going out prospecting anymore."

Enir looked at him in wide-eyed surprise but could say nothing.

"Old Doc just told me that I was all through," Stripe continued in a low voice. "I went over there a day or so ago to get something for my indigestion, and he gave me some pills. I took them but they didn't help me any, so I went over again this morning and he had me strip. Then he went over me with that listening thing of his. After he finished, he told me that I didn't have indigestion. I could tell by the look he gave me that it was something bad, so I waited awhile before I said anything. He didn't say anything either; just sat and looked at me for a minute. So I said, 'How long, Doc?'

" 'I can't tell you that, Stripe,' he said. 'Maybe a year if you take it easy, maybe a day if you don't. I can tell you one thing: You are all through prospecting.' "

Enir waited for the old man to continue, but when he saw that Stripe was waiting for him to say something, he asked, "What are you going to do?"

"Why, just what Doc told me to do, take it easy."

Enir pondered this answer for a full minute. How could an outdoor man like Stripe take it easy? he asked himself.

Stripe raised his feet up onto the bunk, screwed his body around, and lay down with his hands beneath his head. "I think I'll catch a wagon to the end of the railway, then take the train to Regina."

"Then what?" asked Enir.

"Oh, I'll get me a little job at some saloon, I reckon, or some hotel. I'll make it all right." Stripe heaved a sigh and relaxed.

"How much dust do we have left?" asked Enir presently.

"We don't have any dust," replied Stripe. "We changed it all to coin, remember?"

"Oh, yes," replied Enir. "Do you know how much it all comes to?"

"Yep," replied Stripe, "a little over a hundred pounds, about six hundred dollars, all told."

Enir was thoughtful for a minute. "That should hold you over for a while," he said. "Maybe I'll un-

15

cover something when I follow up that lead we struck."

"Oh, yes," replied Stripe, "three hundred will last me quite a while."

"You take all of it," said Enir, but old Stripe cut him off sharply.

"No, I won't; I'll take my part. Three hundred will probably be more than enough for me anyway. Heck, I'll still be able to make a living."

Enir said no more, and after deciding that Stripe had told him all he intended to, he rose and set the kettle upon the coals. He strolled over to the small window, and Stripe spoke again.

"I have a little more to tell you, so sit down and I'll do it while the kettle boils." Enir dropped back onto the stool, and the old man continued, "I didn't tell you this last fall because I wasn't feeling good even then. Besides, you wasn't ready then to hear it. I think you are ready now, but I dare not wait any longer anyway, so here is what I want you to hear: Do you recollect me telling you how I lost my partner?"

"I remember you saying that the Indians killed him," replied Enir.

"Not Indians, Indian," replied Stripe. "Anyway, I didn't tell you near all of it. That spring while we were down stateside, we decided to split up. Both of us would head north, but on separate streams. We figured that our chances would be better that way. So it was agreed that I would take the Keetenany and he would go on and follow up the Flathead. We planned to meet up around the head of the Oldman, then come on in here. Well, it was way along in August when I struck some color on the Elk, or a little stream just before it that run into the Elk. I began to work it, and just about the time it began to look promising, here he come. He said that he had been following me for weeks but had missed me when I turned up the Elk. He had dropped back and picked up my sign, and here he was.

"He told me that not long after he had struck the Flathead, he had picked up a little color in one of the small streams that runs into it. He had followed this lead until he came to a big, high waterfall that he couldn't get by. Right there in the sandbar at the foot of this waterfall, he had struck paydirt. He said that it was the richest placer he had ever struck, and the deeper he went, the better it got. He panned out more than a hundred pounds of pure dust. It finally petered out, though, and it was then that he began trying to get by that waterfall. He said that the walls of that canyon were two hundred feet high and slicker than glass. Since they were almost straight up, he began trying to find a way to get by them. He was certain that the mother lode was above the falls, and he spent a week trying to find a way around them. It was while he was doing this that he discovered a small Flathead village on a little stream quite a ways west of this waterfall. These Flathead had a permanent camp there. Their lodges were built out of stones and logs and covered with dirt. Most of these lodges like that have grass and vines growing all over them and are kind of hard to find. Well, those Flathead seemed kinda friendly, so my partner decided to rest awhile and try to find out how to get to that stream above the waterfall. This valley is called White Bosom Bare, and to the Indians it is a sacred place. I won't go into details, because there is a long story to it, but in this story was mentioned a stone ladder, which is concealed somewhere along the steep circular mountain that almost surrounds the valley. The Indians assured him that there was no other way into this valley, and he knew they were not lying.

"Well, my partner listened to this story again and found out that there was one Indian among them who knew where this stone ladder was. He had been up it and had seen the sacred valley. He kept hanging around, trying his best to find out which one of these Indians had the secret. Finally some squaw pointed him out, but this Indian refused to talk to my partner so he went back and cached his dust, then lit out after me. As I have already told you, it was September when he found me, and I was getting some pretty good looking rocks myself, so we decided that the best thing to do was for him to go down to the edge of the Blackfoot country, pick him up a good stout squaw, come back and get the dust, and hightail it on here. Meanwhile, I would keep after my lead and try to be here by the time he was. Then, in the spring, we would both go up there and see what we could do.

"Apparently, on the way back, my partner got to thinking, what if something happened to this Indian who had the secret of the stone ladder? If he was the only one who knew about it, and if he happened to run afoul of a grizzly or a moose bull, how would my partner ever find it? To be safe, he figured that he'd better get this secret first, then, when we started out the next spring, we could get right after it. So he went on down to the trading post, picked him up a few bottles of hooch, and also a good stout squaw, then hurried back up there. His idea, of course, was to get the old boy hooched up, wrangle the secret from him, then stop by and pick up his cache and make it back here before the weather turned bad.

"When he reached the village, he couldn't find this fellow he was looking for, but finally an old crip-

18

pled Indian volunteered to take my partner to him. I suppose he was getting a little anxious by then, since we had already had a short cool spell. Anyway, he started pouring the liquor to this fellow, and when he thought he had him to about the proper stage, he cut him off for a while. Pretty soon he showed him another bottle and began to put the pressure on him about the ladder. When he did, this old crippled Indian drew his tommyhawk and bashed his head in.

"I suppose you are wondering how I know about all of this?"

Just then the kettle began to boil. "Go ahead and make us some tea," Stripe said. "I need my whistle dampened anyhow." Enir rose and made a pot of tea. After they had drunk a cup or two of the strong brew, old Stripe set his cup down, cleared his throat.

"Well, when I got in, I expected to find my partner waiting for me, but he hadn't showed up. I became worried and decided that if I hurried, I might have time to go see about him. I never did cut his sign, but I didn't have any trouble finding the village he had told me about. I didn't see anything of my partner, but I noticed that the Indians treated me rather cool. One evening a squaw came into my lodge, and I could tell by looking at her that she was a little different from the rest of them. She told me guardedly that she was the squaw who had come there with my partner and that she had witnessed his death. She told me what he had done and warned me that the Indians had figured out who I was. Well, I got out of there so fast that I scorched my moccasins.

"Now, I didn't tell you this story to entice you to try to get into that valley. That would be suicide. If there is only one trail in, there is only one out, and don't think for a minute you can put anything over on that tribe. That's a smart bunch of Indians there at that village. They are not average Indians, not by a long spell. But there are a hundred pounds of pure gold cached somewhere close to that waterfall, and God alone knows now where they are. I don't dare go in there myself, because they know me now, but I thought that maybe you could go look for it. I just want to add one thing. Don't be too optimistic about finding it. I don't know anything about the country around there, but I knew that hell-raising partner of mine pretty well, and it's my guess that that gold is better hidden now than it ever was. But it is all cleaned and packaged, so I think that it's worth a try. There is always a chance that you might stumble onto it."

Enir sat for a long time after Stripe had dozed off to sleep. He went over everything Stripe had told him and found it both exciting and spiced with intrigue. Presently his thoughts settled upon the doctor's report on Stripe's health. This suddenly shocked him out of his dreamy attitude, and he rose and tiptoed from the shack. Enir made his way directly to the doctor's office in the government building. An officer told him that Doc was over at Zeb's store. He arrived at the store just as Doc and Zeb emerged from Zeb's little office. Old Doc took one look at Enir's face and motioned him to a chair.

"Now, son," Doc began, "I don't know what Stripe has told you, but I know what I'm going to tell you. Stripe is bad. I won't answer any questions," said Doc when Enir started to speak, "you just listen. I gave Stripe some pills that will make him drowsy. So don't get alarmed if he drops off occasionally. It is good for him. From what he told me, you don't let him do anything, so keep that up. That may be why he is still alive. Outside of that, just leave him alone. I have known people to go on like that for years. If he feels like talking, let him talk. It won't hurt him. I don't mind him playing cards or chess, that won't hurt him either. But I don't want him getting up and building fires, chopping wood, or going on any hikes. You seem to have more influence with him than anyone else, so try to keep him quiet. I have given him all the medicine I have for his particular ailment, so there is no need for him to come to me again, but if he wants to come, let him, it won't hurt anything. I just wanted to tell you that there is nothing more I can do. It is up to all of us to keep him quiet. He is just as well off here as he would be anywhere, so just go ahead and treat him as if you thought that there was nothing wrong."

Enir sat and looked at the doctor when he had finished. What will I do? he asked himself. I can't go away and leave him. "Is there a chance that he will get better?" he asked the doctor.

The doctor shook his head. "I never knew of it," he said sadly.

When Enir arrived back at the shack, Stripe was still snoring peacefully, so he quietly prepared their evening meal. When the bannock was brown, he sliced some cured sausage into the skillet. As its aroma filled the small room, old Stripe rai head and sniffed.

"Golly, is it suppertime?" he asked. "I do what has got into me, sleeping like that."

"Maybe it's because you got a load off your m replied Enir, "but you've got me to where I don't be lieve I can sleep at all."

"Eh? Oh, you mean about that hidden gold? Oh, yes, you'll sleep. You'll sleep a lot of times before you find that. You might dream a little, but you'll sleep."

"How's your appetite?" asked Enir.

"It's good, I reckon," said Stripe. "Them sausages sure smell good anyway."

"Pull up then. She's ready," said Enir.

After their meal, old Stripe eased back onto the bunk and stretched lazily. "There are a few more things I would like to . . . er . . . call your attention to while you have all of this on your mind," he said. "Just stack those dishes over there on the bench. I'll wash them after a while."

"No, you go ahead and talk and I'll just wash them while I listen," said Enir casually, as he poured hot water into his gold pan.

"Well, if you go over there, and there is no doubt in my mind that you will, I want you to try your dead-level best to make friends with those Flathead. They can tell when you are lying or pretending, so don't try it. I am pretty sure that if you do very much looking they are going to get suspicious, so I wouldn't try to hide your plans from them. I would advise you to tell them that you are a prospector. They understand what a prospector is. What I want you to get firmly into your head is that you are not interested in their sacred valley. And I hope that you ain't. You will just have to forget about that. Then, if they pin you down, you won't have to lie to them. You could never ▪thing out of there anyway, so forget it.

there is one thing that an Indian respects ll others. Courage. Next to courage is ability, eing a good hunter and a good shot with the , adept at trailing and hiding your trail, and being fast on your feet. A fast runner means a lot to an Indian. Now I didn't get too well acquainted there at that village, but I know about other villages. There are always a few bullies in every village, Indian or white, and sooner or later some of them are going to try you out. I have already taught you how to cope with most of their tricks, but remember they know a lot about yours, too. You were telling me about your fights there on the waterfront where you fought with your fists. If you are half as good as you led me to believe, you will certainly have one on them. I calculate by the time you have broken a few jaws, they will respect you plenty. When Indians are just fighting like that, kind of for fun, they do more wrestling than fighting. They are pretty good at it, too, at least some of them are. But, like I showed you, they will break your leg or arm if they can. There are no such things as rules or anything, like there are in our wrestling. They go in to win, so don't pull any punches.

"They have an entirely different set of values from ours. To help a squaw is to insult her. Politeness is a sure sign of weakness, and if you help an old man he will hate you. I can't understand their philosophy and don't try to. If you are going to live among them, be as near like them as you can. You'll get used to it. I reckon that is about all, except I would advise you to take a bunch of those steel arrowheads that Zeb has over there. Some of that catgut cord he has will come in mighty handy, too. And be damn sure to take a bunch of those needles and a lot of that thread. You can get their full value by trading them to the squaws.

"So you think about all of that for a while, and if I think of anything else, I'll tell you later. I think I'll go over and beat Zeb a game of checkers or something, since I seem to have kinda woke up now."

Chapter 4

One day a small band of Indians arrived at the post and made their camp at a bend in the river that was well protected by heavy brush. The group consisted chiefly of old men, squaws, and children. Enir, quick to take advantage of this diversion, drew on his heavy coat and accompanied the post doctor and one of the police officers on their routine inspection. He did not enter the camp but sat down on the grassy bank and watched the procedure. While the doctor and the other officer were checking them for signs of diphtheria, smallpox, and other communicable diseases, Enir took stock of their meager equipment. He saw three bony pack animals, several tepees, and a few buffalo robes. He also saw a large cast-iron kettle, still lashed to a well worn travois; a squaw was busily unloading it. Two more squaws were building a fire while several half-grown children dragged up dry wood. He saw several dogs accompanying the children who were gathering the wood, but he paid little attention to them. He noticed that none of the men offered to help with the camp chores and that as soon as the Doc had finished examining one of them, he would flop back down as if he were exhausted.

Finally the doctor and the officer finished their examination, pronounced them clear of any disease, and started back to the post. Enir decided that he would remain for a while and watch the Indians. By the time the squaw had the kettle unloaded, the other squaws had a brisk fire going. They placed the kettle upon the fire, then dumped two large skin bags of river water into it. The squaws then turned their attention to setting up the tepees, and Enir became interested in their deft and easy way of accomplishing it. Presently one of the squaws walked over and checked the water in the kettle. She placed a few more coals beneath it, then seized a couple of dogs and unceremoniously bashed their heads against a log. She then made a dash at a big shaggy dog who had just witnessed the fate of her two friends. This dog, whose large joints and feet showed that she was hardly full grown, snapped viciously at the squaw, then ducked into a dense chokecherry thicket and escaped. The squaw jabbered something to one of the old men, who merely stared stoically at her and refused to move. Enir continued to watch them until a little Indian girl went over and tried to entice one of the dead pups to play with her. When she began to whimper and point at the blood running from the puppy's head, Enir felt the bile rise within him. As he got up and made his way back to the post, he was beset by mixed emotions. He knew that this bunch was apparently up against it, but why didn't they get out and hunt for game instead of slaughtering the children's pets? "They must be a lazy group," he said under his breath.

When Enir entered the store, he found Stripe and the factor playing cards. Stripe looked up and said, "Well, Enir, did you get your ashes hauled?"

"Not in that bunch," replied Enir rather curtly.

"Old Doc told us they were a lousy bunch," said Stripe.

"Did you see any plews or any good-looking skins of any kind?" asked the old trader.

"No, I didn't," replied Enir, "but I didn't go in. Doc might tell you."

The factor made no reply but turned back to his game.

Enir strolled from the store over to their cabin. Just before he reached it, he saw a dark shadow move swiftly down the trail and disappear around the corner. He sprang quickly ahead and was just in time to see the large shaggy dog that had escaped from the squaw disappear in the sagebrush. He stood there a moment, then turned and made his way back to the store. Old Zeb looked up and asked if he wanted anything.

"Yes," replied Enir, "I want a pound or so of jerky."

"Just go ahead and weigh up what you want, and I'll set it down directly," said Zeb as he picked up his cards.

Enir weighed out two pounds of dried meat and wrote it down in the open book that lay upon the counter.

"I set it down," he said, and Zeb merely nodded.

Enir again approached the cabin. He strew a generous amount of dried beef on the bare ground between two piles of snow, then retired into the cabin and watched through the window until the dog returned and scooped the meat up hungrily. He opened the door softly. The dog raised her head and looked at him for a moment, then turned and again disappeared into the sagebrush. He threw another handful of jerky out into the open spot and retired.

Old Stripe came in before Enir went to sleep, but Enir kept quiet. Stripe slipped out of his buckskins and quietly eased into bed. Enir heard him begin to snore within a very few minutes. He knew it was the medicine that Doc had given him. Enir fell asleep while thinking about the Indian village, the cache, and the bonanza in White Bosom Bare.

A long, drawn-out howl, coming from just outside the door of the cabin, caused Enir to leap from his bunk. This howl continued to grow in volume as strange notes were woven into it. As it reached the peak of its crescendo, Enir felt himself trembling. Suddenly he seized the ax from the fireplace and rushed to the door. He opened it only a crack, but it was enough for him to see the big shaggy dog sitting in the center of the bare spot before the door with her nose pointed toward the stars. He flung the door open just as the dog finished her lonesome howl and saw her slink away into the sagebrush. He glanced down at the ax and at his bare feet, then grinned sheepishly and replaced the ax beside the fireplace.

"It was just an Indian dog howling," he said to Stripe, but old Stripe did not answer. Enir climbed into bed and lay there shivering, not altogether from the cold. Just before he got good and warm, he remembered that he had caught a glimpse of the morning star while he was looking out the door. Gosh, he said to himself, no wonder I'm not sleepy. It's nearly daylight. So he threw the covers off and slipped into his clothes. He went over to the fireplace, punched some coals off the backlog, and piled on some kindling. After it had caught and he had added some dry wood to the blaze, he shouted to Stripe, "Hey, get up and toast your shins. I know that you're playing 'possum. That howl must have woken up the entire village." When Stripe still didn't answer, he walked over and reached for the edge of the covers on his bed. Just before his hand touched them it halted, because he had noticed that there was no rise and fall to them. Very slowly, he placed his hand on the old man's forehead. Stripe was dead. Before Enir realized what he was doing, he had bolted through the door and was running as fast as he could toward the doctor's quarters at the government building. He reached the door to the doctor's quarters and began pounding on it.

"Come in, son," he heard the kindly voice of the doctor say, and as he opened the door Doc continued, "I was just getting things together before I came over there."

"You were what?" asked Enir, and his voice sounded loud in the still room.

Old Doc looked at him and said, "Stripe is dead, isn't he?"

"Yes, sir, I . . . I think he is, but how did you know?"

"Son, I've been a frontier doctor for many years. That isn't the first time that I've heard a dog give the death howl. I knew that someone was dead, and when you came in, I knew that it was Stripe." Just at this time one of the policemen came in and nodded to the doctor. The officer then turned to Enir.

"Let me pour you a cup of hot coffee; it will make you feel better."

Enir felt tears brimming in his eyes, and he turned toward the fire. The policeman politely turned his back and began talking to the doctor.

Chapter 5

Zeb, the old factor, stood in the center of the large open space directly in front of the wide counter that extended half the width of his store. His eyes squinted and his face was thoughtful as he critically surveyed the large broad-shouldered man who faced him.

"Turn around," said Zeb. When the man complied, Zeb reached up and seized one of the straps that crossed between the man's shoulders and deftly tightened it.

"Now shake yourself," said Zeb. While the man obeyed, Zeb cupped his ear into his palm and listened closely. "Nary a whisper," he said. "I'll say one thing, old Stripe sure taught you how to set a pack. He probably did a good job in the other things he taught you, too, but I'd like to mention a few things that I'm sure he didn't think of."

"What are they?" asked Enir.

"Well," said Zeb, "to begin with, that dog that has taken up with you. I know you have taught her a lot of things during the last month that will be very useful to you. But I still think you had better take along a good stout rope to tie her with in case you need to."

"I told you, Bat doesn't need to be tied," said Enir defensively.

"Okay, okay," said Zeb as he looked down at the big dog. "She sure has perked up during the last few months," he continued. "I wonder how much wolf blood she has in her."

"How do you know that she has any?" asked Enir.

"I can tell by the way she carries her tail," said Zeb matter-of-factly. "My guess is that she is half timber wolf and half shepherd. You sure want to be careful while you're in the timbered country."

"Why?" asked Enir.

"Because," said Zeb, "in about a month or two, she is gonna be a doggin'. And when she starts, them big timber wolves are gonna come from near and far."

"I don't believe that they will bother her," said Enir.

"Her, hell," said the old factor, "I wasn't thinking about the damned dog. Have you ever been up close to one of them old "dog" timber wolves?" When Enir shook his head, Zeb continued, "Some of them get as big as a yearling buffalo, and don't ever think that they won't jump you. I have known it to happen time and again. They don't have to be hungry, either."

Enir let his pack slide to the floor as he regarded the factor thoughtfully. "What had I better do about it?" he asked.

"Well," said Zeb, "it ain't likely that they will jump you in the daytime. When she comes in, I'd advise you to hunt you up a cave or a hole of some kind to sleep in until it's all over. And if she runs off with them, just let her go. She'll more'n likely come back."

Enir started to pick up his pack, when Zeb interrupted, "That doeskin belt I sold you. Now, since you're taking a heck of a lot of stuff, you're going to get awfully uncomfortable carrying all that coin. Why don't you leave part of it here so you won't have to be bothered with it? You can't spend it where you're going anyway."

"It feels all right," said Enir as he twisted his waist.

30

"Yeah, I know it does now," agreed Zeb, "but wait until you've walked about forty miles. It'll more 'n likely rub your belly raw."

"Maybe I'd better," said Enir, and he pulled off the belt and dumped about half of its contents upon the counter.

"I'll get your paper and change it," said Zeb as he disappeared into his tiny office. Presently he returned and continued, "That leaves you four hundred dollars here, and since Stripe is gone, there ain't nobody named as your beneficiary in case something happens to you. Who do you want me to put down for that?"

Enir thought for a minute, then said, "Just put your name down there. I have some folks back in England, but there ain't enough there to be bothered with."

"Naw, I don't want to do it that way," said Zeb. "I appreciate it, but it might not look good. You just give me the name and address of some of your people, and the officers over at the post will take care of it."

Enir gave his family's address, and Zeb wrote it down. "Now it is all legal and appropriate." Zeb looked down at the dog again and asked, "What was it you called that bitch?"

"Bat," replied Enir. "I named her that because she can see in the dark."

"Huh," snorted Zeb, "that's the wolf in her. All of them other tricks you've taught her prove that she's smart like a wolf, too. Well, good luck to you, lad. Come back here any time you want to. You will always be welcome."

Chapter 6

When Enir saw the hackles rise slightly at the base of Bat's neck, he silently ducked from the trail and, followed closely by the dog, hastily concealed himself in a nearby thicket of junipers. Motioning Bat to lie down, he assumed a position where he could see a portion of the trail while they waited silent and still. The sharp ears of the dog moved slightly as they picked up the soft tread of moccasins, and without moving a hair, she rolled her eyes to meet Enir's. Presently an Indian squaw passed by their place of concealment, staggering under the weight of a full-grown deer. Following closely behind her came a stalwart brave, who carried nothing but a light bow carelessly looped over his left shoulder.

For several minutes the man and the dog remained motionless. Very carefully, Enir emerged from the thicket, and keeping it between him and the place where the Indians had disappeared, he moved silently away through the forest.

It was not his fear of the Indians that had prompted Enir's stealthy actions. It was that he was not yet ready for his presence in the vicinity to become known to them. Even though this place fitted the description Stripe had given him, he had not yet become accustomed to so heavily wooded country. Most of his experience in this rough and rugged part of the land had been gained in the mountains and upon the streams. To be able to see no more than a few yards in front of him forced him to depend heavily upon Bat's sensitive nose and ears, which he was becoming more and more accustomed to doing. However, he had located what he was sure was the village he was seeking and was now tracing the stream back to where the waterfall was supposedly situated.

Enir found the waterfall, and after looking at the precipitous sides of the narrow canyon, he had no doubts that it was the one he sought. To make doubly sure he decided to do some panning on the sandbar below it, as he was getting anxious to use his gold pan anyway. His first pan showed a trace of color, and the second one produced a tiny nugget. He continued until he had collected nearly half an ounce of dust.

It was here at the foot of the waterfall, when the sunlight caused the bottom of his pan to glitter, that Enir won the first victory over the gold fever. He did this by applying past history and cold logic. For he knew that this sandbar had been panned recently and that the gold he had recovered could have come from but one source. It was then that he reminded himself of Stripe's warning and of the fate of the last man who had attempted to uncover the deposit above the falls. He also reminded himself that he was here to attempt to find the man's cache. "Dead Man's Cache," he said aloud as he tore his eyes away from the top of the moving column of water.

Very carefully, Enir dipped water from the stream and obliterated the signs he had made on the sandbar. He then walked slowly over the polished stones to the mouth of the canyon, where he stood and surveyed the vast array of debris, which was more than a hundred yards wide and extended as far as his eyes could see in either direction along the foot of the almost perpendicular sides of the mountain. "Dead Man's Cache," he breathed again as a feeling of futility stole over him. He shook off this feeling by telling himself that no man, more especially a man who was crowded for time, would carry a hundred pounds of gold very far over this kind of ground. "It will probably take a while though," he said. He glanced down at Bat and continued, "Do you think that you could behave yourself? You had better get ready to, because we're going to that village."

There were several things that worried Enir as he made his way through the forest toward the Flathead village. First was Bat's hatred for Indians. He could only guess at the extreme cruelty they had dealt her as a pup, and he knew that the wolf blood would make her slow to forgive. He would have to rely upon his influence over her to prevent trouble. The second thing that worried him—causing him to keep a sharp watch for human signs and also to watch Bat closely for any warning she might give indicating human presence—was the question of whether or not anyone else was looking for the cache. If the man who made the cache had told that squaw of his intention to seek the stone ladder, it was also possible that he had mentioned the cache. If he had, and this squaw had remained with the Flathead, it was entirely possible that they had already found the cache. It was hard for him to believe that a man who fit the description Stripe had given him would confide his secret to a strange squaw, but it was equally surprising that he had told her of his plans to find the ladder. These mixed-up thoughts caused Enir to worry. The other thing that made him hesitate to enter the village was that he had no way of knowing whether or not these Indians were still friendly with the white man. Neither did he know if this man, whom Stripe had called Wa-neb-i-te, was still the village chief. "I can think of only one way to find out," he told Bat in a whisper, "so in we go."

Enir, accompanied by Bat, had already spent two days and part of two nights scouting this village, and he had familiarized himself with the various trails leading to it. He had also discovered an abandoned lodge about three-quarters of a mile from the village proper. He had examined it in the moonlight and found it in sore need of repair, but he liked its location because it was on the trail that led toward the waterfall. There were the ruins of other lodges between it and the village, which led him to believe that at one time the village had been much larger. If they will permit me, he told himself, I'll repair that lodge and live in it. I'm sure Bat will like that, he thought.

Early the next morning, as Enir moved confidently along the trail that parallelled the river at this point, Bat suddenly raised her bristles and halted in the path. Enir quickly brushed his hand down her back and stood still. Presently a squaw carrying two heavy water bags tied on either end of a tote stick emerged onto the trail before him. As she stopped with her eyes opened wide with surprise, Enir quickly made the peace sign, saying, "I am a friend of the Flathead and I seek the lodge of Wa-neb-i-te, your chief." This young squaw allowed her eyes to travel over Enir slowly, and evidently they liked what they saw because the fright quickly disappeared from them. She steadied the tote stick with one hand and pointed down the trail with the other while she gave him minute directions. Enir thanked her, and she grinned at him as he turned away.

As Enir Halverson strode from the Flathead village after his short conference with Chief Wa-neb-i-te, he was conscious of relief, and considered that a giant step had been taken toward the accomplishment of his mission. He held his head high and pretended not to be aware of the many eyes that were covertly following him. He was proud of the way Bat had performed, but he was still glad that he had the opportunity to live outside the village. He knew, because Wa-neb-i-te had told him to choose his own vacant lodge, that he would offer no objections to his repairing the lodge beside the river.

Without turning his head, Enir let his eyes dart about in a quick estimate of the size of the village. He was surprised at its scanty population and also at the absence of small children around the lodges. It was surprisingly clean, and the odor that was usually present in an Indian village was completely absent. This is very strange, he thought. In a valley like that one, where game was plentiful, especially at that season of the year, every lodge should have been overflowing. He was convinced that this was not just an ordinary Indian village. Well, I'm not going to let it worry me now, he said to himself as he hastened back to where he had secreted his pack.

With his hunting knife, Enir quickly fashioned a handle for his ax, using a tough juniper sapling with a slight curve at the right place. His next move was to clean the debris from the isolated lodge and to remove the shrubs that had sprung up around it. He was delighted to find that the lodge was much roomier than he had at first thought and also that the fireplace was still intact. By working steadily he had soon felled and split enough pine lodge poles to completely renovate the structure, but the work of placing and securing them to roof and walls was slow and tedious. However, after five or six long, hard days, he had the lodge completely repaired. There were just a few details remaining, such as a good

36

solid door, some shelves, some bow pegs, and some stools or benches. In anticipation of this hewing job, Enir spent half an evening searching the stream for a smooth sandstone and sharpening his ax.

Early the next morning he set out into the forest in search of the type of tree from which he intended to construct these things. He found the tree not too far away and set to work immediately. He wanted to get the heavy work over before the sun had heated the humid atmosphere. He had felled the tree and was in the act of measuring it with the notched stick he used for a ruler when Bat raised her hackles and pointed her nose toward the lodge. So I have company, said Enir to himself as he motioned Bat to heel and moved swiftly toward the clearing. When he reached it, he stood still until his breathing slowed slightly, then he carefully parted the brush and peered into it. He saw two large Indians standing before his lodge. One, a broad-shouldered, heavy-muscled young buck, was in the act of sitting down in the open doorway. The other one, who was quite tall and more lightly built, stood leaning his shoulder against the side of the lodge. Enir watched the heavy one relax in the doorway and stare belligerently out toward the forest. He glanced at the tall one and was sure that he detected a look of expectancy upon his somber face. Enir studied the heavily muscled Indian while he finished getting his wind back from his short run. He noted his long arms, scarred face, narrow hips, and thick chest. The bully of the town, no doubt, he told himself. It was then that he recalled a remark Stripe had made: "Their bullies are always pretty rugged characters." A shiver of apprehension passed over him, and he unconsciously flexed his right arm and shoulder. Deciding to postpone it no longer, Enir took himself in hand, and, silently quoting three more of Stripe's words, he parted the bushes and stepped into the clearing. The words he quoted to himself were "Pull no punches."

Enir strolled nonchalantly across the clearing and calmly sank his ax into a stump, then turned to face the two bucks. He noticed that the heavy one rose immediately, and he also noted, with dismay, that his shoulders almost filled the open doorway.

"Welcome to the lodge of Enir Halverson," said Enir.

"Plew!" The big Indian spit into the dust at Enir's feet. "Why you come here?" asked the buck. "Your squaw run away?"

Enir turned to the tall one and said, "Does your squaw always wear breeches and talk like a buck?"

"Hah," said the big buck as he stepped from the doorway rubbing his palms together. "How you like to take this squaw? No?"

Enir looked at him steadily and shook his head. "I never take a squaw whose belly is filled with dog-meat," he said.

This seemed to infuriate the buck, and he started toward Enir with his arms spread wide and his strong hands opening and closing rapidly.

Enir knew that the angrier he could make this buck, the better his chances were, so he leaned forward suddenly and spit squarely into the heavy face. The buck gasped in surprise, then lunged swiftly. Enir had already taken his stance, so he swung his right fist against the Indian's unguarded jaw with every ounce of strength he possessed. The buck's moccasins flew into the air, and Enir felt a tingle in his right shoulder. The big Indian landed on his shoulders, and his head hit the ground with a thump. The tall buck stepped from the side of the lodge, but stopped suddenly when Bat confronted him with her hackles raised to their full height. Enir spoke quickly to Bat, then glanced down at the fallen buck. The wide-open and crossed eyes told him that this buck's nap was far from over, so he advanced upon the tall buck.

"Do you also wish to die?" he asked the tall one.

The tall buck looked down into the contorted face of his comrade, and his eyes opened wide.

"No, Long-Step good Indian, he go back to village."

Enir seized him by the arm, jerked him away from the wall, and spun him around. "You will go fast," he said as he planted a kick on the seat of the Indian's pants that raised his feet into the air.

The tall buck hit the ground and took off like a cottontail, Bat growling and nipping at his heels as he passed her. Enir allowed himself an amused smile as he stepped into the lodge and picked up his gold pan. There was a small amount of dirty water in it, which he had neglected to pour out because of his hurry to get to work, so he walked over and slowly poured it into the buck's face. This failed to revive him, so Enir started toward the spring-fed brook a short way behind the lodge to refill the pan. Suddenly Bat jumped in front of him and raised her bristles. Enir glanced down and saw that her nose was pointed toward a clump of bushes not very far away. As he looked, the figure of a small Indian suddenly darted from the bushes and fled swiftly into the forest. Enir listened while the whisper of flying moccasins slowly died away, then he looked down at the dog and said, "By the blood of Odin, Bat, I do believe that was a young squaw." He quickly advanced to the spot behind the bushes and examined the prints of moccasins, which the flying figure had failed to conceal. "I was right, old gal," he said to Bat as he rose. She should make somebody a good fast squaw, he mused as he continued on to the spring.

When Enir returned with the gold pan filled with water, he noticed an intense swelling of the buck's jaw. Setting the pan down, he knelt and ran his fingers over the swollen place. "Broke," he grunted. As he slowly straightened, he mumbled a waterfront description of the blow: "I knew I handed him a Joe Darter." He picked up the pan and poured some of the cold water into the Indian's face. The buck groaned and stirred. Presently Enir reached down and assisted him to his feet. The buck stared groggily about him for a moment, then his eyes suddenly began to focus and he recognized Enir. He shakily made the peace sign, and Enir returned it, then pointed to the buck's jaw and said, "Broke." The buck stared at him blankly, and Enir said again, "Your jaw is broke, do you understand?" Then Buck blinked his eyes, and Enir said again, "Your jaw is broke, you go medicine man." And he pointed toward the village. The buck again made the peace sign then staggered away toward the village. Enir smiled, then took a drink of water, picked up his ax, and started briskly into the forest.

As Enir started back to the job after this interruption, he stopped by the small thicket of bushes where the Indian girl had concealed herself. He looked again at the tracks where she had crossed the trail and said aloud to himself, "I wonder if that buck brought his girl friend along to watch him clobber me?" He stood looking into the forest for a moment, then turned away. "I'd better get this job done and start looking for that cache while my luck is running good," he said to himself as he made his way back to the tree he had felled.

Enir had finished the work on the lodge and was very proud of the job he had accomplished. It looked much neater to him than did the lodges in the village. He had screened it from the trail by transplanting some blossoming vines, which he planned to train to cover some limb ends that he had driven into the ground.

At present he was working on teaching Bat some new tricks in a new type of hunting. She had quickly learned to herd a deer into range of his bow, and was getting good at trailing a wapiti to his bedding place. Enir was thrilled to know that getting meat was no problem, but there was something else that was worrying him now. Bat frequently warned him that he was being spied upon. At first he had thought that she was merely catching the scent of other hunters, but when it persisted, he was certain that it was someone spying on him. But why? he asked himself. One evening after returning from the hunt, in which Bat had three times warned him of an Indian's presence, he sat down and began to give it serious thought. He decided to mentally review all of the things that could possibly cause the Indians to take this action.

First, there was the squaw whom the prospector had brought here and who had witnessed his execution. She knew that this man had planned to enter the sacred valley. Did they connect him with this man, or did they merely suspect that there might be some connection? Had this man caused them to be suspicious of all prospectors? Were these Indians schooled in the art of mind reading? Had they watched him while he was panning the sandbar below the waterfall? Finally he decided that they had watched him pan the dust below the falls, and, knowing him to be a prospector, they knew that he would figure out where the gold had come from. If that was so, then they knew about the gold in the sacred valley. After thinking this over, he decided that he had to be right.

He suddenly felt a weakness in the pit of his stomach. "Odin help me," he breathed. "I may be walking along the edge of eternity and don't realize it." He began to understand what old Stripe was trying to tell him. Of course they know the gold is up there, he told himself. That folderol about wailing forests, singing snows, and stuff might fool the majority of the Indians, but it wouldn't fool these men. Then another question arose: If they knew it was there, why didn't they cash in on it? What were they saving it for?

I might as well give up, he thought. But I know one thing: They don't know anything for sure or I would have already had it. I will do just as Stripe said, I will forget about it. But Enir knew that he would not exercise that much self-control. No prospector who had ever seen the glitter at the bottom of a gold pan could deliberately forget about anything as certain as that. Anyway, I will have to try, he thought. Well, I still have the cache to occupy my mind, he thought, I'll just have to settle for that . . . at least until I get better acquainted.

For the next several days after Enir had had this serious talk with himself, he kept busy around the lodge. He cleaned and dried skins, made jerky, carved out wooden vessels for dried berries and other fruit, and plaited rawhide ropes to swing his meat up into the trees. While he was doing this, Enir also did a little more thinking. At last he came to the conclusion that Stripe had been a pretty wise old man. He had figured things pretty close, Enir told himself. My only hope is to be exactly what I am, an inexperienced prospector. I will pay no attention to their spy-

42

ing; I will go ahead and look for the cache, and I will pan the creeks in plain sight of them. Yes, I will go on pretending that I have never dreamed that a bonanza exists in White Bosom Bare.

After Enir had finished up all the odd jobs around his lodge, he built his pack and calmly set out in the direction of the waterfall. He did not go directly to it, but made his camp just below the mouth of the canyon on the west side of the stream, which was the side next to the village. He planned on moving back and forth in a quarter circle until he reached a certain landmark. Then he would cross the stream and do the same thing on the other side. He realized that this would be arduous work, so he found a good hiding place for his pack and carried only his bow and hunting knife.

For two long, hot days Enir moved slowly back and forth through the rough, broken boulders and great slabs of limestone. His knees became raw and his shins received many a bump. He kept a close watch on Bat, but never once did she show signs of sensing an Indian in the vicinity. He crossed over the stream and continued his search, but he found nothing, nor did Bat get wind of an intruder.

Late in the afternoon of the third day, Enir found himself at the foot of the steep mountain. The sunlight seemed to bounce off the black rock, and the perspiration ran steadily down his back. Enir felt disgusted. The leg of the doe he and Bat had killed the day before had hampered his movements, yet he had doggedly stuck with his task and peered into a thousand crevices, lifting many large stones that might have hidden the mouth of some small opening. "Ye Gods, but that man was choosey," he said to Bat. "I have found a hundred places where that gold could have been, but nothing else." As he moved along the bottom of the cliff, he found a small tree that had evidently fallen from the top in the distant past. This decided him to make camp here for the night. The edge of the forest was only a couple of hundred yards below, but he was tired, and, besides, he preferred to sleep in the open.

So he hurriedly gathered a bunch of dry chips from around the trees and a handful of the dry grass that grew sparingly among the rocks. He didn't have much time to spare, because the sun was getting low. Hastily he fished his mineral glass from its case and trained it upon the dry grass. In about a minute he was rewarded by a thread of white smoke, and in a few more seconds by a tiny blaze. Quickly he fed the dry bark into it, and soon he was adding larger limbs. It was while he was thus engaged that he heard Bat give a low whine. He dropped everything and seized his bow, but Bat merely sat upon a flat stone and gazed peacefully toward the forest. "What did you see, old girl?" Enir asked, but Bat acted as if she did not hear him. Enir began slicing steaks from the hind leg of the deer when suddenly Bat whined again. Enir glanced at her, but her hackles were not raised, nor had she moved from her rather languid position upon the rock. "What is getting into you, gal?" asked Enir. "You have been acting strange all day." Bat never took her eyes from the spot she was gazing at, nor did she seem the least bit interested in what Enir said. Enir, following her gaze, detected a slight movement behind the small shrubs. While he looked, a large timber wolf walked boldly out into the open. Bat turned her eyes toward Enir and whined again. "Oh ho, so that is it," said Enir. "By the lights of the north and the whiskers of God, you chose a terrible time." Bat whined again, and her eyes seemed to plead with Enir. "Begone and get it

44

over with," said Enir as he motioned her away. Bat slid off the stone and slowly made her way toward the great black shadow that waited at the base of the rock pile. Enir watched her until she reached the wolf, then his heart leaped into his throat. He suddenly realized that at a distance he had misjudged the size of the animal. For Bat, standing beside him, looked very small. Ye Gods, what a beast, thought Enir. I hope Bat knows what she is letting herself in for.

The sun had already set when Enir forced down the last bite of the venison he had broiled. He sat on a rock picking his teeth when a deep-throated snarl smote his ears. It was followed by another one equally frightening, then they began to blend together as they rolled up from the edge of the timber almost below him. Enir's hair stood on end, and he leaped for his bow. He quickly placed an arrow into it, but he made no further move, for the two large animals who waltzed into the open seemed to be intent upon destroying each other, not him. He listened to the clashing of their terrible teeth and gave thanks to Odin that they were not interested in him. "Fight it out, you creepy black devils," said Enir aloud, but his voice was drowned in the thundering snarls of the two beasts. Presently they separated, and Enir was surprised to see that neither of them seemed to have suffered any wounds during the battle. When they loped away in the same direction in which Bat and her companion had disappeared, Enir said, "You had better make friends, because you are going to have to double up on that beast Bat is with." He had noted that these two were smaller than the lone wolf had been.

Enir was awakened twice during the night, but the sounds were always distant so he dismissed them

45

and went back to sleep. When he awoke at daybreak, he discovered that his water bag was empty, so he decided not to rebuild his fire, as he wasn't hungry anyway. He quickly gathered up the few things he had left out of his emergency pack and struck out toward the stream. There he paused only long enough to retrieve his pack, then he began the long hike back to his lodge. He felt that he had seen the last of Bat. She will never make it in a bunch like that, he told himself. She is quite capable of holding her own with dogs, but these things are devils. Eventually they will grow tired of her, and then they will kill her. As Enir trudged along through the forest he was very sad. He felt guilty for having given her permission to join them. But they had not looked so large to him until Bat had joined them. This was the only excuse Enir made for himself.

It was while traversing the heavy forest that Enir realized what a wonderful asset Bat had been to his safety. He caught himself many times glancing down to where Bat had always been, to see if she was warning him of danger. It always gave him a shock when he didn't see her. The times when she had caused him to flee from the trail because of the presence of a rutting moose bull or a grizzly bear were multiplied in his mind until, by the time he reached the place where he knew the trail was safe, he was quite shaken up.

When Enir reached the lodge he was tired, hungry, and worried. He still felt responsible for losing Bat, although he knew that it would have happened eventually anyway. Zeb had said that she might come back when the mating period was over, but Zeb had not seen what he had. The size and viciousness of those beasts left little doubt in his mind that Bat had been torn to shreds by now. At last the clamoring of his stomach drowned out all of his other misgivings, so he rose and built a fire. All the fresh meat he had was the piece of venison he had saved from the day before, but he had wrapped it in the broad, wet leaves of some wild lettuce so it was still untainted. After he had shaved off some tallow into his gold pan and had cut several steaks from the leg of venison, he looked at the remainder of it, then glanced over at Bat's empty bed. Her absence caused another wave of misgivings to assail him. Very slowly he turned to the small table and sliced up the remainder of the meat, heaping it into the gold pan. I might as well fill up good, he told himself, for it might be a while before I have any more fresh meat.

Many thoughts passed through the mind of Enir Halverson as he ate his belated meal. First he realized that he was not in the high country where the presence of man excited enough curiosity in the young buck deer and the yearling elk to prevent their fleeing until it was too late. Also, stalking them there was much easier. Here, where the forests were filled with hunters who had been trained in the art since infancy, it was quite different. There would now be no Bat to herd the deer toward his hiding place, or to cunningly lead him to the thicket where the wapiti slept. Even though game was plentiful it was also wild, and great skill was required to take it. The short bow, which heretofore had been adequate, was nothing to him now but a stick and a string. Although he had become proficient in its use on close targets, he knew that its range was far too short for what he now faced. I must have a longer bow, he told himself, and Enir had never fashioned a bow.

The next morning, while contemplating his next move, Enir suddenly realized he had not visited the nearby village since his brief interview with Chief

Wa-neb-i-te. Maybe I can find a buck up there who has an extra bow, he said to himself. But, on second thought, he said aloud, "If he did have one it probably would be not much better than the one I have." If I had the best bow in the village, it still might not be good enough for me to eat regularly, he mused silently as he began to sort out the things he had brought with him to trade.

Chapter 7

Early the next morning Enir, with a few spools of heavy thread, several steel arrowheads, three or four of his longest catgut bowstrings, and a few well-polished pieces of silver, nickel, and gold, which were placed in separate packages, set out toward the village. He was well enough acquainted with Indians to know better than to make his wants known before he found what he was looking for, so he assumed a leisurely attitude as he entered the outskirts of the village. His intention was to give the impression that he was on a sightseeing tour and not particularly interested in trading for anything. He was well aware that talent existed among the Indians the same as it does in other races. Thus he reasoned that someone in the village was considered to be better at bowmaking than others. This same line of reasoning told him that there were also those who were shrewd at bargaining, so he had to be very careful. It was not the price that worried him, but the quality.

The first two Indians Enir saw upon entering the village were the one whose jaw he had fractured and the one whose rear he had so soundly kicked. Upon seeing them, he immediately began to look about him for a suitable location for the reunion, but to his surprise the two bucks were quite friendly. And when Enir continued his stroll, without being asked, they fell in beside him. Enir had no desire for the company of the taciturn young men, but since they had imposed their presence upon him, he began to wonder how he might be able to wrangle a little information without exposing his purpose. As they strolled about the widely scattered lodges on the outskirts of the village, Enir studied his two silent companions closely. Finally he decided that he had figured out why these two bucks sought his company. They were evidently the only single bucks in the village. He saw a few younger children but no other teenagers. It was when they came to an extra-large lodge, which supported an equally large lean-to, that Enir halted, and, pointing toward it, he looked at the larger buck questioningly.

"I-lip-a-taw's," said the buck.

"Is I-lip-a-taw a chief?" asked Enir as he looked the lodge over again.

"Bowmaker," replied the buck. "He makes warbows."

Warbows, thought Enir as he looked again at the feathery looking shavings that were strewn beneath a large tree.

"I have never seen a warbow," said Enir, and he noticed that the two bucks looked at him strangely.

"You not ever take warpath?" asked the larger buck.

"No," replied Enir, and he saw an accusing look upon both of their faces.

"It is very strange," said the taller one, "that one who fights so well should never take warpath."

Enir had no desire to lower himself in their estimation, so he thought swiftly and said, "I go on warpath with thundersticks." He noticed that both bucks suddenly stiffened and their eyes grew cold.

"You take warpath against Flathead with thunderstick?" asked the larger one.

"No, against other paleface."

This seemed to put the two more at ease.

"Against paleface, there?" asked the tall one, pointing southeast.

"England," said Enir, pointing east and making the wide undulating hand motion that signified, in sign language, the great waters.

A look of understanding quickly appeared upon the faces of the two Indians, and they again resumed their friendly attitude.

"You win, eh?" asked the larger buck.

"Yes, we win," said Enir. "I go now to look at warbow." He turned quickly toward the big lodge. His ears told him that the two Indians had taken the hint and were not following him as he approached the door of the lodge of I-lip-a-taw. As he halted, he stole a glance over his shoulder and observed the two bucks slowly departing over the back trail.

Enir stood before the tightly closed door of the lodge. He had noticed smoke coming from the low stone chimney, and he could also feel unseen eyes upon him. He drew a deep breath.

"Enir Halverson wishes to enter the lodge of Chief I-lip-a-taw to look at warbows," he said.

Almost instantly the door was swept aside, and Enir found himself facing a very beautiful and buxom middle-aged squaw. The smile upon her face, and her light skin and brown hair told him that she was a breed; nevertheless he was quite stunned by her beauty and stood in wide-eyed surprise until she motioned him to enter.

Enir glanced briefly about the interior of the lodge as he went inside, but his eyes were quickly drawn back to the beautiful squaw. He caught a smile of satisfaction upon her face and suddenly realized that she was waiting for him to speak.

"I . . . er . . . would like to see the warbows," he finally stammered.

"I-lip-a-taw is away," she replied, then motioned to a dark corner of the lodge and said, "So-he will show you bows."

Enir's eyes followed her gesture and saw the triangular face of a girl who sat upon the floor in the shadows regarding him with wide-spaced eyes as she hugged a rather large pair of knees tightly beneath her chin. She rose gracefully and walked to a door, which led into the large lean-to, and motioned for him to enter. As she rose, Enir had noticed two things fleetingly. One was a pair of rather large thighs that her short buckskin skirt had failed to conceal. The other was a pair of neat beaded moccasins, which were laced in front like shoes.

As he brushed past her and entered the lean-to, he also noticed that her head came well up to his shoulder and that she possessed some of her mother's buxomness.

As Enir stood erect after ducking through the door leading to the lean-to, he had a hard time bringing his mind to concentrate upon the business that had brought him here. The small feet and pointed moccasins seemed to remind him of something. But when the girl pointed to the long row of unstrung bows that leaned against the wall, they quickly absorbed his attention. They were long, of a beautiful design, and highly polished. He quickly noticed that they were all identical, that none were strung, and that they were longer than he had expected. He stood and regarded them with a rather baffled expression as he tried to picture himself carrying one of them through the dense forest.

Presently the girl turned her wide, fawnlike eyes

upon him and asked in a low, husky voice, "You want hunting bow?"

"Yes," replied Enir, and she turned and pointed toward the opposite wall. Enir turned, and, blinking his eyes in the dim light, he saw another row of bows that were much shorter. There were not nearly so many of them, and he was quick to note that these bows were of several patterns. He noticed that they were all more than a foot longer than the bow he possessed and that they were highly polished and artistically designed.

As Enir walked slowly over to the neat row of unstrung bows, he was acutely aware of his lack of knowledge concerning them. He came to a halt near the center of the row and desperately began to search his memory for some of the things which signified the type of wood from which it was made, and how the curve was formed. He found a slight variation of color and length, but very little difference in their shape. He suddenly realized that he was looking at an enormous collection of the famous Flathead bow. While he stood before them in admiration, the girl suddenly reached out a slender hand and extracted a bow that he had not yet noticed. This bow was darker in color and maybe a few inches longer than any of the others. When she placed it into his hands, he found it slightly heavier than he had expected. He looked at the girl, and she flashed him the smile he had seen upon the face of her mother. He held it across his chest, and, with his arms spread, he tested its spring. As he flexed it, it seemed to come alive in his hands. The girl smiled again, and he turned and re-entered the main lodge where the light was better. As he entered, he saw the woman smile at the girl, and he immediately became suspicious. Suddenly he had an inspiration, and he quickly fished out one of his catgut bowstrings and began to string the bow. While he did so, he kept a close eye upon the two, but saw nothing but interest in their eyes. When he had finished, he drew the bowstring and released it. When he did, he was rewarded with a slightly musical twang, very low and vibrating. He watched the expressions upon the faces of the two females as he repeated this performance, but he saw only satisfaction there. He set the bow on end beside him to accurately judge the length of it, and when he did he caught another glimpse of those tiny beaded moccasins upon the feet of the girl. This time they rang a bell in his memory. The tracks behind the shrub! There could be no mistake. This was the girl who had watched him fight the two bucks. Very carefully, he measured the bow, then flexed it a few more times, noting its friendly feel and the suggestion of power. The girl reached out her hand and touched the bow, speaking a word he had never heard. He looked questioningly at the woman.

"Hi-co-ri," the woman said with a smile. It was the first English word he had heard since leaving Fort Macleod.

He was now convinced that this was a special bow.

"How much?" he asked.

"I-lip-a-taw is away," said the woman. "When he returns, you pay him."

"I take bow," he said as he took a gold sovereign from his belt and extended it to her. "When I-lip-a-taw returns, if he wants more, I will pay more."

"It is well," said the woman, and he noticed that again So-he smiled.

Enir hesitated, then fished once more into the pouches he carried beneath his jacket and drew out a spool of waxed thread and a large needle, which he handed to So-he.

"In my lodge are many doeskins. Shall I bring them to you?"

So-he glanced at her mother, and the woman answered quickly, "Yes, if you wish." Then added, "I-lip-a-taw has little time for the hunt."

Enir glanced at her and said to himself, yes, I can see why. He turned to So-he and asked, "Why did you run?"

So-he dropped her eyes to the spool of thread she held in her hand, and again her mother spoke for her.

"So-he was afraid. She has not yet had a man."

It was Enir's turn to blush now, and to his deep chagrin he found himself doing so in great profusion. Embarrassed by his own embarrassment, Enir said, "I will bring skins," then turned and ducked out the door and walked swiftly away.

Enir was so elated at the performance of his new bow that for several days he dismissed I-lip-a-taw's two women from his mind and concentrated upon practicing with it. Hour after hour he practiced. He practiced long shots, quick shots, and shots at imaginary moving objects. He did surprisingly well from the start. It appeared that the bow was made especially for him, because he never lost an arrow. He tested it against his short bow and marveled at the vast difference of range. The great powers of the small, dark bow caused him to wonder about the lithe Indian maiden who had selected it for him. She is pretty, he told himself, but he could not dismiss from his mind the powerful sex appeal of her buxom mother. Anyway, he said to himself, I cannot afford to get myself involved at any cost. My business here is too uncertain. I don't fancy leading the entire village in a footrace the way Stripe did.

Chapter 8

He made his first kill with the new bow on the evening of the third day, by piercing the heart of a large buck from a remarkably long distance. It was while he was skinning the buck that he was reminded of his promise to the girl, So-he. So early next morning he cut the backstraps from the buck, and after trimming one of its hind quarters carefully, he placed it and the backstraps into the fresh hide, then picked out four or five of his best doeskins, which he rolled tightly around this. After he had made the bundle as compact as possible, he set out for I-lip-a-taw's lodge. He swore violently under his breath when he saw the two single bucks hurrying to meet him. He greeted them with a wave of his hand but did not alter his stride. Just as he feared, they ignored his cool treatment and fell in on either side of him, and the three trudged on in silence. Presently the tall one noticed Enir's new bow.

"Ugh, So-he's bow," he said after looking at it closely.

Enir stopped, as did the two bucks. The heavy one stepped over and scrutinized the bow closely. He reached out and slid his finger over it caressingly, then let his hand fall to his side.

"So-he's," he said, and the tall one nodded.

"I bought it the day we went there," explained Enir, and when he faced them he saw disappointment registered plainly on both their faces. Presently they turned slowly away and left Enir standing alone. What in Valhalla is going on? Enir asked himself, then in a whisper he said, "Well that is one way of getting rid of the dumb leeches anyway."

When Enir sought entrance into the lodge of I-lip-a-taw, he heard movement inside, but the door was not immediately lifted. He waited for a moment and was about to turn away when he saw the door slowly lift from the wooden stays. He stepped up and peered into the dim interior, and for a moment he could not speak. He blinked his eyes several times before he recognized So-he. She was dressed in a form-fitting bleached doeskin dress, which was well beaded and very feminine. The moosetail brush had been well applied to her dark brown hair, and she wore the high-topped moccasins usually reserved for winter costume. She smiled as she bade him enter in a deep, husky voice, and Enir stumbled through the door in a dazed shock.

"I brought the skins," he said, and he was sure that his voice sounded like a fistful of gravel.

So-he's mother stepped forward and received them, giving him a gracious smile and thanking him. So-he motioned for him to sit upon a rawhide-covered stool, and she squatted gracefully beside the fireplace. No one spoke for a moment, while So-he's mother deftly untied the package he had brought. She cooed her pleasure as she held up each skin for So-he to see, but she yelped with delight when she saw the large bundle of fresh meat. She seized the two long backstraps from the buck and held them high while she spoke the words in Flathead that meant both wonderful and beautiful. She placed one of the long backstraps, or tenderloin, upon the small table, then picked up the rest of the meat and disappeared into the lean-to. Enir looked at So-he.

"You are very beautiful," he said. He tried to

58

think of some other words in Flathead which constituted a compliment but failed. When So-he's mother
returned, she crowded between them to stir the
ashes in the fire pit.

"Could we not walk in the village?" asked Enir of
So-he.

So-he looked at her mother, who gave her the sign
that it was all right, and So-he preceded him out the
door. When Enir had joined her, her mother spoke
from the doorway: "Return soon. I will have meat
prepared."

As Enir walked slowly about the village, he was
conscious of the grace, dignity, and beauty of the girl
who walked silently beside him. He did not know the
Flathead language well enough to find the words to
fit a situation like the one he found himself in, so he
just ambled awkwardly along. After a while, when it
became apparent that she was not going to speak, he
asked, "Is there no place where the flowers bloom
beautifully and the water ripples? No place where
we can sit in the shade and listen to the songs of
birds?"

So-he turned her widely spaced eyes to him and
said, "Yes, there are many such places, but they are
far, and my mother said to return soon."

"Maybe another day we can go there?" asked
Enir.

The girl did not answer immediately, and Enir
said to himself, slow down, Halverson, take it easy.
This girl is not a squaw.

"Have you known my father?" asked So-he, and
Enir admitted that he had not. "He will return
soon," she said, and Enir was sure that there was a
hidden meaning behind her statement. He thought
of asking her if she knew the legend of White Bosom

Bare, but quickly decided against it when he remembered the fate of Stripe's partner.

"I will be very glad to know him," he said, and he was sure that he saw her relax.

Enir was conscious of many eyes upon them as they walked through the outskirts of the village. He was also conscious of his dirty buckskins, his scraggly beard, and his all-around unkempt appearance. He admired So-he's spotless dress and dainty footwear and wondered how she could manage to keep it that way in the crowded, messy lodge. Silently he vowed to pay more attention to his own personal appearance thereafter. Why, even the working squaws are neater looking than I am, he said to himself.

When Enir departed from the lodge of I-lip-a-taw that afternoon his head was in a whirl. So-he was a beautiful girl, and her mother was the most alluring woman he had ever met, yet he found himself quite undecided on whether or not he desired to become further involved. The emotions that he was experiencing were completely unfamiliar to him, and he was plagued by apprehension. He found himself wishing that Stripe were there to advise him, for he felt that he was treading upon dangerous ground. Anyway, he told himself, I have made no commitments or promises. Yet he was unable to shake the persistent feeling of uneasiness. He thought of the many strange customs and traditions that existed among the Indians. He knew that certain actions took the place of words among them. He thought of the way the two bachelors had reacted when they discovered that he was in possession of So-he's bow. The expressions on the faces of those he met while walking with So-he upset him also. I guess that I should have stayed in my own lodge and sweated it out, he told himself. Finally he decided to just stay away from the village for a few days and see if anything developed. If I have infringed upon any of their customs, it will surely come to light if I keep away for a while. This was his last silent comment as he entered the clearing before his lodge.

It was sometime close to midnight a few days later when Enir was awakened by a slight scratching at the door of his lodge. He felt in the darkness for his bow and slipped an arrow into it. Presently the sound was repeated, and this time it was accompanied by a low whine. Enir leaped from the bunk and opened the door. There stood Bat, looking hale and hearty, with an expression of joy upon her shaggy face. He caught a glimpse of a huge dark shadow as it disappeared into the underbrush on the opposite side of the clearing.

"Come in, old gal," Enir said, and Bat turned head and whined, then slipped into the lodge. "I hope you told him to get lost," said Enir as he glanced again at the spot where the shadow had disappeared.

Bat showed one of her rare emotional outbursts by licking his hand and emitting short yelps of pleasure. Enir stroked her head and welcomed her back in the low voice he had always been accustomed to using when talking to her. After a while she turned away and walked over to the deerskin rug, which Enir had never removed, and lay down upon it. Bat had come home.

Enir lay back down, also, and smiled contentedly into the soft darkness. He was too excited to return to sleep, because he had long since given up hopes of ever seeing Bat again. He thought about the great wolf who had followed her back to the lodge. Would he go away or would he hang around until some Indian put an arrow through him? Secretly, Enir hoped that he would leave. He had never cared much for wolves, and recently he had come to hate them. But this was a special wolf. He was Bat's mate, and he had evidently protected her from the ferocious pack and had brought her home unharmed. Yes, he was definitely in the family now, and he could not help but wish him well.

Gradually Enir's thoughts drifted around to So-he. What would Bat think of her? Well, if things should come to a showdown, and he should want out, he might be able to use Bat's confirmed hatred of Indians as an excuse. It was then that he remembered telling So-he's mother that she could have the remainder of the deerskins he possessed. He remembered that he had carefully refrained from promising to deliver them, and now he was worried that one of them would come for them while he was busy at the spring, at the meat cache, or out gathering wood. He feared that Bat might attack them. I suppose that now I will have to deliver them, he said to himself, as he gradually surrendered to the drowsiness which had begun to steal over him.

When daylight arrived, he woke and glanced anxiously at the deerskin rug to assure himself that he had not had a pleasant dream. Bat was there, so he rose and opened the door. Bat came over, and he carefully examined her for scars and other signs of rough treatment. Finding none, he said, "Well, old girl, you came through without a scratch, I see." He dropped his arm about her shaggy neck, and together they watched the sun rise above the jagged mountains to the east. A sense of well-being stole over him, and he thought, no wonder the Flathead chose this valley in which to build their village. This is the most beautiful place in the whole world. Game is plentiful, wood and water are handy, there are plenty of fish in the streams, and the wild fruit and vegetables grow in profusion. His mind touched fleetingly upon the dead man's cache, the mysterious valley, the stone ladder, and then he thought of So-he's bow. Quickly he rose, and taking down his new bow, he showed it to Bat. He was disappointed when she showed no interest in it. He thumbed the bowstring, and she pricked up her ears at the musical sound.

The feel of the bow, the joy of being reunited with his dog, and the lure of the silent forest caused Enir to decide that a celebration was in order. "Well, old girl, let's go and see if your romance has affected your hunting abilities," he said. He selected a few of his best arrows and banked the fire, and they struck out at a swift pace toward the north end of the valley, where the feeding grounds of the wapiti lay.

As they followed swiftly along the dim trail, he watched Bat as she gradually assumed her old hunting stance and began to sniff the humid air with interest. They moved rapidly because it was a long way to where Enir wished to hunt, the place where the wapiti usually fed early in the morning. He did not expect to encounter any game for several miles, so he set a swift pace.

They had traveled about seven or eight miles, and Enir was keeping a sharp eye for the dim trail that led off to the right from the one they were following, to the edge of the swamp that was frequented by the wapiti. The few days that he had hunted alone, his familiarity with the location, and the other things that were crowding into his mind caused him to neglect watching for Bat's silent signals. He was swinging along, thinking about the grace of the girl, So-he, when he bumped into Bat, who had halted in the trail. He suddenly became aware that she was desperately attempting to signal him of danger. Just as he bumped into her she snarled viciously, and just as suddenly a huge male grizzly reared up on his hind legs only yards in front of him. Enir's reaction was quicker than his reasoning. His bow flashed, and before he had thought, he had sunk a shaft deep into the chest of the gigantic monster. A deafening roar came from the great mouth of the beast, and he shot forward as if from a catapult. Enir ducked between two trees just as the bear's claws raked the bark from one of them. So close was the blow that the flying particles of bark stung Enir's face. Quickly he sprinted to the base of a nearby hemlock spruce and ducked behind it. He well knew that it would be foolish to attempt to outdistance the grizzly in a straightaway race, for he had once witnessed one pull down a fleeing elk. Silently he berated himself for his impulsive action. He realized that had he taken flight without wounding the beast, it was doubtful he would have been pursued, for man was very seldom attacked by an unprovoked grizzly. He also knew the terrible temper of the grizzly and realized with a sinking feeling that only death would stop him now. The loud roars, and the fact that he was still alive, told Enir that Bat had joined in the fight, and with trembling fingers he placed another arrow into his bow. He peered from behind the tree just as the bear turned broadside to him and reached for the aggravating dog. Acting entirely by instinct, Enir sank another arrow deep into the monster's side, directly behind the right foreleg. The roar of the beast caused the ground to tremble, but the second he wasted snapping at the offending arrow permitted Enir to place another one into his bow. It was a life-and-death struggle beyond all doubt now, and Enir felt the skin tighten at the back of his neck. Bat had also taken advantage of the wasted second to dart in and tear viciously again at the huge leg, just above the knee joint. Like a flash of light, the great beast whirled and lashed out with his forepaw. Bat was also fast in her retreat, but not fast enough. The great claws raked her right hip with a glancing blow, yet with enough force to turn her three somersaults in the air, and her head struck the base of a small tree hard enough to render her unconscious. As the bear started to where she lay inert upon the ground, his left side was presented toward Enir. He stepped quickly from behind the tree and sank an arrow behind the bear's other foreleg with all the power his bow could muster. This time the bear's roar ended in a shrill scream of rage, and Enir was aware of two things as he feverishly slid another arrow into his bow. Bat was out of the fight, and Enir had revealed his hiding place. When the bear wasted another second to snap at the haft of the arrow that protruded from his side, Enir saw a dark shadow flash from the underbrush. A wide mouth closed over the bear's hind leg at exactly the same place where Bat's attack had torn the skin. The clashing of fangs as they slipped from the bear's leg was audible above the din, and the charge that the bear had already started toward the tree where Enir stood was slowed as the great body slumped sideways. Enir saw blood gushing from the bear's open mouth as he turned to glance at this third opponent. He quickly stepped from behind the tree, and while the great head was turned, he let fly another arrow, which pierced deep inside the bear's neck, about midway between his head and shoulder. At the same instant, the black shadow again flashed from the underbrush and once more tore viciously at the bear's hind leg. There was another clashing of fangs, and again the flashing shadow disappeared. The great mountain of flesh suddenly collapsed and lay still. The forest became as quiet as a tomb. Not even the twitter of a bird broke the silence. Enir stood with his last arrow in his bow and stared unbelievingly at his fallen foe. He saw the great mouth sag open and a large purple tongue protrude. The blood ceased to flow from it, and the ugly lips slowly drooped to partially cover the terrible yellow tusks. The great grizzly was dead.

Enir leaned against the big hemlock and trembled. The distant sound of a woodpecker broke the terrible stillness, and it was soon joined by the chirping of other birds as they returned to their nests and feeding grounds, from which they had been frightened. Bat broke the tension of Enir's reaction by staggering to her feet. Enir rushed over to examine her carefully. He found that there were no broken bones or deep wounds. Only four wide clawmarks that oozed a little blood marked her right hip, and there was a growing lump at the base of her skull where it had contacted the tree.

"By jove, old girl, we've both made it," said Enir excitedly, then in an undertone he added, "thanks to your boyfriend." And his eyes quickly searched the surrounding bushes. But the dark shadow had disappeared.

As Enir turned from searching the surrounding forest with eyes still dilated with fear, he watched Bat as she limped slowly around the great furry mound that graced the center of the small open space. He noticed that she kept well back from the carcass as she examined it.

"He is dead all right," said Enir. "I can hardly believe it myself, but did you know that your boyfriend saved the day?" Then a shudder passed over him. "I'll never kill a wolf or shoot a bear with a bow again," he said aloud. His mind pictured once more that great mouth and those terrible fangs that had closed over the bear's hind leg to finish what Bat had started. "I would not have believed it possible for any beast to hamstring a grizzly," he whispered. Then, moving his head from side to side, he said to himself, that was the most hideous face and the wickedest pair of eyes I ever saw on anything, and to think that Bat might bear pups from that monstrous son-of-a-bitch wolf. Father Odin protect us.

It was many minutes before Enir regained enough composure to approach the bear to check for his arrows. He examined the large torn place just above the knee joint of his hind leg. He looked at the mangled end of the great tendon that controlled the lower leg and foot. He found that the hafts of the arrows in the bear's chest and side were all broken off, but the one in his neck remained whole, and its feather stood proudly up almost to the level of the bulging paunch. He took hold of it and tried to remove it but found that it was securely wedged between two vertebrae. "That is really what stopped him," he said aloud, realizing that the sharp steel head must have entered the bear's spine. The amount of blood that had poured from the beast's mouth told Enir that at least one of his arrows had lodged very close to the bear's heart. He glanced again at the large puddles of blood and wondered if there was any at all left inside. "He would have lasted long enough to have taken care of me if that wolf had not hamstrung him and given me a chance to get in that lucky shot that punctured his spine," he mumbled. It is nothing but pure luck that I'm still alive, he said to himself, pure unadulterated luck. And he felt a tingle chase up and down his spine.

Enir drew his hunting knife and took hold on the haft of the arrow which protruded from the bear's neck. He looked at the heavy fur and hesitated. If I cut it out it will spoil the pelt, he said to himself, and Enir had an overwhelming desire to save this beautiful trophy. He let go of the arrow and walked slowly around the carcass. How in tarnation does a man get the skin off of a beast like this? he asked himself. He remembered hearing Stripe tell of skinning a buffalo single-handed, but he had had a horse, and, besides, this was not a buffalo. As he stood with his knife in his hand, trying to figure some way to retrieve this pelt, Bat gave a low whine, and he glanced at her. He saw that she was lying on her side and that the wound on her leg was swelling terribly. He went over to look at it again, but Bat climbed painfully to her feet and limped away to the shade of the tree. He knew that she was bound to be suffering some pain from a wallop like that, but decided that she would feel better presently, so went back to wrestling with his problem. He seized one of the bear's hind legs and tried to roll him over but could barely shake the giant carcass. "By the pure blood of Odin," he said aloud, "it would take three men to skin this brute." But finally he decided to give it a try anyway. So he hung his bow upon the limp of a bush and started to split the hide along the inside of the hind legs. He worked very carefully. I want a good pelt or none at all, he told himself, and the feel of the thick, dark fur caused his eyes to shine with pleasure. He had straightened from his task of splitting the skin along the inside of the hind legs when he noticed that Bat was sitting up with her ears alert. It must be her boyfriend coming back to check on her, he thought, but suddenly her bristles began to rise and she limped over to take her stance between him and the trail which led to the north. "Indians," he whispered to himself as he ducked quickly for cover. He could tell by Bat's actions that they were quite a long way off yet, but they had to be moving in his direction if they were following the trail. "I will just move down that way and take a peek at their haircuts," he whispered to himself. If they are Flatheads, he thought, I might be able to get them to give me a hand. I will have to move quite a ways toward them, he thought, because if they get close enough to see this bear they will take off, and the carcass is visible from the trail. So, cautioning Bat to silence, he moved parallel to the trail as fast as Bat could travel. He could tell by her actions that there were several of them, and this caused him to double his caution. I have to get a look at their hair, he told himself, for it could be a Blackfoot war party, since they are moving toward the village. As he proceeded, he soon decided that they were moving too slowly for a war party, yet he still could not afford to take a chance. He found a suitable place for him and Bat to hide, where he could see the trail plainly, and settled down to wait. It was only a few minutes before he saw a tall Flathead man moving silently down the trail quite a way ahead of the main band. This satisfied him, so he ran swiftly ahead of the limping dog, and when he reached a position nearer the carcass of the bear he gave the signal used by Flathead hunters who had made an unusual kill and desired assistance. He waited a few minutes and repeated the signal. When Bat limped in with her hackles raised, he knew that the Indians were nearby. He waited silently, and presently the tall Indian he had seen stepped into the clearing with his eyes opened wide with surprise. Enir quickly gave the peace sign, which the Indian reluctantly returned. Two more braves then stepped into the opening, and Enir called Bat to heel and repeated the peace sign, which the two also returned.

While the three stared at the carcass of the big grizzly in wide-eyed surprise, Enir studied them closely. The tall one who had arrived first was by far the most intelligent looking one of the three. He had a high forehead, long arms, and very sharp eyes. One of the others was both crippled and disfigured. His left shoulder was dropped to well below forty-five degrees, and his left arm and hand were twisted and useless. One side of his face had been horribly mutilated, and when it had healed, it had left his great jaw teeth, which reminded Enir of the teeth of a horse, fully exposed, so that saliva continually drooled from between them. His nose was half torn away, and one nostril looked like a small cave. There was also a large scar on the side of his scalp, which had not healed properly, and the naked spot was covered with what appeared to be a large bloody scab. The rest of his body seemed uninjured, and it showed that at one time he had been a powerful man. Enir noticed that his eyes were both sharp and intelligent and that he wore the badge of a medicine man. Enir quickly removed his eyes from his disfigurement, and then he gave the sign that acknowledged his respect for his rank. The cripple quickly returned his response, and Enir saw his eyes light up, which told him that the Indian had not expected recognition from a paleface and also that it pleased him. The third member of the trio was a very stalwart young

70

brave who showed no signs of extra intelligence. In fact, his attitude seemed slightly belligerent as he met Enir's eyes. From the tall Indian's attitude, Enir could easily recognize him as the leader, so it was to him he spoke.

"I am Enir Halverson," he said, "and I have the permission of Chief Wa-neb-i-te to live in your village and to hunt in your forest." When the three eyed him in silence he continued, "I have slain the great grizzly, but I desire only his pelt and his claws. If my Flathead friends have a desire for the meat, it is theirs."

The Indians made no reply, nor did Enir expect any. He stood by after making his speech and watched the tall Indian read every sign in the torn earth of the tiny open space. He watched his eyes travel to the severed leader on the bear's hind leg, then flash to Bat's half-open mouth. He watched him stoop low and examine closely the haft of the arrow that protruded from the bear's neck, then move to the bloody stub of the arrow behind the bear's foreleg. He looked at the places where Enir's knife had slit the hide on each hind leg, then spoke in a low voice to the dumb-looking brave. The brave left and returned in a very short while with four husky squaws. The tall Indian immediately commanded the squaws to skin the bear and drew his hunting knife and extended it to one of them. Enir and the other two Indians did likewise, and the tall one led the way to the shade of the hemlock spruce, behind which Enir had, a short time earlier, taken refuge.

While Enir sat on the damp earth beneath the tree and watched the four squaws wrestle effectively with the carcass of the great beast, he noticed that the eyes of the tall Indian had never ceased their intense scrutiny of the immediate area. He wondered what he was looking for, and it was only a few moments before he had his answer. For suddenly the Indian rose to his feet and advanced toward the shrub on which Enir had hung his bow, where the sunlight did not bear directly upon it. The tall Indian halted a few paces away from the bow, and Enir saw his back suddenly stiffen. His hand reached out quickly and grasped the bow, then he turned to Enir and his eyes held a baleful glitter.

"How is this that I find a strange paleface in possession of So-he's bow?" he asked. Both of the other Indians jumped to their feet, and the squaws became motionless.

Enir rose and said, "I bought it from the squaw of the great bowmaker, I-lip-a-taw. So-he, herself, selected it for me." Enir saw the gleam of anger fade from the eyes of the tall Indian, but the young brave leaped forward.

"You lie," he shouted. "You, like all paleface, speak nothing but lies." Suddenly he turned and snatched a knife from one of the squaws and advanced toward Enir. "Now, paleface, you will die because of your lies." All eyes were turned upon Enir as he stepped back in surprise at the young Indian's intense anger. "Get your knife, paleface," said the young brave. "I will grant you permission to die honorably."

Enir hesitated. "I thirst not for the Flathead's blood," he said.

The angry brave whirled toward the tall Indian and said, "Let I-lip-a-taw speak."

I-lip-a-taw, thought Enir, and he looked again at the tall Indian. So this is So-he's father, he said to himself. Then he began to understand the young brave's anger: He was another of So-he's suitors. Enir looked at I-lip-a-taw and thought that he saw a shadow of contempt in his dark eyes. Slowly, I-lip-a-taw folded his arms across his chest, closed his mouth tight, and took one short backward step. I-lip-a-taw had spoken. Enir realized that his subtle attempt to force the brave to fight without weapons had failed, and his mind worked very swiftly. He glanced at the knife in the hand of the Indian and noted that the blade was short but very sharp and pointed. Since he had never been taught to fight with knives, a type of combat that in England was considered an act of cowardice, he quickly decided that he would have a better chance to win if he kept both hands free. This would tend to give the Indian over-confidence, which might possibly invite carelessness. Also the quick temper of this particular brave could easily be agitated by gibes and insults, which would also rob him of some of his skill.

"Get your knife, paleface," repeated the Indian in a trembling voice.

Enir drew himself to his full height and said, "Enir Halverson disdains the use of weapons to fight with one who has so little honor. Were you not made a brave for killing old men and squaws?"

"You will die slowly now, paleface, and while you die, you will think upon all of your dirty lies." He advanced, holding the knife low like he knew his business.

Enir began to circle, keeping his eyes upon the Indian's movements. Suddenly the brave began to leap shortly to the right, then to the left; each time he slapped the ground smartly with the flat bottom of his heavy-soled moccasin. Enir realized that this would effectively distract his attention.

"You dance very awkwardly, eater of dogmeat. It is small wonder that So-he hates you," said Enir.

The Indian's eyes became wild with hatred. "Now you die, die," he screamed as he lunged forward.

Enir seized the brave's wrist, but the Indian's strength was terrific. Enir was lifted almost clear off the ground, but he suddenly released his grip, which threw his opponent off balance. As he staggered, Enir followed up his advantage with a neat uppercut to the brave's chin. Although the blow did not have the power it would have had if Enir had had solid footing, it still packed enough force to spin the brave around and cause him to fall heavily upon his stomach. He grunted very loudly when he landed, but he started to rise, then suddenly his arms gave way and he fell back upon his stomach. His legs jerked several times and he lay still. Enir, who had stepped up with his right arm cocked for a haymaker, stared at him curiously, then he stepped back. He must have a glass jaw, he told himself, but he watched him closely for a moment because he knew that the blow had not landed quite solidly enough to suit him. Presently he turned to face I-lip-a-taw but saw that the Indian had already motioned the squaws back to work. The crippled Indian grunted and also turned away. They all seemed to ignore the sleeping brave, except Enir. He well knew that there was no broken jaw this time and fully expected the brave to recover presently and resume the fight.

A few minutes passed and still none of the Indians did more than glance at the prostrate form of the fallen brave. Enir joined them and became interested in watching the squaws handling the carcass of the big bear. He soon saw how they intended to manage the job. They were going to skin the upper half, remove most of the meat from it, then turn him and skin the other half.

Suddenly, a loud, uncanny howl broke the stillness. The high plaintive notes caused the squaws to gather in a huddle, I-lip-a-taw to leap high and slap his empty knife scabbard, and the crippled Indian to draw his tomahawk. Enir, alone, showed no excitement, but merely turned slowly around. All eyes were turned upon the source of the unearthly wail, and what they saw was Bat's ugly muzzle pointed toward the sky as she sat at the edge of the open space. When she had uttered the last wailing notes, she rose and limped dejectedly into the underbrush.

"She wakin," mumbled the medicine man in a deep-throated murmur, and the squaws all began making signs that were supposed to ward off evil spirits.

I-lip-a-taw looked at Enir and asked, "Is your dog possessed of the evil spirit?"

"No," replied Enir, "she was only telling us that the brave is dead."

I-lip-a-taw hurried over and rolled the brave onto his back, and there, protruding from just below his breast bone, was the bloody hilt of the knife. I-lip-a-taw slowly straightened and looked strangely into Enir's face.

"You knew?" he asked presently.

"Only when I heard the cry," replied Enir, "because I have heard it before."

I-lip-a-taw studied him for a full minute in silence. "Does your dog always cry like that when you kill people?" he asked in a hushed voice.

"She always cries when someone dies, whether I killed him or not," replied Enir.

I-lip-a-taw looked down into the face of the dead brave, then he suddenly reached down and drew forth the bloody knife. He straightened up and tossed it to the feet of one of the squaws, saying sternly, "Go back to your work. Did you think that one who alone slew the great bear would himself be slain by such a one as Ba-ep-o-lic?" The squaws made haste to obey, but as they worked they glanced often at Enir Halverson. In them were no longer gleams of suspicion and hatred but rather looks of stark fear.

No words were spoken for several minutes as the squaws worked steadily at their difficult task. Enir longed to pitch in and help, but he remembered the code of the Indian, so he held back. Presently I-lip-a-taw turned to the medicine man and said, "Na-bab-i-ti, your legs are strong. Would you go to the village and bring back four husky squaws to carry the meat and the body of Ba-ep-o-lic?" The medicine man made no reply but turned and started toward the trail. "You should tell them to make haste," continued I-lip-a-taw, "or we shall have to travel in darkness." The crippled Indian still did not speak, but Enir saw him strike a long swinging trot as soon as he reached the trail.

Enir grew tired of the stabbing glances of the squaws and the silence of I-lip-a-taw, so he strolled away into the forest in search of Bat. He looked under the spreading limbs of the creeping juniper and in the deep shadows of the trees, but Bat was nowhere to be found. As he slowly circled the location, he began to think again of the great wolf who had so graciously risked his like to save him from the bear. Was it me or Bat he wished to protect? he asked himself. He probably thought he was avenging the death of his mate, he finally concluded. Enir was sure now that Bat had joined him somewhere in the forest, and he began to worry. The wound on her leg was still swelling, and he feared that by now she had become unable to walk. Even if the great wolf found her, he could not carry her to water or attend her wound. Just as he was about to appeal to I-lip-a-taw to stop the work and let the squaws help him search for her, some strange objects attracted his attention. They appeared to be three large bundles of sticks, which had been bound tightly by rawhide thongs and hidden beneath the low-hanging limbs of juniper bushes. He approached them and examined them closely. There was a wide flat rawhide strap attached to each end of the tightly bound bundles, and the wood was of a nature that was strange to him. He bent down and looked closely at the bundles and at the soft leather straps. Pack straps, he said to himself, then he reached down and hefted the end of one of the bundles.

"Bow wood," said a voice almost beside him, and he turned quickly to face I-lip-a-taw.

"Where did they come from?" asked Enir to hide his surprise.

"From far, far," replied I-lip-a-taw as he pointed southeast. "From the land of the Comanche."

"Er . . . did you carry them all the way?" asked Enir.

"Leave pony on other side of mountain," replied I-lip-a-taw. "Pony no good here. Too much snow, too much wolves, bear, and cougars."

The other side of the mountain, thought Enir, then roughly estimated that they must have carried them almost a hundred miles.

"I cannot find my dog," said Enir. "I fear that she is down somewhere near, because her wound has been getting worse." He waited for a moment, hoping that the Indian would offer to let the squaws help hunt for her without his asking. I-lip-a-taw turned and started back toward where the squaws were working.

As they walked around a thicket of heavy brush, they both detected movement and halted at the same time. Almost immediately a great male timber wolf strode boldly out into the open and stared directly at them with large green eyes that caused a creepy tingle to chase up and down Enir's spine. I-lip-a-taw started to unsling his bow, but Enir laid his hand gently upon his shoulder.

"He is mine," he said. "He is the mate of my dog."

I-lip-a-taw stood still and his eyes went from Enir to the great wolf, who stood within easy bowshot. The wolf dropped his head and peered beneath the tangled limbs, glanced once more at Enir, then loped away into the forest. Enir hastened forward and raised the low limbs of the juniper, and there lay Bat, trembling and whimpering softly. He saw that her leg was terribly swollen, so he stooped and gathered her into his arms and hurried to where the squaws were.

"She is very hot," he said to I-lip-a-taw, and the Indian turned to one of the squaws and asked if there was any water left in the water bag. The squaw hastened to where the bow wood was left and returned with a large bag fashioned from the stomach of a moose, which contained about a gallon of tepid water. Enir bathed Bat's face and helped her to drink a few swallows, and she seemed to improve. By the time Na-bab-i-ti had returned with the squaws, she was again able to limp about.

The meat, which had been cut into large chunks, was quickly loaded upon one travois, while the body of Ba-ep-o-lic was placed on another, and the rest of the meat that was not discarded was speared on rawhide thongs and lashed to the bundles of bow wood. One plump squaw was ordered to carry the hide, but it was so heavy that Enir volunteered to help her.

All went well for a mile or so, but because of Bat, Enir and the squaw began to fall far behind the others. Finally, Bat became unable to walk at all, and Enir flattened a place in the center of the huge pelt, then placed her upon it. He carried one end while the squaw carried the other and they made much better time.

Once, while they were resting, the squaw explained to Enir the best way of preserving the large skin.

"It must be painted with the thick bark solution and rolled tight for three days," said the squaw. "Then it must be stretched and ground with sandstone to clean the inside. It must be painted again with the tarry bark solution, rolled again, and left three more days.

"It must then be rubbed well with the salt dirt and rolled again. After two days it should be scraped again with sandstone and painted with the bark tar and left for five days. After this, it should be cleaned and worked with the hands until it is soft. If there are hard spots in it, it should again be painted and left for several more days, when it should again be worked with the fingers until it is very soft."

Enir's mouth dropped open and he was about ready to tell her that they would just leave the pelt in the forest and go on home, when a thought struck him. He fished a silver dollar from his belt and offered it to her, saying, "Would you, who are so skilled in the art, do this for me in exchange for the metal picture?"

The squaw showed her snaggled teeth in a wide grin as she reached for it. "It shall be even softer than the wapiti skin in the lodge of Wa-neb-i-te," she answered.

When they reached Enir's lodge, he carried the softly whimpering dog into it and bathed her swollen leg gently with cool water. He also let her drink her fill of it and then helped her to get comfortable upon her deerskin bed. When he returned, the pelt and the squaw were gone. Enir dropped to one knee and skylighted the trail. He could just barely distinguish the figure of the stout, bow-legged squaw as she moved slowly around the curve in the trail and on toward the village. He felt just a tiny twinge of guilt as he watched her stagger out of sight, then he smiled. Who said that money has no value amongst the Indians? he said to himself.

It was near noon the following day when Enir, returning from the spring with a bag of fresh water, saw two Indians approaching from the village. He recognized one as I-lip-a-taw, the bowmaker, but the other one was a stranger to him. It was the strange Indian who held his interest, because he appeared to be arguing with I-lip-a-taw as he gestured wildly with both his hands in an apparent attempt to win the approval of the stoic bowmaker. When they approached nearer, Enir could see that this strange Indian was in the throes of terrific anger. His eyes blazed, and he stomped the ground occasionally like an angry buffalo bull, but I-lip-a-taw paid him no mind. When Enir hung the water bag upon the wall and strolled out to meet them, the angry Indian came forward swiftly and confronted him.

"You lying, tricky-tongued paleface," he shouted. "You, who are not man enough to possess a squaw, give big work to other man's squaw. I am E-lay-i-te, mighty fighter with the knife, and I have come to kill you, paleface. You killed my uncle's son by trickery, then you give big work to my squaw, who will no longer prepare my food. You are the son of a dog and the brother of a buzzard." The Indian halted directly in front of him. Enir glanced at I-lip-a-taw and saw that there was a rather serious look upon his calm face.

"I did not know—" Enir started to say to the Indian.

The Indian interrupted him. "Speak not your filthy lies to me," he shouted. "Speak to the Great Spirit, whom you soon shall meet." And his hand flashed to the hilt of the long, wicked-looking knife he carried. Enir did not hesitate. He had already taken his position when the Indian stopped before him, so he threw a right to the man's exposed jaw, putting all his weight behind it. The knife that E-lay-i-te had drawn, sailed off to one side just as his moccasins passed by Enir's face. The sharp smacking sound echoed from the silent tree trunks, and E-lay-i-te landed solidly and lay quite still. Enir felt the familiar thrill travel up his right arm and shoulder, a sensation which told him that he had just broken jaw number two.

I-lip-a-taw stepped up to look down at E-lay-i-te's crossed eyes and grunted. Enir picked up the long knife and carried it over to a large rock with a crack in its center, then stood looking at the rock while he balanced the knife in his hand. Presently he turned and glanced up into the branches of the large tree that stood before his lodge. Suddenly he threw the knife with all his might, and it sank deep into the trunk just above the bottom branches. He then turned to face I-lip-a-taw and noticed that he still wore the serious expression he had seen upon his face.

"You think twice," said I-lip-a-taw. "Why?"

Enir pointed to the inert body of E-lay-i-te and said, "Maybe he has a right to be mad."

"Hump," grunted I-lip-a-taw. "He mad because you kill Ba-ep-o-lic. They big friends. E-lay-i-te all time fight with squaw."

"Why did you come with him?" asked Enir. "Do you also think I did wrong?"

"I come for another reason," replied I-lip-a-taw. "He catch me up the trail, and I let um come, teach um lesson."

Enir was thoughtful for a moment. He was afraid to ask the bowmaker what his reason was for this visit, but decided there was no reason to postpone it, so he said, "What is this other reason?" And he looked squarely into the serious eyes of the tall Indian.

"I like to talk. We go by front of lodge where none can hear."

Enir looked down at the prone E-lay-i-te and said, "He won't hear."

"Mebby hear pretty soon," replied I-lip-a-taw as he led the way to the front of the lodge.

Enir followed him and motioned to a flat stump, and when I-lip-a-taw was seated he chose one close by and asked, "Of what does I-lip-a-taw wish to speak?" I-lip-a-taw did not answer immediately but looked deep into Enir's eyes for a full minute.

"You talk straight talk?" he asked.

Enir returned the tall bowmaker's prolonged stare and said, "I talk straight or I do not talk at all."

"Good," said I-lip-a-taw. "You know prospector with white stripe in whiskers?"

Enir thought swiftly. How did they connect him with Stripe? He had already decided that Na-bab-i-ti, the crippled medicine man, was the one who had done in Stripe's former partner. Some Indian must have remembered seeing him with Stripe the previous fall. Anyway, he had promised to tell the truth, so he answered, "Yes, I knew Stripe. I was his partner. He is dead."

I-lip-a-taw nodded slowly as if he were contemplating his next question. "You search for yellow metal?" he asked.

"Yes," replied Enir.

"Did Striped Beard tell you to look in White Bosom Bare for yellow metal?"

"No. He told me not to go into White Bosom Bare." I-lip-a-taw stared at him for a second.

"He said the valley was sacred grounds."

"White Bosom Bare sacred to Striped Beard?"

"No," replied Enir, "he said that it was sacred to the Flathead, and for me not to go into White Bosom Bare." He would not lie because he had given his word.

"Why you come here, Enir Halverson?" asked I-lip-a-taw.

Enir remained silent. I-lip-a-taw rose slowly to his feet and extended to Enir the gold sovereign that he had given to the Indian's squaw.

"You take, and give me So-he's bow."

So-he's bow again, thought Enir. He had killed a man over it, he had killed a grizzly bear with it, and now it seemed to have become a part of him.

"You take," said I-lip-a-taw, his voice rising slightly.

Somewhat reluctantly, Enir motioned I-lip-a-taw back to the stump, ignoring the gold piece.

"If I talk straight to I-lip-a-taw, will he not hate me?"

I-lip-a-taw slowly resumed his seat, and Enir thought that he caught a flicker either of amusement or of achievement in his sharp eyes.

"I will not hate you. You talk," he said.

"Will I-lip-a-taw promise not to tell others what I shall tell him?"

"You talk first," replied I-lip-a-taw. "I do not know."

Enir hesitated. He did not want to leave this valley, and he knew that if he did not make his story convincing, he would surely have to, so he decided to make a clean breast of everything. If he could not trust this honorable Indian, there was nobody he could trust, so he told him about Dead Man's Cache. He also told him that he was the only living person who knew of its existence, which was his reason for asking him to keep his secret. I-lip-a-taw listened silently, and for several moments after Enir had finished, he sat and stared at the toes of his moccasins.

Presently he asked, "Did Striped Beard tell you before he died that there was gold in White Bosom Bare?"

"Yes," replied Enir.

"And if you not find cache, you look there?"

"Why is the yellow metal so important to the valley?" asked Enir after some hesitation. "Why did the Great Spirit put the gold in White Bosom Bare, if he did not want men to find it?" he asked when I-lip-a-taw did not answer.

"It is not for I-lip-a-taw to say why Great Spirit do things," replied the Indian presently. "But Great Spirit give the valley to Flathead. Flathead believe that He make valley sacred so he can use it for breeding ground for his animals. Flathead need these animals for food and clothing. If the yellow metal is found there, many paleface come, bringing with them thundersticks and death. They would destroy the animals and defile the valley. I came for your word, Enir Halverson, that you will not attempt to enter our valley. Let Enir Halverson speak."

Enir sat in silence. He knew that the ax had fallen. If he refused, he would either be slain or driven out of the valley. He also knew that if he gave his word, he would keep it. No longer could he dream of a bonanza above the falls. On the other hand, life in the valley was pleasant. With So-he's bow, he would always have meat. And if he did not give his word, the bow would be taken from him. He would never see So-he again. Very slowly he rose, and I-lip-a-taw rose with him. He looked the tall bowmaker straight in the eyes.

"I-lip-a-taw has Enir Halverson's word that he will not attempt to secretly enter the valley of White Bosom Bare," said Enir.

I-lip-a-taw, who had watched every expression upon Enir's face, was fully aware of the struggle he had gone through. His eyes softened, and he laid his hand upon Enir's shoulder but said nothing. Presently he sat back down on the stump, and Enir did likewise, but he did so rather dejectedly.

"Tell me, I-lip-a-taw, how well did you know Striped Beard and the man who Na-bab-i-ti killed?" asked Enir.

"I only knew Striped Beard by sight," he replied, "but his partner was a rascal. He tried to trick his way into the sacred valley. He gave a brave much firewater because he had been led to believe that this brave knew the secret of the stone ladder. That is why Na-bab-i-ti killed him."

"Did you know about the yellow metal he found by the waterfall?"

"Yes," replied I-lip-a-taw, "but I did not know it was so much. I did not know about the cache until you told me."

"Will you tell others of it now?"

"No, Enir Halverson. You have given me your word; now you have mine."

"Do you suppose that anybody knows about it already?"

"Nobody knows," replied the Indian. "Indians do not keep secrets such as this from each other."

Enir thought for a minute, then asked, "Where is the squaw that this man brought with him?"

"We send her back to the Blackfoot, where she belongs," replied I-lip-a-taw.

"When?" asked Enir.

"The next day after Na-bab-i-ti kill paleface," he replied.

"Now wait," said Enir. "Striped Beard said that squaw was still here when he came to look for his partner."

"No," replied I-lip-a-taw. "I tell you this: One time when I go for bow wood, I find this man and Striped Beard down in Teton country searching for the yellow metal. When he come here I know him, but he did not know me. I told Wa-neb-i-te who he was, but Wa-neb-i-te's scout told him that Striped Beard was alone up north at the time. When Striped Beard come later looking for partner, we not sure that he knew about what this man had found and what he was trying to do. So one night I send my squaw to Striped Beard's lodge, and she tell him story and warn him we knew he was this man's partner. When, next morning, I find Striped Beard's tracks very apart in trail, we knew that he know about gold."

"How long have you known about the gold in White Bosom Bare?" asked Enir.

"I do not yet know," replied I-lip-a-taw. "I only know what this man and others have said."

Enir was silent for a while, but his mind mulled over what this Indian had told him. So this was not the first time that the golden arrow had pointed to White Bosom Bare. Stripe's partner was probably not the first prospector who had lost his life because of it either.

At this moment a loud snort brought both Enir and I-lip-a-taw to their feet. They looked at each other guiltily, for they had both forgotten about E-lay-i-te. They rushed over and found him vainly trying to raise himself to a sitting position. Enir walked over and picked up the water bag from where he had hung it, then stepped into the lodge and returned with his gold pan. When I-lip-a-taw had assisted the half-conscious brave to his feet, Enir stepped up and dashed about half a gold pan full of water into his face. The Indian snorted, jumped sideways, and broke wind all at the same time, but it had the desired effect. Almost immediately he began to blink owlishly at them. Enir set aside the gold pan and moved closer. E-lay-i-te squinted at him, then awkwardly made the peace sign. Enir returned it, and I-lip-a-taw guided the man to the trail and started him toward the village. They watched until he had rounded the bend in the trail, then returned to their seats.

"Tell me, Enir Halverson," said I-lip-a-taw, "why do you thirst so much for the yellow metal? If you found it, would you hasten to the place where the lodges are very close together and where the wind stinks? Would you drink the poison firewater and gorge yourself until your belly became like that of an expectant squaw? Would you build a big lodge with many beds and make men pay you to let them sleep in them? Would you worry your hair white for fear somebody would steal it from you? Do you need it to make you big name among the paleface? Would you enjoy eating while others went hungry? Do you think it would make your mind stronger and give you the right to tell others what to do? No, I think not, Enir Halverson. I think that you are much happier hunting for it than you will be when you find it. Have you ever thought about that?"

Enir stared long into the eyes of the bowmaker and searched his soul for an answer to his many questions. He could think of none, so he remained silent. I-lip-a-taw looked down at the gold sovereign, which he still held in his hand, then slipped it back into his medicine bag.

"I will go now, Enir Halverson," he said. "When you are tired of thinking, come to the village and walk with So-he." Then I-lip-a-taw walked slowly but proudly up the trail to his lodge.

For many minutes after I-lip-a-taw had departed, Enir sat upon the flat-topped stump and reviewed his conversation with the amazing bowmaker. The profound wisdom he had expounded had not only surprised Enir, but had also touched him deeply. The many startling truths he had revealed were quite shocking to Enir. The mentioning of scouts and the fact that Chief Wa-neb-i-te knew exactly where Stripe was prospecting at a certain time led him to believe that this village was something other than what it appeared to be. Old Stripe was certainly right when he told me these Flathead were not stupid, he thought. He also thought of how the bowmaker had twisted his arm. He sure got what he came for, he said to himself, but what good is gold to a dead man?

The longer Enir thought about it, the less certain he became that he really wanted to locate the bonanza of White Bosom Bare. It was easy for him to see why the Indians would be apprehensive of what such a discovery would do to their valley. If a large strike was made there, this whole valley would be exploited. The thought of this beautiful valley being

88

turned into a pigsty by the trash who always followed in the wake of every big strike caused him to shudder. I am glad that I gave my word, he said to himself. I am also a fool for not realizing this before. The longer Enir's mind dwelled upon this ethnological problem, the greater became his compassion for the Indians. For the first time, he began to realize they had made great sacrifices to preserve this beautiful continent that the white man was now so determined to exploit. "I am glad that I am out of it," he said in an undertone, as he wrenched his mind from the distasteful thought and rose to his feet. He glanced up into the lower branches of the big fur tree, where the handle of E-lay-i-te's knife was barely visible in the shadows. I wonder if he has missed it yet, he asked himself, as he hurried into the lodge to check on Bat.

Four days passed. Bat was improving but was still unable to use her hind leg. Enir became worried because he was almost out of meat. He was afraid to leave Bat alone at the lodge because of her lingering hatred for Indians. He contemplated using a rawhide rope and tying her inside the lodge, but he discarded the idea because Bat had never been tied. At last he decided to design a latch whereby the door of the lodge could be fastened from the outside. When this was accomplished he made plans to leave early the next morning in hopes of making a quick kill. That evening, after giving Bat the last of his meat, he ate only a handful of dried berries and retired early.

"There is nothing wrong with your appetite," he said to Bat, after watching her swallow the meat and beg for more.

Enir was sleeping soundly in the early morning hours when Bat woke him with her persistent whines. "What's the matter, old girl?" he asked as he reached for his bow. He made his way to the door, and opening it a tiny bit, he peeped out. Bat whined coarsely, and placing her nose in the opening, she attempted to force her way past. "So, it is your boyfriend," whispered Enir as he opened the door and let her out. I figured that he would eventually be around, he said to himself as he watched Bat limp toward the shadows of the big fir tree. When his eyes became more accustomed to the darkness, he was able to see the outline of the great wolf. The picture that it brought to his mind caused him to shudder. With his bow in readiness, he stepped outside and saw the dark shadow blend with the deeper darkness. He called to Bat, whose form he could barely distinguish in the dim starlight, but she failed to respond. He called again, and she answered with a low whine. Alerting his senses and holding his bow in position, he proceeded slowly to where she stood.

What he saw caused him to pass his hand over his eyes and look again. For there at the edge of the deeper shadows was the body of a full-grown doe. He reached down and felt it and found it to be still warm. When Bat whined with pleasure, he said, "Don't thank me, thank your boyfriend." As he dragged the doe to the center of the clearing, he looked up and checked the position of the stars. Why, it is almost daylight, he said to himself, and entering the lodge, he quickly dressed and then sought his knife. An hour later there was a thick steak broiling over the coals, and the aroma of fresh venison filled the lodge. Enir smiled as he looked down at Bat and said, "I'll bet that I'm the only man in the world who is guilty of sponging off a wolf."

With his supply of meat miraculously replenished and with a lattice door for the lodge strongly constructed of slender boughs bound together by rawhide thongs, Enir decided that it was time for him to go walking with So-he. He could feel his heart pounding beneath his ribs, and his stride automatically lengthened as he approached the lodge of I-lip-a-taw. He freely admitted to himself that this attractive Indian maid had never been completely out of his thoughts since she had handed him the bow. "So-he's bow," he whispered, then to himself, I wonder . . .

As he neared the lodge, he saw the tall form of the bowmaker emerge from its door and come striding to meet him. Enir stopped and gave the customary greeting sign of the Flathead. I-lip-a-taw returned the sign and said, "Come with me to the lodge of Na-bab-i-ti. When we return, So-he will be waiting." Enir obediently turned and walked beside the bowmaker to a lodge only a short distance away. Na-bab-i-ti rose from where he had been sitting in the shade of a large tree and came to meet them. When they had exchanged greetings in the sign language, Na-bab-i-ti, the crippled medicine man, laid his right hand upon Enir's shoulder and said in the strange voice that his deformities forced him to use, "Welcome to my lodge, Enir Halverson. You will always be welcome here." Enir was taken by surprise at this gesture of friendship, but he quickly gave the recognition sign of Na-bab-i-ti's rank. "I thank the great Na-bab-i-ti," he said, and took a seat upon the log that the medicine man had indicated.

When they were all three seated, I-lip-a-taw said, "Enir Halverson, this is the only living man who has returned from visiting White Bosom Bare. Would you like to hear his story?"

"I would be both delighted and honored," replied Enir. I-lip-a-taw signaled to the medicine man, and he began without preliminaries. His deep-chested voice, which his disfigured mouth forced him to use, plus the monotony of the Salish tongue, caused an eerie feeling to creep over Enir as this strange story unfolded.

"A messenger of the Great Spirit is chosen with care. He must be tested for strength, wisdom, courage, and endurance. His mind must also be trained to hear the commands of the Great Spirit. I was so prepared. Tar-wa-ba-te, who was the messenger at that time, was very old and almost blind. He was my teacher. The period of my training was very long and hard. There were times when I thought that I would surely fall, but the Great Spirit gave me courage and I continued. The last part of my training was that I should be placed for one moon in the Canyon of Loneliness. There, during this time, I could speak to no one but the Great Spirit, who would answer me through the voices of his lesser creatures, which I had to learn to understand. To reach this Canyon of Loneliness, I had to travel far and I had to shun all people and let myself be seen by no one. In the Canyon of Loneliness there are no people. The Great Spirit has placed a curse around it, and only the ones who have his permission may enter. Before I departed from Tar-wa-ba-te, he explained to me the location of the stone ladder. It was not until I had been in the Canyon of Loneliness for many days that I realized I had stood at the foot of it many times without being aware of its presence.

"My first task, after leaving the Canyon of Loneliness, was to reach this ladder and ascend it without being seen by anyone. To do this, I had to travel by trails that were strange to me and sometimes very dangerous because I had to travel them in darkness. I had to seek and ascend this ladder while the moon was small, and at this time the wailing forest wails its loudest. As I climbed, the wailing was constantly in my ears, which caused my fingers to tremble and my step to falter. I reached the summit of the curved mountain, on whose northern slopes the forest is located, just at daybreak. The forest had ceased to wail, and I was able to pass through it while it was silent.

"My shadow had begun to grow long before I reached the stream that forms the north boundary of this forest. I had to mark my trail well in order to be able to find the top of the ladder on my return. I was thankful for the silence and the fresh, cool water, and also that the great moose bull, whose antlers resemble the roots of a mighty tree, gave no heed to my presence. I carried my bow, but the Great Spirit had commanded me to slay only the grouse and the water rat, which I needed for food.

"When I stood on the banks of the stream and gazed at the colorful valley before me, my heart grew very large. I was greatly impressed by the enormity of the great meadow which lay between the stream and the distant snow. Even though I had already traversed the wailing forest, the peaks were still very far away. Never had I dreamed that the valley was so vast or that the peaks were so high.

"I crossed the stream on a beaver dam, and by sunset I was lost in the vast sea of tall grass. Even though the Great Spirit assured me, I found myself unable to conquer my fear. The grunting of the wolf, the screams of the cougar, the thoughts of the beast whose tracks I had seen in the mud of the stream, and the sounds of unknown beasts who crashed through the tall grass above me caused my knees to become weak and turned my blood to water. With the presence of death all around me, I turned and fled back toward the stream. But before I reached it, the forest began to wail. At last I stumbled out of the

93

tall grass and upon the spongy strip of bare ground which separates it from the stream, and there I fell upon my face and earnestly invoked the aid of the Great Spirit. Finally I ceased to tremble, and I was able to hear the voice of the Great Spirit, which told me to go to the beaver dam, where I would find many dry sticks. Then, in the center of this strip of spongy ground that was bare of grass, I should build a small fire, and in its light I would be safe. He added that I had to keep the fire burning until daybreak and would need many pieces of dry wood. He warned me that only the light would frighten away his beasts and that I had to keep it burning brightly.

"I obeyed these orders, but when my fire began to burn brightly, a great host of demons gathered in a half-circle in the grass about me, and I found myself between a great wall of flashing eyes and the eerie wail of the demons of the forest. The skin upon my head grew very taut, and my hands and chin trembled uncontrollably. I placed more wood upon the fire, hoping to frighten some of them away, but more gathered instead. So I began my death chant. I ceased when a great cloud obliterated the stars. In the deep darkness, other eyes joined those that were there, and I began to hear vicious snarls and shrill screams, and I resumed my death chant. At this moment the sound of distant thunder was heard, and then the snows began to sing. I ceased my death chant and listened closely to this strange sound, and to my surprise the sea of flashing eyes began to disperse. As the sound grew in volume, all of the eyes disappeared, and when it ended there was not a single pair of eyes before my fire. The wailing of the forest also became dim and muted, and a great breath of cold air settled upon me. Shivering from cold, I piled more wood upon the fire and drew my blanket close about me.

"The silence grew very oppressive, and the cold continued. Before I realized it, my supply of wood had run out. I was afraid to leave the fire to go in search of more, so I drew my blanket over my face and lay very still. The cold gradually subsided and I slept. I do not know how long I slept because the clouds continued to hide the stars, but I was awakened by a loud grunting sound, and the first thing I noticed was that my fire no longer burned. I started to rise, and it was then that I became aware of a terrible beast towering above me. The starlight was very dim, but I could see that the monster stood upright and that his splayed feet were as large as doeskins and his great claws left deep grooves where they were buried in the spongy earth. I glanced up and saw that his head was among the stars and that his terrible eyes gleamed wickedly, reflecting the light from the dying embers of my fire. I was convinced that I was looking upon death, and my first thought was to die bravely. So, in disobedience to the command of the Great Spirit, I quickly raised my bow and sent an arrow into his breast. I was conscious of a dreadful roar just as my spirit left me.

"I do not know how long I lay there beside the ashes of my fire, but when I woke there were two suns just above the tops of the distant mountains. My clothing was caked with blood, and I was too weak at first to rise. I felt no pain, but there was a numbness throughout my entire body. My left arm refused to do my bidding, and when I looked, I saw that it was no longer an arm, but only a piece of broken and shredded flesh. My head felt strange, and raising my right hand, I found that part of my scalp was dangling loosely about my ear. As my hand explored my numb face, I found that the right side of it had also been torn away. It was then that I asked the Great Spirit for death, for I no longer felt a desire to live. The Great Spirit's answer came quickly.

" 'Na-bab-i-ti, you are my messenger,' it said. 'Your legs are sound, and so is your right arm. Go into the water, put meat into your injured mouth, and swallow it with the water. Then go quickly to the stone ladder before your eyes become swollen. I will guide you. You are my messenger.' I remember no more, but they say that I was found the next day and escorted here."

After Na-bab-i-ti had finished speaking, he sat staring into the distance, and Enir was convinced that he was reliving his dreadful experience. Enir's mind raced back over the strange story, touching upon the wailing forest, and the singing snow, then back to the mysterious stone ladder. He remembered that the old Indian had said he had stood beneath it many times without knowing that it was there. Had Na-bab-i-ti also been searching for the stone ladder? he asked himself. He longed to ask some questions but knew that it would be both useless and dangerous. Although he had given his word never to enter the sacred valley, he still could not dismiss from his mind this mysterious stone ladder. I wonder what it looks like? he asked himself. Was it really a ladder or just a series of ledges? It must be easy to climb, he thought, or anyone as badly injured as Na-bab-i-ti evidently had been could not have climbed down it. His own experience with a big grizzly reminded him of how a similar beast would appear to a frightened Indian. But the singing snow and the wailing forest were not so easy to account for. There must be something to it, he said to himself, or this legend would not have survived so long without alternation. But what?

I-lip-a-taw put an end to Enir's mental abridgments by rising to his feet. Enir did likewise, then turning to the medicine man, he said, "Enir Halverson thanks the great Na-bab-i-ti for honoring him with his story." He then handed him a silver dollar, which he had fished from his belt, saying, "Would you accept this metal picture as a gift?" Na-bab-i-ti accepted the coin without a word and began to examine it curiously. Enir then turned and overtook I-lip-a-taw, who had already started back toward his lodge. He fell into step beside him, and they walked along in silence. Enir was convinced that I-lip-a-taw had had a reason for bringing him here, and he thought he knew what it was. This wise old Indian knew that his curiosity concerning the sacred valley was far from satisfied, and he wished to make sure that this curiosity would not cause him to break his promise before he had made any final decisions about it. So he silently resolved that he would be careful to drop no sign, token, or word that would lead I-lip-a-taw to believe that he had not succeeded. But he also resolved that sometime in the future, after all suspicions concerning him were allayed, he would find that stone ladder if it were visible to the human eye.

During his walk with So-he, Enir found that, although she was familiar with almost every part of the great valley, she knew very little about the business of Chief Wa-neb-i-te and his followers. She had been to the great waterfall and had seen the rubble at the foot of the curved mountain, but she gave no hint that she had ever heard the stone ladder mentioned by anyone. Enir was careful to ask no pointed questions concerning the sacred valley, but he did try to find out the reason for this village being so vastly different from other villages. Why were there no small children, young men, dogs, rubbish pits and cluttered pathways, and so few beaten trails? So-he, having lived most of her life in this village, did not realize that it was different from other villages, so Enir decided that he would have to get the information from some other source.

Chapter 9

Bat soon recovered enough to accompany Enir on short hunts, and the exercise caused the soreness in her bruised leg to diminish rapidly. Enir took advantage of the opportunity to stock up on meat against the time when she would again be incapacitated. The great dark wolf, to whom Enir had given the name "Shadow," had ceased to bring his offerings when meat began to hang from the tree limbs. Each day, though, he grew bolder, and finally he made no attempt to hide his presence from Enir. Nor would he flee into the forest when he came near him. Enir made no attempt to make friends with him but would often talk to him in the same soft voice he used when talking to Bat. He would always use the name "Shadow" when speaking to him. The wolf would sometimes cock his head slightly when his name was mentioned, but Enir never caught a gleam of friendliness in those steady green-gray eyes.

One day while Enir was busy slicing meat for drying, Shadow emerged from the forest and lay down less than a hundred feet from where he stood. This was the closest he had ever approached, and Enir took the opportunity to study him while pretending not to notice his presence. A few minutes had passed before Enir realized that the wolf was also studying him. Presently Shadow rose and quickly disappeared into the forest. Enir saw him glance up the trail as he crossed it, and following his glance, he saw a strange animal standing motionless in the path some hundred yards away. He reached quickly for his bow, but the animal moved, and he recognized it as E-lay-i-te staggering under the weight of a loosely rolled bearskin. He resumed his labor but hid a broad smile when E-lay-i-te approached. This smile was prompted by two reasons. First, E-lay-i-te was walking stooped over to balance his load and at the same time was endeavoring to keep his eyes glued upon the spot where he had seen Shadow disappear. Second, the Indian's chin was pointing about ten degrees off center, which told Enir that his jaw had been improperly set. Enir did not raise his eyes from his work until he heard the bearskin hit the ground in the clearing. When he looked up, he found E-lay-i-te standing with his back toward him, gazing intently into the forest where Shadow had disappeared. When he turned, Enir was aware of a deep scowl upon his face, so he gave no friendly greeting. After gazing sullenly at Enir for a few seconds, the Indian said, "You look good at bearskin." Enir stepped over to untie the loosely rolled bearskin and examined it closely. It was very soft and pliable, and he wondered how such a job had been accomplished under such primitive conditions. He stepped back and looked with pride upon the huge skin, which seemed to cover half the clearing.

"Tell your squaw that she did a fine job," he said. E-lay-i-te asked sullenly, "Can I have knife now?" Enir, who had forgotten about the knife, glanced up into the lower branches of the tree under which they stood. E-lay-i-te looked also, and his sharp eyes remained fastened upon the tip of the knife's handle, which was almost invisible. Just at this instant, Bat appeared in the open door of the lodge, and baring her teeth she growled menacingly. E-lay-i-te whirled around, and when his eyes rested upon Bat, they grew round with fright. Enir spoke to her softly and she subsided. E-lay-i-te stood in the center of the clearing, looking first at Bat then off into the forest, but he said nothing.

Pushing by Bat, Enir entered the lodge and reappeared with his ax. He handed it to E-lay-i-te, saying, "You go cut long pole and get knife." E-lay-i-te took the ax but stood still, looking questioningly at Enir then off into the forest. "He is the mate of my dog," said Enir, "he will not bother you." E-lay-i-te took two halting steps toward the edge of the forest then stopped. "How do you know that he won't bother me?" he asked. Enir was silent while he looked into E-lay-i-te's scowling face. "Do you have anger in your heart for me?" he asked. E-lay-i-te stood for a moment looking down at his toes, then replied, "I have anger only for my squaw."

Enir thought for a minute, then asked, "Why do you have anger for her?"

"Squaw she fight like hell. She make me carry bearskin. She say if she carry it, she not bring knife." Enir smiled and said, "I will go with you." So together they recovered E-lay-i-te's knife, and the scowl immediately left his slightly crooked face. He turned toward the trail, then he looked again into the forest, saying, "Very big wolf."

"Yes," replied Enir, "he is mine. You tell other braves that he is mine and that they are not to harm him." E-lay-i-te stared into Enir's eyes for a moment, then whirled and walked briskly up the trail.

Enir constructed a strong lean-to on the back of his lodge, and upon its dirt floor he placed Bat's bed. She seemed to appreciate her new quarters, and one day, while he was working at the spring, Enir saw Shadow slip from the bushes and inspect it through the wide outside door. Enir was pleased when he refused to enter it, but he noticed that a day seldom passed now that he did not visit Bat.

One night during a heavy rainstorm, Bat gave birth to four roly-poly pups, two males and two females. She seemed proud of her accomplishment and whined with pleasure at Enir's excitement. Enir spoke softly to her and stroked her head while his eyes closely examined each pup. He noted that the wolf markings were dominant in all of them, but the largest male seemed to have heavier bone structure and a wider head than the others, which caused him to resemble a dog pup much more than the other three. "I will name him Wo-dan," he said, "and he shall be the king of all dogs."

Bat was a jealous mother and refused to let Shadow come near the lean-to. For several nights Enir was awakened by her vicious snarls, and he knew that Shadow was getting anxious to meet his family. Enir paid them no mind, for he was determined not to interfere with their arrangements. There was one thing that worried him, however. Shadow seemed to always be nearby, and each day he grew bolder. He would approach very near when Enir took one of the pups from the lean-to, and Enir watched with interest as his sharp eyes examined it closely. Enir realized that he had unconsciously ceased to regard Shadow as the dangerous wild beast he was, and had allowed himself to think of him as another member of his household. This will never do, he told himself. Suppose a stranger should come to his lodge while he was away? So-he, for instance. What would be Shadow's reaction? The thought caused him to shudder. He thought of some of the things that the old factor back at the trading post had told him and worried even more.

Enir's anxiety over not being able to tell So-he

about the arrival of the pups soon came to an end, for when the pups were three weeks old, Shadow's visits became less frequent. So one morning he went to I-lip-a-taw's lodge and told her of his good fortune. So-he immediately begged her mother for permission to accompany Enir back to his lodge to see them. Her mother finally gave her consent, with the stipulation that she would not tarry long nor would she enter Enir's lodge. So-he quickly agreed, and Enir was conscious of a guilty blush. When they arrived at the lodge, So-he preceded Enir round the corner and surprised Shadow, who had just deposited the body of a fawn near the door of the lean-to. He did not retreat but bared his terrible fangs and snarled defiantly. So-he shrank back against the wall of the lodge, pale and trembling with fear. Enir quickly stepped between her and the wolf and began speaking to him in the soft voice that he habitually used. He called his name repeatedly, and Shadow ceased to snarl, but his cold green eyes remained fixed upon So-he. He fell back at Enir's unhesitating approach, but So-he remained pale and trembling. Enir assured her that everything was under control, an assurance he far from felt when he turned his back to single out Wodan for So-he to meet. He noticed that Shadow had halted at the edge of the brush, which was only a few yards away, and it was plain that he intended to retreat no farther. Enir tried his best to ignore him, but when Bat followed him out and bared her teeth at So-he, he felt a bit shaky. He spoke reassuringly to Bat and quickly pushed between her and So-he, then handed So-he the pup. So-he momentarily forgot her fear at the sight of the chubby little puppy and sank to her knees, cooing over it and stroking it gently. Wo-dan yawned, and seizing one of her fingers in his toothless mouth, he wagged his stubby little tail. Bat

103

watched So-he pet the pup for a minute, then she came slowly forward and licked her fingers. When she did this, Shadow turned and disappeared into the thick brush, and Enir breathed with relief, for he was convinced then that So-he was accepted.

When Enir returned from seeing So-he home, he placed his gold pan upon the coals in his fireplace, and into it he tossed a loin from the small deer Shadow had provided. While it was sizzling, he sat down upon his bunk and began to seriously contemplate his future. I came here, he told himself, to search for a dead man's cache. A cache no living person besides myself knew existed. Then his eyes traveled to the bow that hung upon the wall beside the bunk. "So-he's bow," he said aloud, then dropped back to his silent meditation. Because of this bow, he had killed a man. With it, he had accomplished a feat that had astounded an entire tribe of Indians. It had also placed him under the suspicion of an influential person who had divined his intentions and had effectively moved to block them. Furthermore, this person had used the bow to wrest from him the secret of Dead Man's Cache.

Strangely enough, it was not these things that caused his present worry. For he no longer experienced that feeling of bleak disappointment when he thought about the promise he had made. When he considered the lives that would be lost, the havoc wreaked in this beautiful valley, and the price others would have to pay for his success, he lost his desire to search for the bonanza above the falls. The task that immediately faced him was one of making a decision. A decision upon which his entire future was delicately balanced. Was his desire for So-he, which caused his heart to swell and his loins to tremble, strong enough to still forever the call of distant

104

horizons? Would it suppress his desire to search for gold and erase from his mind the pictures of riches and grandeur that flashed into it when he saw the glitter in his gold pan? He realized that he must make this decision soon, for this desire must either be satisfied or forgotten. To forget, he must go away immediately. He must not only go far away, but he must go alone and soon. He must leave Bat with Shadow and do as Stripe had done, make footprints far apart in the trail. He must cross over the mountains and on the other side forever remain. I must be strong in my decision, he told himself severely. I will not take her and love her, then leave her in tears and disgrace. I must find another place, where the deposits of gold in the stream beds have no ties with my conscience.

It was at this point that two things happened to disturb his thoughts. Bat, who had smelled the odor of the cooking meat, scratched upon the door just as Enir's eyes locked again upon So-he's bow. Very, very slowly he rose to his feet. With the bow balanced delicately in his hand, and taking long, purposeful strides, he walked to the door and threw it open. "Come in, old girl," he said. "I am glad you called, for I fear that I was losing my reason." He then walked briskly to the fire and turned the meat. His heart felt light and his head slightly dizzy as he sat back down upon the bunk. "How could I ever look into her eyes and give her back the bow?" he asked aloud. And where, he asked himself, could I ever find a girl half so beautiful, gentle, and obedient? Who cares for gold when one already has something that all the gold in the world cannot buy? If my desire to roam overcomes me, we will roam together, for tomorrow I will speak to I-lip-a-taw.

It took a long time the next morning for Enir to decide on how to approach I-lip-a-taw on the subject he had in mind. It took still more time for him to gain enough courage to do so. At last, he decided upon the approach that was in harmony with his character, blunt and direct. However, when he reached the lodge and found I-lip-a-taw alone outside, busily sorting bow wood upon his crude work bench beneath the large tree that grew some fifty yards from his lodge, many questions began to pop into his mind. What if he should disapprove because Enir was a paleface? What if he should tell him that So-he was already promised? What if So-he, herself, should refuse to take this final step? Although he was well aware that the girl had but little voice in such matters among Indians, he was also aware of I-lip-a-taw's concern about his daughter's welfare. Well, he told himself, if I am going to get turned down, it will be less embarrassing if we are alone. So he forced himself forward with determined strides.

I-lip-a-taw continued to work upon the bow wood, pretending that he did not see Enir until he entered the shade of the big tree. When he finally raised his eyes, Enir asked bluntly, "Do I have your permission to wed So-he?" For a full minute I-lip-a-taw gazed into Enir's eyes, then his shoulders seemed to sag as he leaned upon the crude bench where he had been measuring and sorting bow wood. Enir forced himself to stand erect and refused to lower his eyes while he awaited the bowmaker's answer.

Presently I-lip-a-taw drew a deep breath and said, "You are a strange man, Enir Halverson. You slay the great bear, tame the great wolf, and slay our strongest braves with your bare hands. Yet you speak to me as a child would speak to his father. Tell me first, what Enir Halverson, who talks so straight and strikes so hard, would do if I should say no?

Would he go sulk in his lodge and lament to the Great Spirit? Would he go weeping from the village like a whipped child? I think not, Enir Halverson. So what is there for me to say?"

"You could say yes, and we would remain friends," replied Enir. "But she is your daughter."

"Then that is what I shall say, Enir Halverson, yes. But there are also many other things I would say." He moved over and seated himself upon the bench, motioning Enir to sit beside him.

I-lip-a-taw let his shoulders sag slightly as he gazed out into the forest. Presently he began to speak softly, supplementing the beautiful Salish language with the universal sign language.

"So-he's mother is half French. For some reason, our three sons died in their infancy. So-he is our only child, and we love her very much. I have promised my squaw that she will be the only squaw I will ever have, so I will never have a son. So-he has led a sheltered life. She works with her mother making clothes, preparing skins, and storing food, but she has never carried heavy burdens, dug for roots, or dragged in the wood. She has helped me with my work and understands it well, but we have never allowed her to do the heavy work. You must be prepared for this, Enir Halverson, and do not blame her for not knowing. There are other things that I will also tell you. You, who have no fear, have lived a dangerous life. Much more dangerous than that the Flathead live. I realize that in doing so you have gained much knowledge of the wilderness and will always supply plenty of meat, but do not expect So-he to share your bravery. Last night she woke us screaming that a great wolf was in our lodge and was attacking her. Upon questioning her, I found that she had witnessed you, with no weapon in your hand, face down a mighty wolf, whose fangs were longer than her finger and whose snarls were more vicious than a cornered cougar's. She also watched from the forest while you knocked one man senseless and raised another high into the air with your foot. She helped E-lay-i-te's squaw prepare the skin of the great bear you slew, then that night she dreamed that it had come alive in the lodge and woke us with her screams. She listened while a squaw told of witnessing your fight with Ba-ep-o-lic and of how you slew him with a single blow as easily as one picks up a stick. She thinks, Enir Halverson, that there is nothing that you cannot do. But you and I know that upon the field of battle, when the arrows fly as thick as angry hornets, they are no respecter of persons. So-he has never seen a scalp taken, nor witnessed the carnage of battle. Neither has she seen a wounded buffalo bull suddenly come to life and rise among a group of squaws and children who were busy skinning and preparing meat. She has never seen the bloody horns as they toss people right and left, nor heard the screaming squaw whose entrails trail her in the grasses. All of these things, which are common to you, she knows nothing of. And it is because of this that I warn you. I know that you cannot change Enir Halverson, nor would I have you do so, but I beg you to be kind to my daughter. It sometimes makes me sad when I realize that she has given her heart to one who is so quick to gamble his life, for, you see, we love her very much. But if you are compelled to do these things, Enir Halverson, I beg you to remember that I give unto your care our gentle So-he. If you love her, think deep upon these things and be not so quick to risk your life. I-lip-a-taw has spoken."

For several moments, Enir remained silent. He realized that I-lip-a-taw had sorely overrated him, but he also knew that if he attempted to straighten him out, he would only add the virtue of modesty to the already tremendously bloated image the Indian held in his mind, so he said nothing. While I-lip-a-taw sat in silent meditation, Enir made a mental list of all the heroic deeds that the bowmaker had given him credit for. What if I should tell him that I accidentally provoked the great grizzly by an impulsive and stupid action, which I deeply regretted until the last blow fell, or that the great wolf was not tame and that he tolerated my presence solely because of the sex of my dog. I could also tell him that Bat alone was responsible for my great success at hunting and that while she was disabled, I lived by sponging off of a wolf. While these thoughts were flashing through his mind, another statement stood out in bold relief. "So-he thinks that there is nothing that you cannot do." Father Odin, help me, prayed Enir silently, then to himself he said, what am I letting myself in for?

Presently, I-lip-a-taw heaved a great sigh and said, "We will go now to talk with So-he's mother. She will be delighted, but there are also some things that she has been waiting to tell you." As Enir followed I-lip-a-taw to the lodge, he thought this last statement over. So they have been waiting for it, he said to himself. It was then that he remembered the smiles that were exchanged when So-he's mother saw him emerge with the bow. Who won whom? he asked himself, then immediately he experienced a feeling of guilt. Enir Halverson, you are becoming vain, he thought. Then he warned himself to be careful not to let himself believe all of these things which I-lip-a-taw had so generously given him credit for.

In the serious conversation with So-he's mother,

Enir learned many things. First, that it took a tremendous amount of dried or cured meat to last throughout the long winter months. Second, he learned that the stormy weather would soon be upon them and that it was necessary for all of this to be prepared before the snow came. He was told that there were usually many rain storms and much unsettled weather preceding the snows and that this would make preparing winter food more difficult. Therefore he should bring all of his meat to I-lip-a-taw's lodge so So-he's mother could help her prepare it. He was shown the location of the root cellar and told to report any field of root-bearing plants he should discover.

"Is there no fresh meat in winter?" he asked I-lip-a-taw.

"Snow get very deep," replied I-lip-a-taw. "Goose go away, and the deer, wapiti, and moose hide well in the deep forest. The wolf and the cougar catch all the rabbits, and the bear go to sleep. Not much hunt in winter."

Enir brought all of the meat he had swinging to So-he and told her where he had located a large field of bulbous roots. He also told her where he had found a small field of late berries. His next move was to build a door for the lean-to, shut the pups inside, and put Bat back to work. Bat, who was now thin and supple, seemed to enjoy working, and Enir brought so many carcasses of deer and wapiti to I-lip-a-taw's lodge that at last So-he's mother reluctantly told him to bring no more.

Because of the slightly mysterious rank held by I-lip-a-taw in his village, Chief Wa-neb-i-te announced that So-he's wedding would be celebrated by a feast. This ceremony was traditionally reserved for the wedding of chieftans and the birth of their children, but because the people in this tiny outpost seldom had the opportunity to attend one of these celebrations, Wa-neb-i-te decided to forego this tradition and honor I-lip-a-taw's daughter with a local celebration. He set the time for the full moon of October. Enir promised to furnish a wapiti for the feast, provided that some of them would help him build a small room, or lean-to, on his lodge. The arrangements were made, but the squaws refused to help because of Bat and Shadow. So the task was eventually accomplished by Enir and I-lip-a-taw.

Although the scheduled feast was yet a long way off, the squaws were already bustling about making plans for it and took delight in making obscene remarks to the blushing So-he. Enir was also busy decorating and cleaning up his lodge. He built some shelves and crude furniture for the new lean-to, enlarged his bunk, and filled a new doeskin mattress with soft, springy moss.

He had worked all day and was sleeping unusually soundly when he was suddenly awakened. He quickly rose to a sitting position and was passing his hands over his face trying to figure out what had woken him, when a tremendous thunderbolt seemed to jar the entire valley. He quickly rose and was feeling his way to the door, intending to take a look around, when another bolt of thunder smote his ears and large raindrops began to splatter on the roof. He had reached the door and opened it a tiny bit when a flash of lightning almost blinded him and his entire body seemed to feel the prick of a thousand needles. Blended with the terrific thunderbolt that accompanied the flash was another crashing sound, which seemed to be in the back of the lodge. Enir was partially stunned for a few seconds, and when his ears stopped ringing, he heard the muted yelping of a puppy in distress. The rain was falling in torrents, but he could still hear the yelping of the pup, and he knew that it was coming from the tiny lean-to on the back, which he now called his doghouse.

Without hesitating, Enir quickly pushed his way into the storm. The heavy sheets of rain almost halted his progress, but after he had gained the protection of the wall of the lodge he was able to make it. When he reached the back of the lodge, he shielded his eyes from the rain with both hands and stood astounded at what the wicked flashes of lightning revealed. A bolt of lightning had struck a nearby tree, and half of its severed body had fallen squarely across the doghouse. The walls had buckled and partly collapsed. The torn roof hung awry on top of the teetering structure, which trembled violently at each jarring thunderbolt. The frenzied yelping which came from this rubble caused Enir to disregard the danger, fall to his knees, and begin to feel about in the stygian darkness. He found a pup who was pinned to the muddy floor by a small lodgepole. He quickly released him and the yelping stopped. He felt around over the flooded floor of the wrecked hut and listened closely, but there was no trace of the other pups. So, hugging the wet, bedraggled puppy in his arms, he backed out of the rubble and fought his way to the door of the lodge. Laying the puppy upon the bunk, he felt his way to the fireplace and began searching in the damp ashes for some live coals. The rain had fallen down the chimney, but over against one wall he succeeded in finding a few live coals. He slid his kindling box over near them and carefully coaxed a tiny flame. He then lit his tallow-pot and hurried back to see about the pup. It was Wo-dan, and he was fast asleep. Enir examined him closely but found no mark or bruise upon him.

He was deeply worried about the other pups, but the storm seemed to have increased its intensity, and he knew that until it had abated, there was nothing he could do.

Enir discarded his wet underclothes, and gathering the sleepy puppy in his arms, he lay down upon the bunk to wait. The pup immediately wriggled free, then curled up beside him and went back to sleep. For perhaps an hour, Enir lay listening to the raging elements, and then the thunder slowly receded and the rain began to settle down to a steady downpour. Deciding that he could stand it no longer, Enir drew on his moccasins to protect his feet, and, with the rest of his body naked, he stepped out the door and again felt his way to the wrecked doghouse. The lightning, though hardly so brilliant, was yet frequent, and Enir was able to verify his former diagnosis of what had happened. He thought that he saw movement in the low shrubbery a few yards below and went down to investigate it. What he found was far from encouraging. The ravine was now a raging torrent, and in the flashing light, Enir saw great masses of debris, several floating logs, and large masses of dirty foam swirling rapidly by. He watched for a minute, then turned and sadly made his way back to his lodge, convinced that he knew what had happened to the other puppies. The shock had thrown them into confusion, and when the hut collapsed, they had made a dash for safety and had been swept away by the angry stream. Bat was probably trying to save them, but he had scant hopes for her success.

Enir was rudely awakened the next morning, just after daybreak, by two awkward paws being pressed against his naked breast. He opened his eyes, and the sight of Wo-dan's gangling form reared up on the bunk caused the memory of the night before to strike him like a dash of cold water. He leaped to his feet, expecting his newly tidied lodge to be changed to suit the fancy of an active pup, but was surprised to see everything still in place. Suddenly there was a scratching sound on the lodge door, and he quickly opened it to see a very, very bedraggled and leg-weary Bat standing before it. When she came into the lodge, Wo-dan began to leap about joyfully, but Bat turned her tired, sad eyes toward Enir. Enir dropped to his knees and began to stroke her head and talk to her in the soft voice he habitually used. "I know that you did your best, old girl," he said, then began to massage her tired legs. Bat went over to the corner where her bed used to be and lay down. Her pitiful condition caused Enir to experience a lump in his throat. He quickly caught Wo-dan and put him outside, then drew on some dry clothes and went out to survey the damage the storm had done.

After he had fed the dogs, pressed his wet buck-skin suit, and eaten a huge breakfast, Enir started the arduous task of cutting away the fallen tree and rebuilding his doghouse. For two long days he labored, and the strenuous activity helped him forget his great loss. Bat left the lodge each of these mornings before Enir rose and returned late in the evening tired and weary. Enir felt deep pangs of sorrow for her. It was not so hard for him to resign himself to the loss of the pups, because Wo-dan was underfoot so much that he was forced to tie him to a tree, but it broke his heart to see Bat so disconsolate.

Early in the morning of the third day after the storm, Shadow appeared at the edge of the clearing. He and Bat greeted each other by sniffing noses, and Wo-dan made herculean efforts to break the rawhide rope with which he was tied. Presently Shadow approached to within a few yards of the struggling pup and examined him briefly, then he and Bat disappeared into the forest. Enir, who had been secretly hoping that maybe Shadow would succeed in finding the lost pups, could tell by his actions when he greeted Bat that his efforts, too, were vain, so he went back to putting the finishing touches to the camouflaging of his new doghouse.

After deciding that Bat and Shadow had been gone long enough to prevent Wo-dan from attempting to follow them, he started over to untie him. It was then that he saw the tall form of I-lip-a-taw coming down the trail. As I-lip-a-taw walked over without a word and inspected Enir's reconstruction job, Enir smiled to himself. He knew well that every detail of what had happened was known to the Indians, and also that there would be very few questions asked. "You lose other puppies?" asked I-lip-a-taw, and Enir answered with a brief nod. "Mebbyso good," replied I-lip-a-taw callously. Enir watched the sharp eyes of I-lip-a-taw inspect the tracks of Bat and Shadow in the soft mud near the trail, then rise to survey the nearby forest. He saw him study the remains of the tree that the lightning had struck, then move to the neat pile of firewood that Enir had stacked beneath the overhanging limbs of the low juniper. "Very bad storm," said I-lip-a-taw, then he turned up the trail toward the village, walking briskly. It was not until he had passed from sight that Enir realized that he had not spoken a single word during I-lip-a-taw's brief visit. "Mebbyso good," he said to himself as he went ahead and untied Wo-dan.

Chapter 10

Since he could think of no other pressing duties to perform, Enir decided to go on a short hunt. But when he tested his bow, he found it to be just a little bit out of tune. Upon inspecting it, he found that the bowstring had absorbed enough moisture to cause it to stretch just a tiny bit, so he thought it best that he put on a new one. Selecting a new string, he carried it and the bow out to his favorite stump in front of the lodge and began the tedious task. He was almost finished when he saw I-lip-a-taw come into the clearing and, without waiting for an invitation, plop down upon a nearby stump. While Enir was finishing the job, he noticed a faraway expression in I-lip-a-taw's eyes as they gazed intently at the bow, so he asked, "Why does everybody call this So-he's bow? Did she fashion it?"

"She think she did," replied I-lip-a-taw. "So-he was very small, but she help. She rub with tiny sandstone." Then, after his eyes, still retaining the faraway expression, had wandered about over the distant mountains and forests, he began this very interesting and touching story.

"When my squaw say we have son, I put this bow to season. We have son and he die, so I leave bow to season. Squaw say again we have son; I look at bow but do not finish yet. When this son also die, I leave bow to season. Then squaw say again we have son, but when this son die, I forget about bow for many, many moons. Then, after many winters, squaw say again that we have son; I think of bow, but I do not go to look. This time it was So-he, and she was very little. She was also beautiful, and I think maybe that she also die, but she was healthy, and we loved her very much. When she was still small, she go with me to work on bows, and she would talk to me much while I worked. When she grow large enough to understand, I take this bow from season, and together we finish it. I gave the bow to her and told her that it had been many years to season. For many summers we talk about her bow. I told her that this bow was of special wood and was much better than other bows, because it had been longer to season. That it should be the bow of a mighty hunter. It is true that this bow is better than any bow I ever made. When So-he began to dream about her lover, she would often tell her mother and me that he would be a mighty warrior and with this bow he would bring home much meat. Her mother would ask her many questions about this great warrior, and So-he would answer them. This amused her mother, and she would always tell me of the things she said.

"The summers sped by swiftly, and So-he was no longer a child. My work took me far away, and each time that I returned I could see that she had grown taller and more beautiful. We began to worry much about her future. For here there are few young men who do not have squaws. I spoke to Wa-neb-i-te about going to another village, but he told me that he needed me here. It was because of the great number of soldier paleface which were, and still are, pressing toward our country. I tell him that even I could not make a bow to outshoot the paleface's thunderstick, but he said it was a bad time to move. That I should go far away to a place where I knew was much bow wood suitable for making the powerful warbow. Before I start on this journey, I ask So-he to describe this lover of hers once more, so that if I should find him, maybe I could bring him back. She described you, Enir Halverson, you, who had not yet come into this valley."

I-lip-a-taw paused so long at this point in the story that Enir thought it had ended. But since he could think of nothing to say he remained silent and thoughtfully strummed the bow. The musical sound of it seemed to bring other thoughts to the tall bowmaker, for after a moment he began again, taking up the story where he had left off.

"On the way back we stopped to leave ponies with the Flathead who live on the other side of the mountains and who hunt buffalo with ponies. There I met Ba-ep-o-lic. He was born in this valley and went with his family over the mountains to join the buffalo hunters many years ago. He asked permission to return with us, giving as an excuse that he wished to visit with his uncle and his cousins. He never mentioned So-he's name to me, but the squaws who were helping me told me that So-he's beauty was talked about by many young men among the buffalo hunters. I knew then what his intentions were, and I will say that I was not pleased. Ba-ep-o-lic was a fool. He was also cruel and very much disliked among the young men with whom he hunted. It was for that reason that I did nothing to stop the fight. I knew that you would slay him, but I expected you to use a knife. I did not want to be the grandfather of Ba-ep-o-lic's children."

Enir said nothing for several minutes, hoping that I-lip-a-taw would continue, but as the silence deepened, he asked, "How did the scout who saw me with Striped Beard describe me?"

"He described you as a tall, strong, boy," replied

I-lip-a-taw. "I did not know that it was you, nor did anyone. The scout said that there was no dog with you." Enir was silent. He felt a cold lump rise in the pit of his stomach. I could have lied my way out of it, he told himself. I could have had So-he and the gold, too. Or could I? he continued in silent thought, for somehow So-he and the gold did not embrace the same thought. Well, I have given my word, anyway. Now that I think of it, I can't say that I'm sorry, he silently concluded.

While I-lip-a-taw's eyes were again surveying the distant horizon, Enir's thoughts traveled back over the astonishing things he had learned about the Indian's way of thinking and also over the things he had heard concerning their way of life. He decided that while I-lip-a-taw was in a talking mood, he would ask a few questions which might possibly concern his own future. He had already discovered some surprising facts about the intelligence of the Indian, and he wondered how many more surprises were in store for him.

"Tell me, I-lip-a-taw," he asked, "why is it that the Indian and the paleface are at war? Why does the paleface kill the Indian with the thunderstick, when there is plenty of room for both the paleface and the Indian? Why do they fight?"

I-lip-a-taw looked long at the toes of his moccasins. Presently he said, "Paleface claim that this land all belongs to them. They claim that Indians are like wild beasts, same as cougar, bear, and wolf. They do not understand Indian's wisdom. Indian strive to protect this land, paleface seek to destroy it. Where streams were once clear, the plow of the paleface has made them muddy. They destroy the grass where the buffalo feeds, destroy the forest where the wapiti, the deer, and the moose breed, and they kill much game when they do not need it. If Indian say stop, then they kill Indian. The thunderstick will shoot much farther than the bow, but the paleface cannot see farther than his nose. Very soon there will be no buffalo, no deer, no wapiti, and no moose. Then someday there will be no more forest, not any more room, even for the paleface to live. The water will be too filthy to drink, the air will stink, and the people will be so many that they will run over one another.

"Long ago the Indian saw that this would happen unless we were careful. Long ago our forefathers knew that too many people was not good. They also knew that it was necessary that only the wisest and the strongest should survive. Then we would always be assured that the wise would govern and that their decisions would be just. The children of the Indian must be healthy to survive. He must be shrewd to prosper, quick to think and act, or he will surely die. This way we have strong race. The paleface cannot yet see this. They defile the water and ruin the land because this will give them more gold to increase their power. Someday, maybe before your grandchildren are dead, the land will be so wasted, the water will be so poison, that sickness will be everywhere. This beautiful land will rot, the air will become poison, the streams will dry up, and all the people will sicken and die, because of the stupidity of the paleface. I-lip-a-taw has spoken." He then came slowly to his feet and walked silently away toward the village.

Enir was thoughtful for several minutes after I-lip-a-taw had departed. He said to himself as he watched the tall Indian disappear up the trail toward the village, I think I-lip-a-taw speaks more with anger than with wisdom. But he thought long on some of the things that the wise old bowmaker had said. He is right about one thing, he said to himself, the white man does treat them as if they were beasts. Then his thoughts drifted to what I-lip-a-taw had said about So-he's bow. The best one he ever made, he said to himself, and So-he thinks that she helped make it. Then another thought struck him: So So-he's beauty has traveled over the mountains. He looked again at the bow, which he still held in his hands, and said aloud, "As I remember it, I had started to go hunting." Wo-dan chose this time to rouse himself and come over to Enir to be petted. Enir was fondling his large ears when Wo-dan broke away from him and looked up the trail toward the village. Enir looked and saw So-he coming purposefully down the trail. He quickly rose and started to meet her.

After they had embraced, So-he broke away, saying, "I gave my promise not to tarry. I want to take the puppy Wo-dan to our lodge. There for the next few days he will be happy to play with me and the strange things that he will find there. This will make him forget his brothers and sisters, and he will not grieve over them so much."

Enir smiled at the thought of Wo-dan grieving but said, "I thank you very much for making such a sacrifice of your time, and I am sure that Wo-dan will be pleased. Does your mother approve?"

"Oh, yes," replied So-he. "Would you please catch him for me? I must hasten back before the others see me and will make a big laugh about it tomorrow."

Enir gathered up the big, gawky puppy and placed him into So-he's arms. As she hurried away, he smiled broadly at the awkward position in which So-he held the gangling pup. His huge jointed legs protruded on either side of the slender girl, while

Wo-dan struggled desperately, not to get free, but to nuzzle So-he's face and catch her streaming hair.

The village, it seemed, had conformed with Chief Wa-neb-i-te's wish that this coming event be celebrated with gaiety and feasting. Everybody appeared to be happy and well pleased. But there were two who inwardly refused to respond to the spirit of festivity. These were the two young single men with whom Enir had first fought. The largest one, whose name was Wa-sa-sa-ti, and was known as "Stout-Boy," felt a much deeper resentment than did his slender companion, whose name was Lu-se-i-tic, and was called "Long-Step." Long-Step was unhappy chiefly because of Stout-Boy's silent grief. He, like many more, had expected Stout-Boy to eventually win So-he's hand. But Stout-Boy, who had seen no reason to do otherwise, had been content to wait until he had an opportunity to compile some facts concerning his strength and bravery to present to I-lip-a-taw before he made his bid for So-he. He was now secretly disillusioned and resentful. This strange paleface had unexpectedly appeared and quickly distinguished himself with deeds of strength, skill, and bravery, until even the great I-lip-a-taw looked upon him with wide-eyed admiration. So, alone, deep in the silent forest, Stout-Boy fingered his crooked jaw and meditated.

Stout-Boy admitted to himself that Enir Halverson had earned the praise of all the Flathead by his accomplishments. No other person to his knowledge had ever slain the great bear single-handed, tamed the great timber wolf, or slain men with his bare hands. Yes, he deserved much credit, but he did not deserve So-he. So-he belonged to him, Stout-Boy. Had he not watched and waited for her to grow into a beautiful maiden? Had he not loved her even before

122

she had learned to swim? This strange paleface had no claim upon her, and he, Stout-Boy, intended to do something about it. At last a scheme began to take form in his frustrated mind. This scheme did not exactly suit him, but it was the only one that he could think of that promised a chance for success. So, as he made his way back to the village, his mind worked desperately to perfect the details of this plan. Time was swiftly running out.

The first part of Stout-Boy's plan was for him and his friend Long-Step to gather all of their valuables and place them in a pack, which Stout-Boy carried in a hurried trip over the mountains. There he bargained for all of the firewater he could, and upon returning, he hid the firewater in a place he had previously chosen. Then he brought his canoe up very near the village and hid it beneath the overhanging limbs along the stream, where in the evening the shadows would be very deep. With these details attended to, Stout-Boy awaited an opportunity to put the rest of his plan into effect.

The second phase of the plan was to lure So-he to a certain place near the outskirts of the village, overpower and bind her, than row silently down the small stream to a predetermined spot. From there he would carry her on a marathon hike over the mountains and then to the northeast, to the land of the Blackfoot. There Stout-Boy had an aunt who was the squaw of a Blackfoot brave, and there he hoped to join the Blackfoot tribe and live out his days.

One evening just before sunset, Long-Step came hurriedly to Stout-Boy and told him that So-he had just departed for Enir's lodge to return the puppy that she had been keeping for the last few days. Stout-Boy acted immediately. He told Long-Step to pass out the firewater, while he gathered the things that he thought he would need, such as rawhide thongs, light provisions, and a gag, which he had carefully constructed. He then hastened to the place where the trail forked, which he knew would be well shadowed, and sat himself down to wait.

Chapter 11

Wo-dan had enjoyed his visit with So-he much more than So-he's mother had enjoyed his company. It had taken him but a short while to realize that he could do things here that he would be soundly slapped or tied to a tree for at home, and he had joyfully taken advantage of this discovery. The only punishment he had received here was the time that I-lip-a-taw had booted him out of his bowroom. But So-he's mother had had enough of him. So, on the afternoon of the third day, she told So-he that she should take him back to Enir's lodge. So-he had never owned a pet, nor had she had the pleasure of other children to play with for a very long while, so she was loathe to part with the playful pup. She argued with her mother that Enir was probably off on a hunt and that because of Bat and Shadow she was afraid to take him home unless she was sure Enir was there. Her mother finally told her that she could wait until evening but no longer. So, just before sunset, So-he gathered the ungainly pup in her arms and set out for Enir's lodge with her mother's warning ringing in her ears.

When So-he reached Enir's lodge, she put Wo-dan down but told Enir that her mother had made her promise not to linger. But time passed very swiftly under the circumstances, and when she at last broke away she discovered that it was almost dark. She departed swiftly up the trail, and Enir had to overpower Wo-dan to prevent him from following her.

"You loose-jointed wolf imbecile," he said to the pup affectionately, "I bet that I have to tie you to a tree tomorrow to keep you out of my mother-in-law's hair."

Enir had retired for the night when he heard I-lip-a-taw speak his name just outside the lodge door. He sprang from bed and opened the door. I-lip-a-taw entered promptly, which took Enir by surprise. He hastily lighted the tallow-pot and looked at I-lip-a-taw questioningly. I-lip-a-taw let his eyes wander around the lodge, then he said, "So-he not come home. Where is she?" Enir felt a wave of fear strike him like a breath of cold wind. His first thoughts were of Bat and Shadow, but he quickly discarded them because he knew that they had both accepted So-he as belonging to the family. But stray bears, rutting moose, cougars, and angry wapiti bulls trooped through his mind in slow motion as he hastily donned his clothing. He seized the tallow-pot, pushed I-lip-a-taw out the door, and, shutting Wodan up inside the lodge, started toward the trail. I-lip-a-taw, who had been convinced that So-he was with Enir, now began to share Enir's apprehension.

Enir proceeded swiftly to the place where he had last seen So-he running up the trail, and holding the tallow-pot close to the ground, he said to I-lip-a-taw, "I saw her running right about here." A few yards farther on they both saw the plain imprints of So-he's moccasins. I-lip-a-taw snatched the tallow-pot from Enir's hand, and holding it very low, he moved rapidly up the trail. Presently he halted and threw out his arm to stop Enir. Enir could see over I-lip-a-taw's shoulder what appeared to be signs of a struggle in the partially bare trail. I-lip-a-taw continued to hold Enir back while his sharp eyes studied each tiny mark. "Blackfoot," he whispered, then a few seconds later he said, "no, Flathead brave." Then, handing Enir the tallow-pot, he said, "You wait. I go tell Wa-neb-i-te, we get trackers." He then dashed away toward the village.

While Enir nervously waited, he lowered the tallow-pot, and by its flickering light, he studied the signs in the trail. Gradually his eyes began to make out what I-lip-a-taw had seen at a glance. One thing in particular attracted his attention. This was an extremely large moccasin print that was clearly outlined in the shallow dust. Enir was pretty well acquainted with most of the braves in the village, but he could think of none whose foot would fit a track like that. "Must be a stranger," he whispered as he continued to search for other tracks.

For perhaps a quarter of an hour Enir waited there in the silent forest. He had unlimited confidence in I-lip-a-taw and expected a group of trackers to arrive at any second. But at the end of fifteen minutes, his anxiety had overcome his patience, so, setting the tallow-pot carefully aside, he struck out for the village to see what the holdup was. But when he reached the village, he found everything very quiet, and the only sign of activity he saw was a dim light in the round lodge, or community hall, so it was to it he ran.

What Enir encountered when he stepped into the round lodge caused him to stare in amazement. Four Flathead braves lay in the center of it tied hand and foot, and he could see that they were evidently very drunk. He recognized E-lay-i-te among them, and he started toward him. Suddenly a deep rumbling voice, which he recognized as belonging to Na-bab-i-ti, the medicine man, came from the shadows. "You wait outside Enir Halverson," it said, and Enir recognized a ring of authority in it. Enir turned toward

127

the voice and saw Na-bab-i-ti standing in the shadows with his tomahawk in his good right hand.

"What is going on here? Where is everybody?" Enir asked, striving unsuccessfully to keep his agitation from his voice.

"They go hunt Long-Step," replied Na-bab-i-ti, "you wait." Enir felt a surge of resentment rise within him, only to be replaced by cold logic. These Indians considered this their business and were attending to it in their own way.

"What has Long-Step got to do with it?" he asked more calmly.

"You wait," repeated Na-bab-i-ti. Enir was spared a long wait, however, for it was only a matter of a few minutes before a group of men, headed by I-lip-a-taw, appeared, dragging the now thoroughly frightened Long-Step. No one spoke to him, nor did the fierce expression in their eyes invite conversation.

Long-Step was immediately relieved of his moccasins and strung up by the thumbs, and a small fire was kindled beneath his writhing feet. This method was very effective, for within a few minutes, the entire plot, so far as Long-Step's knowledge of it went, was disclosed. Stout-Boy was named as the culprit. He had left with So-he in a canoe headed downstream. He also confessed his part in the plot and named all the braves to whom he had distributed the liquor. Chief Wa-neb-i-te ordered him cut down, bound, and placed beside the four drunken braves. He then held a quick conference among his scouts, and they began to leave one by one as they received their assignments.

Enir, who had been ignored in this conference, went over and stood beside I-lip-a-taw. After the last brave had departed, I-lip-a-taw, who had discerned the disappointment in Enir's face, laid his arm gently across his shoulders and said, "Do not be disappointed, my son. It is just that the trackers fear that you, not understanding their methods, would hinder them. When Indians track by night, they go chiefly by sound and smell. It will soon be morning, we will wait." Wait, said Enir to himself, that is all that I have done all night, and I have began to detest the word. "Let us go to our lodges and get the things we might need to be ready," continued I-lip-a-taw, and he departed abruptly. Enir watched him disappear, then fell to thinking over what he had just said. He was forced to admit that the old Indian was right, he would be more or less in their way. But there was one word that I-lip-a-taw had mentioned that rang a bell in his mind. It was the word "smell." He stood rooted to the ground for a few seconds, then turned and started purposefully toward his lodge.

When Enir entered his lodge, the first thing he noticed was that Wo-dan had resented being left behind and had shown it by attacking everything he had found loose inside it. He quickly set the now-burned-out tallow-pot on its shelf, booted Wo-dan outside, and began to put things back into place. He also discovered that, despite his agitation, he was hungry. He threw some kindling upon the smoldering embers of the fire, set his gold pan upon it, and threw some meat on to cook. Then, disregarding Wo-dan's pleas to be admitted, he set about making preparations to put the plan that had been forming in his mind into effect.

While the meat was cooking, Enir selected several of his straightest and best-balanced arrows, checked his bow, and drew his knife many times across the whetstone. He then sat down upon the bunk and began to concentrate upon what he had heard of Long-Step's confession. Stout-Boy's plot to abduct So-he had not been formulated on the spur of the moment. It had been planned for several days. That he had also chosen a destination and a way to hide his trail, Enir had no doubt. He realized that Stout-Boy was not intelligent, but he never doubted his cunning. He was an Indian, which meant that he knew all of their tricks and had planned his escape accordingly.

Enir forcibly put aside his anger and frustration, while he coolly began to consider what Stout-Boy's plans might be. First, he could not have planned to go very far in the canoe. There were many rapids not far to the south, and also many shallows. He could not go west, because in that direction he would soon encounter barren country with sand and thorny shrubs. He could not continue south on land, because he would soon be in open country where his discovery would be certain. This left only east or northeast over the mountains. He also realized that Wa-neb-i-te's trackers were aware of this, and he had no doubt that the search would center in that direction. But he also realized that the ground there was rocky and hard and that Stout-Boy had many miles of such country in which to hide his trail.

Presently Enir rose and checked the meat upon the fire. Finding it near enough to ready he divided it into three chunks. One he tossed to the whining Wo-dan, and with another portion in his hand he stepped outside and called Bat. Bat did not respond, so he went to the doghouse and checked: She was gone. Enir felt a sharp pang of disappointment. He walked a few steps into the brush and called again, this time much louder. Still Bat did not respond. As Enir stood with the piece of half-raw meat in his hand, his eyes detected a dim track in the trail. It was not yet complete daybreak, but there was enough light for him to recognize the long, familiar footprints as Shadow's. Enir's heart sank. What an inopportune time for him to appear, he thought.

While Enir stood lost in an overwhelming wave of disappointment, he felt two overgrown paws pressed against his leg as Wo-dan reached for the piece of meat he held in his hand. Enir quickly raised it out of his reach and looked down at the gawky pup. Why not? he asked himself as another thought entered his mind. Wo-dan is very fond of So-he, and his nose is as strong or stronger than Bat's. Yes, why not?

As Enir turned slowly back to the lodge, the thought gradually grew brighter. He will be slow, Enir thought, but that might be better. He will probably give out and have to be carried, but I can let him rest. Stout-Boy will not be traveling fast, burdened as he is. He will be of little value when we overtake them, but if he can find their trail, I will do the rest, he said to himself.

So, with little more ado, Enir called Wo-dan to heel, and by the time the dawn broke over the mountains, he was traveling determinedly toward the southeast. Enir planned to circle the village and intercept the stream a few miles south of it. He knew that it would be useless to start his search within miles of the village, because Stout-Boy would surely take advantage of the swift water to carry him as far as possible. He thought that he knew to within a few miles where Stout-Boy would make his break for the mountains. He was not too well acquainted with the country that immediately parallelled the stream, but he had hunted deer along the sparsely timbered ridges and remembered that there was ample covering there for Stout-Boy to hide his trail among the rocks and gravel. So, thinking thusly, he headed straight south at as fast a speed as Wo-dan could muster.

For several miles, Enir held this pace. Wo-dan's tongue protruded, and he panted heavily. "You will soon get your second wind," Enir told him, and he refused to slacken his speed. Sure enough, within an hour Wo-dan was running easier and panting less. Enir now kept a sharp watch for partially submerged rocks, strips of solid gravel, and other places where it would be easy to hide one's tracks when leaving the stream. He found several such places, but searching around them revealed nothing either to him or to the panting pup. I will just have to slow down and let him rest a little, Enir thought as he slackened his pace.

Enir had discovered several tracks along the edge of the stream, but he had not encountered the large moccasin prints he was searching for. He knew that the tracks he had seen were those of the braves who were also searching, so he paid them little mind. I am not looking for tracks anyway, he said to himself as he pushed ahead. What he was searching for was a very rocky bar, a series of large stones, or any place where it was possible for one to leave the stream without leaving tracks. He had found only a very few of these, and those he had found all ended in a place where one's tracks would surely become visible. What he was searching for was a place where it would be possible for one to travel a very long way without leaving tracks, and thus far he had found no such place.

Presently Enir came in sight of a steep, rocky ridge, and below it he heard the sound of rapids or a low waterfall. This has to be it, he said to himself as he slowed to let Wo-dan get his wind back. As he moved carefully along, he saw a steep bench near the shoulder of a rocky rise, and he studied it closely. Wo-dan went ahead of him, and as Enir watched, the pup held his nose to the top of a large flat rock and whined coarsely. Enir's heart sprang into his throat. He knew that he had found it. He sprang ahead to Wo-dan's side and said, "So-he." Wo-dan looked all about and whined again. Enir pointed to the rocks beyond and again spoke So-he's name, but the pup only looked about them. Enir followed the chain of rocks for several yards, stopping at intervals and letting Wo-dan search for scent, but Wo-dan showed no interest. After they had followed the rocky ridge for a long way, and Enir was about ready to turn back, Wo-dan suddenly stopped on top of a large stone, placed his nose against it, and whined coarsely again. "I have hit it," said Enir in a deep whisper as he plunged ahead. He had not gone very far when Wo-dan sniffed another rock and whined. "So-he." Enir motioned toward the mountains. "Yerrumph," replied Wo-dan, and forged awkwardly ahead. They had traveled quite a long way without any encouragement when Wo-dan suddenly raised his long wolf nose and sniffed the air. "So-he," said Enir, and the pup whined again and started ahead, still holding his nose high. With his heart thumping like a war drum, Enir followed.

Presently they came to an open place where there were the unmistakeable signs of a struggle. Wo-dan ran about yelping excitedly, and Enir saw the deep imprints of very large moccasins leading toward the nearby peaks. "Go after her, Wo-dan," Enir shouted, and started running forward. He saw where Stout-Boy had stumbled and fallen, and once more Wo-dan yelped loudly. Enir suddenly realized that it was now past midday and that they had been traveling for several hours. Stout-Boy overestimated himself, thought Enir as he studied the rocky slope before him. He knew that Stout-Boy had either seen or heard them, because he now made no effort to hide his trail. He also knew from the signs of recent struggling, that So-he was hindering him more. Wo-dan was yelping almost continually now, and Enir's whole body felt as light as a feather. As he ran forward, Enir studied the rocky hill in front of them. He saw that he could cut across and possibly come up in front of them, so, leaving Wo-dan behind, he sprinted forward. But just before he reached the shoulder, for which he was certain they were headed, he came upon a very deep gorge, which separated him from the main shoulder by several hundred feet. At the same instant, he saw Stout-Boy and So-he struggling at the foot of a ledge that parallelled a very steep bluff. He heard the sound of gravel, which they had dislodged, as it fell into the gorge before him, and he felt fear grip his heart. What if So-he should fall? he asked himself as he quickly drew his bow. Placing his hands beside his mouth, he shouted, "Stop, Stout-Boy." Stout-Boy released So-he and whirled to face his back trail.

"You stop, Enir Halverson. You stop or I will throw her over the bluff. Do you hear me, Enir Halverson?" Enir saw that Stout-Boy still had his eyes on his back trail, and suddenly he knew why. When he had cut across in his effort to head them off, Wo-dan had stayed on the trail. It was Wo-dan's yelping and thrashing about that Stout-Boy had heard. Enir realized that he dare not show himself, for if he did, Stout-Boy might carry out his threat. Very carefully, he placed an arrow in his bow, and with the full power of his arm he sent the arrow speeding across the gorge. He had acted almost entirely by instinct in timing his shot. Automatically he had considered Stout-Boy as a large buck deer standing in an open spot, and he had aimed his shaft according to the estimated distance between them, at a point some three feet above Stout-Boy's head. He held his breath as he watched the flight of the arrow. For a fraction of a second it looked as though it might fall short, but suddenly it seemed to gain speed as it plunged into Stout-Boy's side just below his armpit. Stout-Boy's knees slowly began to buckle as he turned and tried to speak to So-he. But black blood began to gush from his mouth, and he began to clutch feebly at the bunch-grass which grew along the edge of the bluff. Very slowly his grip began to weaken, and he plunged over the bluff. Enir's hand trembled as he placed his bow back into position behind him. He was conscious of a wave of relief passing over him, which left his knees also trembling. He carefully ascended the gorge and climbed slowly up to where So-he lay. He found that she was weeping as he carefully drew his knife and cut her bonds. Just then, Wo-dan came lumbering up the slope and began to nuzzle her face and yelp with joy. It was only then that Enir realized he was almost completely exhausted. So-he pushed Wo-dan aside and threw her arms about Enir's neck. "I knew that you would come, Enir Halverson," she said sobbing.

"Did he hurt you, So-he?" asked Enir gently.

"Oh, no," she replied, "he was very gentle. He told me before he died that he would not have done it."

"Done what?" asked Enir.

"Thrown me over the bluff," replied So-he. "He told me while he carried me away that even when we were children playing in the water, he had loved me. He said that as long as he was alive I would not be your squaw. I believe him, Enir Halverson. For I remember that when we were small he would let no one tease me. He also brought me many presents from the forest. It had never entered my mind before, but I know now that he loved me. Although he was not bright, I cannot feel it in my heart to repay his love with hatred. Do you not see, my Enir? He did what he did because he could not help it. He knew not that he was stupid. It makes me very sad to know, now, that he loved me, and yet I had to watch him die. I wish that I could hate him, but I cannot. I have never witnessed death before."

Enir gazed down into the dark gorge for a moment, then said, "You also know that I had to do the thing I did, too, don't you?"

So-he pressed her body against Enir's and said, "Yes, my Enir, I know. Let us try to forget it for now. We are all three at peace. My father told me long, long ago that Stout-Boy would soon die because he was stupid. But I did not then know what death was."

"I am sorry now that I had to do it," Enir said.

After a moment's pause, So-he said, "It is like killing an angry moose bull when you are not hungry. It is something that has to be done. Let us try to forget it."

The sun had long before set when Enir Halverson staggered down the trail that led to the village. Upon his back rode the exhausted So-he, while in his arms he cradled a gangling, leg-weary pup. They stopped at his lodge, where they drank cool water and rested. They ate a few bites of rich deer-tongue pemmican, and then, leaving Wo-dan asleep, they slowly made their way to the village. The darkness was deep in the shadows, for large clouds hid the moon, but their hearts were light even though their feet were heavy. So-he led the way to I-lip-a-taw's lodge, but it was empty. They then made their way down the winding pathway to the lodge of Chief Wa-neb-i-te. There was a light inside, so Enir unceremoniously pushed aside the rawhide door and entered. There before a single candle sat Chief Wa-neb-i-te, I-lip-a-taw, and four scouts. As Enir and So-he entered the circle of light, every eye was widely open and every mouth agape, but no word was spoken. Enir halted, and looking about him, he said in a tired voice, "You will find the body of Stout-Boy at the bottom of a cliff far to the east, near the mountain of white stone. You will also find my arrow in his heart. Enir Halverson has spoken." And he sat down tiredly beside I-lip-a-taw.

Silence reigned for a full minute inside the lodge of Chief Wa-neb-i-te. I-lip-a-taw was the first to move. He rose suddenly to his feet and drew So-he into his long arms. "I am all right, Father," So-he said. "Stout-Boy did not harm me." By this time everyone was on their feet, but Chief Wa-neb-i-te raised his hand for silence. Then he said to Enir, who had also came wearily to his feet, "You followed a trail that my best trackers could not see, Enir Halverson. How?"

"I followed no trail," replied Enir. "I followed the son of the great wolf I call Shadow. He followed the trail." The Indians gazed at each other in silence, and So-he slid her arm gently around Enir's waist.

Chief Wa-neb-i-te stepped into the center of the lodge and said in a loud, resonant voice, "The feast will be held tomorrow evening." Then, turning to the four scouts, he said, "Go, summon everyone to the feast."

Chapter 12

Enir and So-he's honeymoon was quite in accordance with the Indian custom. Between the rainstorms, Enir stored a large supply of wood, while So-he decorated the interior of the lodge with buckskin lace and beaded bones. She also proved very adept at feathering arrows and kept Enir's knife sharp enough for him to shave every day. She was highly skilled in the culinary art, as well, and Enir ate better than he had since leaving his home in Liverpool.

Because Wo-dan worshipped So-he, Bat accepted her, but she still considered herself first in Enir's life. During the few fair days before the snows came, Enir gave Wo-dan some long hours of training. He taught him to work with the rawhide rope that he used when trailing the wapiti. But at other times, while hunting the deer, he let him run free with Bat. She, being intelligent enough to understand what Enir wished, soon had Wo-dan fairly well trained. Enir had taught Wo-dan to obey the same commands he gave to Bat, and he had responded beautifully. *I wonder how long it will be before he takes off after a bitch wolf?* Enir asked himself one day as he watched him assist Bat in herding a deer toward his hiding place.

One morning Enir woke with a strange feeling. He lay still while he tried to decide why this morning was different from other mornings. He could hear no wind or any other sound, so he rose to take a look outside. Being careful not to awaken So-he, he tiptoed to the door. When he opened it, his eyes could see nothing but a veil of whiteness. He stood for a moment and was gradually able to discern the dim outlines of the surrounding forest. As the daylight increased, he could see a myriad of gigantic snowflakes as they settled silently upon the earth. He stood fascinated as he watched the floor of the tiny clearing slowly rise. It was very beautiful. He felt the freshness of the air, but the cold was hardly noticeable.

Enir returned to the bed and woke So-he. "Come and look," he said, "it is the strangest sight that I have ever seen. The snow is falling so fast that we will soon be buried."

So-he rose and followed him to the door. She stood for a moment looking, then turning to Enir, she asked, "Is it the first time you have watched it snow in the valley?" Enir admitted that it was. "It is always beautiful," she said. "But you will grow very tired of it before it goes away."

"Yes, I know," he replied. "I have seen it snow upon the prairie, but it was nothing compared to this."

"It will not seem so long now," said So-he, "because you are here. But before you came, the winters were very long and lonesome."

Enir glanced up into the almost invisible branches of the large trees and said, "I see now why you thought that the meat was not high enough."

The snow continued for two days, then the bitter cold arrived. The lodge was almost completely buried, and Enir worked with his wooden spade, making a tunnel to the doghouse and to the firewood. "We must be very careful not to get the fire too hot," said So-he.

"Why?" asked Enir.

"Because we will be sick," replied So-he. "My father always made me get used to the cold by staying outside for a while each day. He said that if you do that, it will make you strong."

"I did not know that," said Enir. "I will let you keep the fire and say when it is warm enough."

So-he said nothing for a moment then she said, "It will take a very small fire when the snow is deep, you must also keep the chimney open, or it will make much smoke."

The first winter in the valley held many new experiences for Enir. Shadow visited them on several occasions, but it was not until late in the winter that he would partake of the food Enir offered him. When the air was still and the cold very deep, Enir and So-he would listen to the distant wolf calls late in the evenings, and Enir imagined that he could hear Shadow's voice among them.

When the snow began to melt and the honking of geese began, Bat ran away with Shadow. When they returned, Wo-dan had to relearn much of what Enir had taught him. But he did this quickly. He had grown so much during the winter that Bat seemed to have grown smaller. Bat seemed to have become more fond of So-he, and even Shadow no longer shied away at her approach. Wo-dan still worshipped her, but he had much more respect for Enir. It was Enir who always meted out his punishment, and it was Enir whom he obeyed.

One day, So-he told Enir that his son would be born in early summer. Enir seized his head in both hands and sat down upon the bunk. Babies, thought Enir, must have milk, medicine, diapers, and a score of other things. And there were none within a hundred miles. "Father Odin, help me," he groaned.

"Where does your father live?" So-he asked. "I

have heard you speak to him as if he were here with us. I like his name. I think O-din is a pretty name. I am sure that he will be proud of his grandson."

"Oh, you sweet, innocent child of the wilderness," groaned Enir as he took her gently into his arms.

"I am very glad for you," she said. "There have been so few babies at the village. Mother was so proud that she shed tears."

"What did I-lip-a-taw say?" asked Enir.

"He said for me to tell you that he was saving four bows," replied So-he. Enir groaned silently, and silently he again appealed to Father Odin.

Spring came swiftly, and soon flowers replaced the snow in the open places. Wo-dan became very proficient in the hunt and seemed to enjoy it immensely. Bat became very heavy, and one day she disappeared with Shadow. This irked Enir at first, but when he thought of the fate of the other pups, his anger abated. I can't blame Shadow, he told himself. He missed Bat for a while, but his concern for So-he consumed most of his worries. Her mother was now inside the lodge most of the time, and Enir spent many hours sitting upon one of the several stumps before it, listening to the bluejays, magpies, and various song birds, whose songs were often interrupted by the hoarse honks of mating geese. As the sun grew warmer, strange song birds arrived in the forest, but Enir was not happy.

One day a rather coarse voice bounded from the door of the lodge, and, as the birds in the surrounding trees hushed their songs, Enir rose three feet above the stump upon which he sat. "Waa, wahhhh," the voice sounded, and Enir ran to the door of the lodge, only to be met by So-he's determined mother, who pushed him away and shut and latched the door. Enir beat upon the door and threatened to tear it down, but only a low laugh answered him.

After what seemed hours, the door was opened and Enir rushed in to stare into So-he's smiling eyes. Gently she turned back the doeskin blanket, and Enir had his first glimpse of his son. He was dark, wrinkled, and withered, and Enir's knees suddenly felt weak. To him, he looked more like a wolf whelp than a baby. "Waa . . . what is the matter with it?" he asked shakily. A broad smile creased the face of So-he's mother, and she said, "There is nothing the matter with it. He is a fine strong boy."

"Why he is almost black?" asked Enir. "And look how small he is."

"His head is very large," said So-he weakly.

"Have you ever seen a small baby before?" asked So-he's mother. Enir confessed that he had not, and she continued, "In a few days, he will get lighter. Very soon he will be white, He is a very large and healthy boy, and his voice is strong. He is much longer than most babies." Enir became slightly pacified by her confident voice and evident pleasure.

"You go now and tell I-lip-a-taw. Tell him all of the things I have said." Then, pointing to Wo-dan, she continued, "And take that dog with you, before I bash his head. So-he needs rest." Enir slipped the hunting leash over Wo-dan's head and obediently took the trail to the village.

When I-lip-a-taw's long fingers carefully lifted his grandson for the first time, his eyes shone with pride. "He is a very tall one," he remarked, and thus did Enir Halverson, Jr. obtain his Indian name,

142

"Tall-One." I-lip-a-taw looked closely at the baby's long arms and wide forehead, then spoke again: "He has the head of a chieftain and the body of a warrior. He will cause you to be very happy but will grieve you much. I fear that he will be another Enir Halverson." Enir did not know whether to feel complimented or offended, but when So-he looked at him and smiled, he knew that it was meant for a compliment. She had often told him that I-lip-a-taw loved him like a son.

Although there was no milk, medicine, or modern conveniences, Tall-One did not seem to notice. He squalled loudly in his coarse voice which frightened the birds from their nests, burped, and soiled his doeskin diaper at regular intervals. He soon discovered that if he kicked persistently, he would eventually fall from the bed. This was in itself a thrill, but if he bellowed loudly, Wo-dan would rush into the lodge and pass his broad tongue delightfully over his face, which was an even greater thrill. One day So-he came into the lodge and found him gnawing upon an old moldy bone that Wo-dan had brought him. She insisted that Enir put an automatic shutter upon the lattice door. This he accomplished by means of a large stone and a slender rawhide rope passed through a tiny hole he had carved in the wall of the lodge.

Because Tall-One's appetite ranged from dirt and pebbles to small pieces of wood and the dung of chipmunk, Enir was forced to build a primitive playpen to place him in when they were both busy or absent from the lodge. The wild carrot or turnip, which the Indians called the windy weed, when scraped very thin, proved to be a great delicacy for Tall-One. But soon mashed berries, the eggs of ducks, well-pounded meat, and strong broth supplemented the breast, and Tall-One continued to grow steadily. He eventually learned to upset his playpen, and Enir had to tie several stones about the bottom of it to prevent this from happening.

Chapter 13

Bat returned several times during the summer but, her visits were always limited to a few hours. She showed no interest in Tall-One and very little in Wodan. She made it plain that Enir alone prompted these visits, and she always remained near him while there. When he would talk to her in the soft, guarded voice he had developed while on the hunt, her eyes would shine with delight and she would obey his every command.

Enir could see that somewhere off in the forest Bat was raising her second family, and he knew that she and Shadow had chosen for them to be wolves, so he made no attempt to locate them. When these short visits gradually grew less frequent and finally stopped altogether, Enir could not help feeling a deep pang of sorrow as his mind recalled some of their adventures in the past. He held a very deep love for Bat because she had been his friend when he needed one. She had guided him through the forest while it was yet strange to him. She had guarded him from danger and risked her life to protect him. He knew that the presence of So-he in the lodge, their love for Wo-dan, and possibly the arrival of Tall-One had each contributed to her making her decision to spend the rest of her life with Shadow. He wondered if she had had this in mind when she had so carefully trained Wo-dan to assist him on the hunt.

Enir missed the presence of Bat for sentimental

reasons only. For her training of Wo-dan had been very thorough, and due to his wolf instincts, his greater speed, and his strength, he far exceeded her on the hunt. His senses of smell, sight, and hearing were almost uncanny, and his wolf instinct, which enabled him to divine the actions of different animals and to move to block them when it was necessary, enabled Enir to bring in so much meat that the entire population of the village was astounded, and So-he's eyes would shine with pride.

Enir, himself, had now reached full maturity. His strength, speed, and stamina were very close to the maximum of mankind. Because the menial tasks about the lodge no longer called for his attention and only a small part of his time was required to furnish meat, most of his days were free and he used them to explore the far reaches of this unique valley. During some of his extended trips, his eyes beheld things that even the Indians had not discovered. He also found many things that brought to his mind some of the subjects he had been taught in school back in England, such as volcanism, mineral deposits, the formation of mountains, and the glacial period. He did not know enough about these subjects to become deeply interested, but his mind touched upon them frequently as he polished his gold pan in the numerous small streams.

There were two things that were always present in Enir's mind during these excursions. One was Dead Man's Cache and the other was the mysterious stone ladder. Many times he had sat upon the shores of the stream below the high waterfall and striven to place himself in the dead man's shoes, but no inspiration had visited him, and he had failed to find Dead Man's Cache. His eyes had carefully studied the entire length of the curved mountain, but he had found no place where he could scale it. He had viewed the debris at its bottom and the dangerous slides, and on two occasions had felt the mountain tremble, but he had found no trace of the stone ladder nor had he heard the wailing forest or the singing snows.

One day, while returning from a trip to the northwestern part of the valley, he was forced to circle a vast field of broken stone and other debris, which he knew to be moraines of some prehistoric glacier. As he crossed a narrow brook, which was fed by springs flowing from beneath this great vine-covered mass of broken strata, he saw a track that was almost as familiar to him as his own. He stooped low and examined it closely. Farther down the stream he found many smaller tracks. "Bat and her pups," he whispered, and he felt a strange swelling inside his breast. He followed the stream for some distance and found more of the same tracks, only this time the long tracks of Shadow were present, also. He stood upon a high stone and let his eyes travel over the several square miles of tangled, shrub-covered wasteland, and whispered to himself, "What place could be better for a wolf to have his den?" He quickly called Wo-dan and placed the rawhide rope upon his neck, saying, "I'm afraid you will run across your pappy and he might fail to recognize you." He lingered in the vicinity for several minutes while he marked it well in his mind, then he turned and hurried away, saying to himself, if Bat wishes her pups to be wolves, I shall not interfere. Yet, the longing to see her once more tugged strongly at his heart.

Chapter 14

The snows came early the next autumn, and every sign pointed to a very severe winter. The geese left the lakes early, the deer and the wapiti departed to the deep forest, and the tracks of the bear were no longer seen. "It very bad sign," said I-lip-a-taw. "The Great Spirit has spoken to the animals, which means that he will freeze the ground deep. It is well that you have plenty, Enir Halverson."

Enir thought of the private root cellar that So-he had insisted he dig and wondered if the Great Spirit had not spoken to her also. He looked at the frozen meat he had swinging high in the trees and thought of the dried meat, roots, berries, and other dried wild fruit that So-he had stored in this cellar. Enir felt secure.

One evening, while he and So-he sat watching Tall-One battle with the lattice fence that Enir had placed before the fireplace, a faint sound reached his ears. Recognizing it as a wolf call, he stepped to the door, and opening it a tiny bit, he listened closely. When the cry was repeated, he thought that it sounded different from the usual wolf call and imagined that he could detect a note of hunger in it. He stepped outside the lodge and listened until the call was repeated once more. He was certain of the complaining note this time, and he also became aware that it came from the direction in which he had found the tracks of Bat and her pups. He went back to So-he, but for the remainder of the evening the call haunted him.

Enir rose very early the next morning, and without awakening So-he he slipped into his fur coveralls and put some dried meat into his travel sack. Then, with his bow and snowshoes in his hand, he stepped quietly outside. He went to a certain tree from whose branches hung the carcass of a very large buck deer. The buck had been old, and Enir had saved it for Wo-dan to eat. He quickly laced the hind feet of the deer's carcass tightly together and adjusted it to fit his shoulder. Next, he thoughtfully slid into the tunnel and quietly closed the door of the doghouse. I am sorry, he said silently to Wo-dan, but you can't go this time.

With the heavy carcass of the deer upon his back, Enir made slow progress as he moved away in a northwesterly direction. When he reached the open forest where the shrubbery was more sparse, he donned his snowshoes and began to make better time. He arrived at the edge of the ancient moraine about midday and immediately began to look for wolf tracks in the light wind-driven snow that covered the heavier crust. For a long while he found nothing; not even the funny little tracks of the ferret showed upon the desolate, drifted snow. He kept moving carefully into the rougher part of the great field of rubble, and after a while he saw the long tracks of a timber wolf. After he had followed them for a time, he decided that they had been made by Shadow. He rested for several minutes, then laboriously climbed to the pinnacle of a small mountain of broken stones. From this position, his eyes commanded a view of a large section of the moraine, and here he sat down to wait.

He knew well that if Shadow was within a reasonable distance of him, he would soon be around to investigate. Only about ten minutes had expired when his eye caught the flicker of movement behind a cluster of shrubs not far from the base of the mound upon which he sat. "Shadow," he said in the voice that he knew would identify him. Quickly a large, dark head appeared from behind the shrubs, and two yellow-green eyes gazed steadily toward him. "Hello, Shadow," said Enir as he rose and lifted the heavy carcass above his head. With both arms he heaved with all his might, and he watched the carcass come to a stop a short distance from where the wolf stood. "Take it to Bat, Shadow," Enir said in the same soft voice. The great wolf regarded him for a minute, then quickly approached the carcass of the deer. Once again he regarded Enir with those long, slitted, yellow-green eyes, then Enir watched him seize the deer with that terrible mouth and disappear swiftly into the broken field of stone. "It is only a small payment on what I owe both of you," Enir whispered as he slid from the mound and began the long trek back to his lodge.

Enir's legs ached with fatigue, for he had not yet become accustomed to the awkwardness of travel with snowshoes, and, besides, since the days were so short, he had had to hurry home before nightfall. While he rested, he explained to So-he what he had done and how Shadow had eagerly seized the meat. He also retold Shadow's part in the slaying of the great grizzly, whose hide now covered their floor. "You see, I cannot let him starve," he said. "He saved my life." So-he came forward and slid her arms about his neck.

"Of course you can't, Enir Halverson," she said, "nor your faithful dog Bat, either. They are Wodan's parents you know." Enir realized more plainly than ever the depth of So-he's love for the wolf-dog Wo-dan. I am glad that he loves her, too, thought

Enir, for Wo-dan bid fair to become even stronger and more formidable than Shadow, and such a beast could only be governed by love.

Later that winter, Enir went to the lodge of Chief Wa-neb-i-te and said to him, "I have many frozen bodies of deer that I shall not need. If any of the people should need them, send men to carry them to the village."

Wa-neb-i-te rose and looked long into Enir's eyes, and said, "I thank you, Enir Halverson. Should any of my people get hungry, I shall accept your offer." Then Enir turned and walked away, while Wa-neb-i-te gazed at his retreating back. "Mebbyso squaw man," he said, "but nobody better not say."

Chapter 15

The following spring came as abruptly as had the winter. The sun shone warm, and the ducks and geese returned in great flocks. The snow receded swiftly, and all the streams gurgled with pleasure. Within a few weeks, the forest began to hum with bird songs and the chatter of rodents, which induced the feeling of peacefulness that would last for several months.

Enir sat upon a stump at the far side of the tiny clearing, happily plucking a brace of geese while he listened to So-he croon an Indian love song to the groggy Tall-One, who was waging a losing battle with sleep. As his fingers tore great bunches of feathers from the two unfortunate birds, his eyes wandered from the feather bag to the cloud-shrouded peaks of White Bosom Bare. Only the outline of the two peaks was visible, but in his mind he could see the entire picture clearly. For, even before he had entered this great valley, he had paused many times upon the peaks to the east and had closely studied this mysterious pageant of nature. He had acquainted himself with every tiny detail, and he remembered now almost every bend in the two small streams that ran in opposite directions to converge in the center and form the stream where the waterfall was. This waterfall lingered in his mind as he finished plucking the two large birds and waited for So-he's song to stop. Dead Man's Cache was somewhere near these falls, and somewhere above them, where the stream cut through the curved mountain, he believed, was an undiscovered gold deposit that would stagger the imagination. The rough nuggets that he had panned at the bottom of the waterfall told him that they had not been washed along a stream bed from very far, and when his pulse began to quicken, he solemnly reminded himself of the promise he had given.

When Enir had first heard the story of White Bosom Bare, he had scoffed at the idea of such a place being inaccessable to man. The stories he had read about mountain climbers, explorers, and other daring adventurers made such a myth seem preposterous. But, after having carefully surveyed the base of the circular mountain several times, felt the ground tremble beneath his feet, and studied its bulging sides and precipitous walls, he had become pretty well convinced that no lone prospector could ever hope to scale the curved mountain. There were several things about the strange legend of White Bosom Bare that were very cloudy in Enir's mind. First, if the Great Spirit used the sacred valley for a breeding ground for his animals, how did they get down into this valley? He was unable to picture in his mind a bull moose descending a ladder. Second, how could a blind Indian explain to another person exactly how to find this ladder when that person had never seen it? Yet, according to the legend, Na-bab-i-ti had found it and climbed it on a moonless night. Not only that, he had descended it with his head half skinned, his arm torn up, and one ear torn nearly off. Enir looked down at the two naked birds and slowly shook his head. If he could find out the answer to this first question, he decided, it would more than likely answer the rest of them.

So, when Tall-One at last yielded to slumber, Enir carried the two geese to So-he and told her that he was planning an overnight trip and that he would need Wo-dan. He then suggested that she take Tall-One and spend the night with her parents. When So-he hesitated, he said,"I would feel much better if you would go."

"Then I will go," said So-he, and Enir knew she was aware that he was thinking of Stout-Boy, but he said no more, for this was a subject that had never been mentioned by either of them, and he was content for it to remain that way.

They rose early the next morning, and Enir helped So-he get the things together that she would need. But he did not accompany her to her parents' lodge, because he did not want to answer any of the questions that he feared I-lip-a-taw would ask. He did not have a guilty conscience, but he did intend to search again for the stone ladder.

Enir arrived at the waterfall before the sun had reached its zenith. He was slightly winded, and Wodan's tongue was beginning to get long, but after they had both drunk from the cool, clear stream, they were ready to continue. Enir decided to turn back to his left and follow the edge of the curved mountain to search for the tracks of animals or any other clue concerning the so-called ladder that might present itself. Due to the density of the vegetation in some places and the numerous thorny vines, Enir had been wont to skip or hurry over this particular part of the location, but since he was determined to study every square foot of the ground along the base of the curved mountains, he forced his way through it. But when he reached the strip of bare ground that invariably lay adjacent to the bulging walls of the mountain, he found it, like all the other places he

154

had examined, devoid of hoofmarks or any other type of footprint.

As his eyes wandered up the steep incline, a tiny thread of green attracted his attention. He noticed that this green line was roughly parallel with the base, but in places it ascended sharply. In attempting to get a better view of it, he began to look around for some place of vantage where the bulging lower crags would not interfere. Presently he spied a long sliver of stone that protruded from a tangled mass of vines at a rather sharp angle. He thought that if he climbed upon it, he could trace this dim line better. So he worked his way to the foot of this stone and started to walk up it. He had taken only about four or five steps when the stone slowly settled. He quickly backed up a step or two, and the stone rose again. "Huh," he said, "a balanced rock." He repeated this performance and obtained the same results. He wondered what the stone was balanced on, but he could not see from where he stood. He climbed down and tried to lift the heavy end of it, but it would not budge. He found a large square-shaped boulder and placed it upon the slender tongue of stone, then began to inch it forward. Presently, it slowly lowered, and Enir stooped and peered beneath it.

What he saw was a neatly stacked pile of rawhide bags, all about equal in size. These bags were made of deerskin and appeared to be tightly stitched. "Dead Man's Cache," he whispered with bated breath. With trembling fingers he lifted one of the bags and untied the slender rawhide thong that closed it. The glitter of raw gold caused his breath to become very rapid and shallow. Dropping to his knees, he counted twenty-six bags with the one he held in his hand. When he hefted it, he judged it to weigh in the neighborhood of five or six pounds, "I have found Dead Man's Cache," he whispered again, as another thrill chased up and down his spine. I have passed by it many times, he said to himself, then his thoughts went to the tiny green thread he had seen on the mountainside. "I'll bet that the dead man was doing the same thing that I was when he found this balanced rock," he whispered, and Wodan, who lay curled up beside him, cocked his head and eyed him strangely.

Enir reached out and scruffed his neck, and said, "No, I'm not losing my mind, but you might as well listen to this. Suppose that I had found this cache before I went to the village? Before So-he handed me her bow? There would have been no So-he, no I-lip-a-taw, and no Tall-One in my life. Had I not had the bow, then I would not have killed the bear, so there would have been no Shadow and no Wo-dan either. What do you think of that? Eh?" He reached out and scruffed Wo-dan's neck again. Enir frowned deeply and silently continued pursuing the thought. I would, at this very minute, be where the wind stinks. Now that I have the gold, I don't know what to do with it. If I take So-he and Tall-One out of this valley, she will be known only as my squaw and Tall-One as a bastard. I would be known as a rich squaw man and laughed at behind my back. Then, looking again at Wo-dan, he said aloud, "And you would be looked upon as a wild timber wolf, and I would be forced to keep you in a cage. What do you think of that?"

For several minutes, Enir sat in silent meditation as a frown formed upon his forehead, and his eyes traveled many times to the handmade buckskin bags so neatly stacked beneath the balanced rock. Suddenly he rose, and after retying the bag he held in his hand, he placed it back upon the stack. The dead man was neat in many ways, he thought as he straightened up and glanced again toward the tiny thread of vegetation upon the side of the curved mountains. If that fellow was looking at that, he surely must have checked it out, so I will not bother to do so, he thought. He then walked over and pushed the boulder from the balanced rock and watched it settle gently back into place.

Enir built his campfire close to the stream that evening, and after he took a couple of thick steaks from his pack sack, he placed one over the coals to broil and tossed the other to Wo-dan. While his steak broiled, he sat down beside the fire and frowned deeply into its embers.

Strangely enough, as Enir relaxed there by the fire, his thoughts were not concentrated upon the Dead Man's Cache, but upon some of the thoughts that the finding of the cache had triggered. He called to mind some of the things that I-lip-a-taw had said while they were seated upon the stumps there before Enir's lodge. He realized that the eyes of the wise old bowmaker had beheld many things as he roved the country in search of bow wood, and the conclusions he had reached were very disturbing. Were these conclusions accurate? Was the fate of the Indian already decided? He recalled many things that he had seen during his trip through eastern Canada, then jumped to some of the tales he had heard about battles with the Indians in the States. Yes, he conceded, it is true. The freedom of the redman, who for thousands of years had striven to preserve this beautiful continent, was swiftly coming to an end. Even Tall-One would probably some day feel the lash of the arrogant destroyer's slave whip. Suddenly Enir's body began to tremble with indignation, and he rose quickly to his feet. "We will fight these selfish, bigoted, and destructive aggressors with what weapons we have until the last one of us dies," he shouted to the silent forest. Wo-dan leaped to his feet, and with his hackles raised looked about for some hidden enemy. Enir glanced down at him, but he did not smile as he rotated the broiling meat. His thoughts were centered upon the safety of his loved ones and their inevitable fate. He now understood the Indians' philosophy of life, their utter unselfishness and their naturally gentle nature, and he also considered himself one of them. Henceforth, their troubles would be his also.

After he had eaten the steak, Enir's anger began to cool, but he was no less resentful of the aggressiveness of the white man. He also reminded himself that he had entered the play during the last act, but he was determined to do what he could in defense of his wife, family, and friends. He began to think of some other things that I-lip-a-taw had said to him. Was the wise old Indian trying to offer him a way out when he asked for the return of So-he's bow? When he told him of the inevitable fate of the Indian, was he also trying to tell him what to expect if he married So-he and cast his lot with them? He realized that even if this were true, he still had no regrets. But his reasoning told him that his first responsibility was to them and that he must make every provision possible should all of this happen as soon as I-lip-a-taw had predicted. And he forced himself to concentrate upon this. First, he had to teach them the predominant language of the paleface, which was English. Second, he had to teach them how to live in a world where it was everyone for himself instead of all for one and one for all. He must teach them selfishness, greed, and other traits of the pale-face. These thoughts caused Enir to shudder, even though he had been brought up under these same principles.

Finally Enir's thoughts drifted back to Dead Man's Cache, and as he settled back upon a soft bed of leaves and gazed with sleepless eyes far up into the ocean of stars, the foundation of his plans was laid. He went over them many times, striving to erase all thoughts of selfishness, but at last he consoled himself with the idea that he was doing the best that he could in the discharge of a duty he had assumed when he shouldered the responsibility of So-he and their children's future. It was only then that Enir relaxed. Confident that he would be watched over by the wolf-dog Wo-dan, he slept the deep, dreamless sleep that the whispering forest suggested.

When Enir rose the next morning, he sought the piece of doeskin in which So-he had so carefully wrapped his meat. With it in his hand, he went straight to the balanced rock. For many minutes he marked many measured steps and sketched several piles of stone upon this piece of doeskin. When he was satisfied with his crude sketching, he returned to his fire, and with a hot arrowhead he traced the dim lines left by the sharp thorn he had used for a pen. After satisfying himself that the crude map was both plain and correct, he went to the large cluster of canelike grass that he had seen growing beside the stream, and from the center of it he extracted one of the largest stalks. In a joint of this stalk he inserted the drawing. When this was accomplished, he set out on his return trip to the village.

When Enir reached the place where the dim trail

forked, he took the one on his left. He did this for several reasons. First, it was the nearest route to the village. Second, it led by the place where he had slain the great grizzly. This place would always hold an interest for him for many reasons. Here he had first met I-lip-a-taw, first slain man, and made history by fighting alongside the most vicious timber wolf that the forest could produce. It was here also that So-he's bow had stood the supreme test and that I-lip-a-taw had given him the chance to prove that So-he's judgment of him had been correct. As Enir's thoughts reviewed I-lip-a-taw's action, he whispered to himself, "I wonder if I-lip-a-taw can play poker?"

By the time Enir reached his lodge, the outline of his plan had been completely formulated. The details of it would be considered as they arose, and his mind was at ease. The cane tube inside his pouch, which had been acting as a strong magnet to his thoughts, had gradually been rendered inactive and securely placed into the niche that cold logic had slowly hewn into the walls of reason. It would be held in reserve, as a safeguard for the future of his family should he lose his life in the defense of their freedom.

He wasted little time in his lodge. He hurriedly stored his bow and meager equipment then went on to the lodge of I-lip-a-taw. So-he's mother seemed quite amused at their greeting and smiled sadly as she said to So-he, "I want you to remember the long absences of your father when he went for bow wood. Compare them with two short days and consider how fortunate you are." Tall-One shrieked with joy when Enir tossed him, which also seemed to amuse his grandmother, who was not accustomed to seeing such emotional outbursts from small children. Tall-One had inherited none of the Indian stoicism, nor had he inherited the trait of indifference which usually prevails among the small children of the Indian. She had become upset when Tall-One had been so persistent in his desire to investigate everything strange that he found in the lodge. So-he had been forced to put him on a leash.

When they arrived at their own lodge, the antics of Wo-dan caused So-he's Flathead reserve to crumble, and she laughed gayly. "Slow down Wo-dan," she said, "before you run over somebody." Then to Enir she said, "I wonder how much larger he will grow. He is now almost as large as Shadow, yet he still grows."

"He will be larger than Shadow," replied Enir, "because his bones are larger. I do not know how much he will grow, but he resembles Shadow more each day, except his head is slightly wider and his nose a little shorter." Wo-dan begged to see Tall-One, and when Enir set him on the ground he sniffed him over carefully, then seized him by his single garment, which was a doeskin diaper, and carried him ahead of them into the lodge.

"He is getting much stronger, too," commented So-he. Enir said nothing, but his mind traveled ahead to the time when Wo-dan would reach full maturity. He could not help but wonder what would happen when he needed to be corrected. He shook his head slowly as they followed him into the lodge.

So-he was both surprised and pleased at Enir's attention during the following weeks. She postponed the making of doeskin garments and stored away the several bent-twig patterns her mother had so laboriously constructed. She devoted her entire time to preparing food and going on picnics and swimming parties with Enir. He was always in such a joyous mood that So-he's heart also sang loudly, for never was a woman more in love with her husband.

One day, while Tall-One slept, she accompanied Enir on a short hunt. He told her that he wished to show her how well he had trained Wo-dan. At the outskirts of a meadow only a few miles from the lodge, Enir suddenly drew her into the concealing branches of a spreading juniper. He whispered for her to be still and watch. Presently she glimpsed Wo-dan as he slithered through the underbrush far across the meadow. A few moments later a large doe passed very close to them. She held her head high, with her eyes upon the form of Wo-dan. Enir remained motionless and let her pass. So-he looked at him and asked why he did not use the bow. "Did you not see that she has a fawn?" replied Enir. "I never kill a doe who has a fawn."

"I love you Enir Halverson," said So-he, and thus ended their hunt.

One day later, while So-he worked upon doeskin garments, Enir selected a large scrap of skin and asked her to construct for him a very small bag. When she had done so according to his directions, he presented her with a small joint of wild cane, which had been meticulously sealed and highly polished. "Place this into the bag and sew around it with many stitches," he said.

"What is it?" asked So-he.

"I will tell you when it is finished," replied Enir. When she had finished it to his satisfaction, he said, "This is for you. You must put it into your medicine bag and wear it at all times, even when you sleep. You must never lose it or allow it to be in possession of any other person, not even your parents."

"But why is it so important?" asked So-he.

Enir smiled and said, "It is a trail. By following its

directions, it will lead you to the most powerful medicine that there is among the paleface. It will make them respect you and if you will use the medicine right, they will hasten to do your bidding."

"But why do I need the medicine of the paleface?" asked So-he.

There was a strange expression upon Enir's face when he answered, "Someday the paleface will come with many thundersticks. They might take the life of I-lip-a-taw and myself. Or they might come while we are both away. If such should happen, you will take Tall-One and Wo-dan and flee through the forest to the large village by the great lake in the south. Somewhere in that village, or near it, is a lodge presided over by a learned and friendly old paleface whose name is Father DeSmith. Him, you shall seek. When you find him, you will tell him about Tall-One and myself. Him you will tell everything. You will tell him that Tall-One's paleface name is also Enir Halverson and that I am your husband and Tall-One's father. You will also tell him that the Great Spirit of the Flathead is the same Great Spirit whose name is in his book. Then you will give to him this bag, and tell him that in the name of this Great Spirit I, Enir Halverson, ask him to find this medicine and teach you its use. This I command you to do should such a thing happen. You will remember this and think often of what I have said. I, Enir Halverson, your husband who loves you, has spoken."

So-he stood silently and watched the strange expression leave Enir's face and the boyish smile return. She glanced down at the small package she held in her hand, and a troubled look came into her eyes. Never before had Enir spoken or acted in this manner. "Do you think that the paleface will come with thundersticks?" she asked.

"I do," replied Enir as he folded her into his arms. "Each day they come nearer and each day they grow stronger," he said huskily. "I have often thought of taking you and Tall-One and fleeing to the northwest, but I cannot desert our people. I-lip-a-taw and I have talked of it, but you are not to mention to him the things I have said, nor the things that I have told you. Let us now forget about all of it until the time comes to think of it. Let us continue as we have, for the Great Spirit smiles upon those who are happy but frowns upon those who worry."

So-he placed her arm about Enir's neck and said, "It shall be as you say, Enir Halverson, but you shall tell me when the time comes to worry."

One languid day in autumn, they were watching the wild geese form in large V formations and circle the valley several times before they disappeared to the south. Most of the duck had already departed, and the song of the locust was very muted. "It is very beautiful when the forest begins to prepare itself for winter," said Enir.

"You are going to have another son," said So-he.

"What?" Enir almost shouted, "when?"

"Mother said that it might be before the snow goes away," replied So-he.

"Why have you not told me before?" asked Enir.

"My mother said not to tell you until I was sure," replied So-he. "But today she said that I should tell you." Enir glanced at the lowering sun, then at the empty tree limbs.

"But I should have known so that I could bring in extra meat," he said.

"The root cellar is filled to overflowing," said So-he, "and it is not yet cool enough to hang meat in the trees." Enir ran his fingers through his long, dark auburn hair and silently agreed with her.

"Does I-lip-a-taw know?" he asked presently.

"No," replied So-he, "Mother said that I should tell you first."

Chapter 16

It was during a blustery blizzard, when the winter was grasping frantically for another grip upon the land which spring was dragging away, that a tiny daughter was born to Enir and So-he. She was a very beautiful child, both strong and healthy, yet she seemed very tiny and as delicate as a flower. Whispering-West-Wind was her Indian name, but Enir suggested that they name her Sa-ra, a name that was easy for Tall-One to pronounce. When I-lip-a-taw looked upon her for the first time, his sharp eyes sought those of his wife's and he whispered, "So-he." His wife nodded, and they both smiled. Enir was so proud of her that he could hardly take his eyes away from her, and each time her tiny voice sounded, Wodan would cock his great head and whine coarsely.

Both So-he and Tall-One could now speak English well enough to carry on a conversation, so Enir established the rule that English would be the language used at all times within the lodge. This proved to be much more difficult for So-he than for Tall-One, who seemed to speak it plainer than he did Salish. I-lip-a-taw surprised them all by demonstrating his ability in handling the English language, and he confessed that he used it constantly while on his long trips for bow wood. But what surprised Enir was that So-he and her mother could converse well in French. French was the language her mother had been taught in childhood.

When summer arrived, Enir began to make preparations for a trip back to the trading post on the fork of the Oldman River, where he had wintered with Stripe. He debated long on whether or not to take Wo-dan with him. But when So-he informed him that she planned to spend most of the time during his absence with her mother, he quickly decided to take him along. He gathered the thirty-odd beaver pelts and all of the gold he had panned and decided that this, plus the money he had left with the old factor, would purchase all he would be able to carry back, for it was quite a long way to carry a heavy burden.

When Enir arrived at the trading post near the Oldman River he was surprised at the additions that had been made during his long absence. New buildings had been added, and great stacks of firewood, several wagons, large stacks of lumber, and a small herd of cattle greeted his eyes. Getting to be a regular town, he told himself as he went on to the trading post. When he stepped into Zeb's store, he found that it had changed very little, but when Zeb came out of his tiny office to wait on him, Enir noticed that he had aged greatly during the four years he had been away. "What can I do for ya?" Zeb asked, and Enir was forced to smile at the familiar voice. Old Zeb eyed him for a moment, then recognition showed in his faded eyes. "By gad," he said. "You're Enir, ain't ya? Boy, what a trappin' man you made." He came from behind the counter with his hand outstretched. Wo-dan stepped in front of him and the old man almost fell backwards. "Great jumpin' Judas," he said. "If it ain't a full-grown timber wolf."

"No, this is one of Bat's pups."

The old factor stared at him blankly for a moment, then said, "You mean that is a cross between that wolf-dog bitch you left here with and a timber wolf?"

"Yes, sir," replied Enir.

"Lord of mercy, get ahold of him," said the factor. "I don't like the way he's lookin' at me."

"He is perfectly gentle," said Enir as he reached down and patted Wo-dan's neck.

"Lordy me," said the factor as he looked again at Wo-dan. "So he's one of her pups and his daddy is a timber wolf."

"Yes, and what a timber wolf he was," replied Enir.

"Yeah, I can imagine," said the old factor. "I believe that is the damnest lookin' thing that I ever saw in the way of a dog. You'd better do somethin' with him before somebody takes a shot at him."

Enir produced a slender rawhide rope and slipped it over Wo-dan's head, saying, "I did what you advised me to with Bat. I broke him to a rope." The old factor's mouth fell open as he watched Enir lead the obedient Wo-dan across the room and tie him to a rickety old billiard table. "He is all dog," he said. "He just doesn't look it."

"I'll drink to that," the old factor said. "He damn sure don't."

Enir decided that, because of Wo-dan, it would be better to make his visit with Zeb as short as possible. He talked with him awhile and found out that all of the policemen that he had known had been rotated and that the old doctor had returned to England. He also learned that a town site was being developed at the post and several families were expected to arrive here in the near future. Enir took Wo-dan and went to visit Stripe's grave and look over some of his old hunting ground. When he returned, he asked Zeb to evaluate his beaver pelts and to weigh the dust he had brought. When this had been attended to, he asked him about the money he had left with him. When Zeb had checked his book and given Enir an exact total, Enir began to make his purchases. He selected two new rifles, one handgun, a bundle of needles, and almost all of the thread Zeb had on hand. He chose a couple of bolts of durable cloth, a box of arrowheads, a few pencils, and several writing tablets. He then ordered a tremendous amount of ammunition for the two rifles.

"You are sure gonna have a load here," said Zeb.

"Yes, sir," replied Enir. "I am going to have to hire some packers." He went ahead and added an inch and a half wood auger, a heavy ax, and a cast-iron meat pot to the pile. "Let's see how much that leaves me," said Enir.

Zeb figured for a moment and said, "Forty-five dollars, or there about."

"Lay on six of those four-dollar blankets," Enir said as he pointed to a stack of Hudson Bay blankets on the counter.

"That leaves you about twenty-one or -two dollars," said Zeb. "That should be enough to hire a couple of packers."

"Do you know where I might find them?" asked Enir.

The old factor thought for a minute, then said, "There is a bunch of Indians camped over by the fork. You might find 'em there. I hear tell that they're a pretty clean looking bunch. Why don't you run over there and see while I cook us a batch of grub? But take that damn wolf along with you. I don't trust him."

"And him tied?" asked Enir.

"Tied, hell," said Zeb. "Don't try to tell me anything about timber wolves. Why, he could eat that rawhide rope you have on him then beat you to the door."

"I'll take him," Enir said. "But he wouldn't try to get loose. You see, he doesn't know that he's a wolf."

"Yeah, and there's liable to be hell to pay when he finds out, too," said Zeb.

At the Indian encampment, Enir found two middle-aged squaws who agreed to carry his packs to the edge of the Flathead country for five dollars each plus guaranteed protection from any roving Flathead braves. During the dickering, Enir discovered that neither of them knew exactly where this edge was located, so he made the bargain. The greatest trouble he had was assuring them that Wo-dan was not a wolf, but a very large dog who closely resembled one. He was forced to demonstrate Wo-dan's obedience several times before they were fully convinced.

Upon returning to the post, he informed the old factor of this, and Zeb said laughingly, "Boy, you got it made. Once you get them squaws in the bush, you can make them do anything by threatening to sic that wolf on 'em."

"By jove," said Enir. "I hadn't thought of that. I can make them carry that stuff right to the door of my lodge."

"You got a lodge?" asked the factor.

"I have an old one that I have repaired and put in shape to live in," replied Enir.

"I was wondering what you wanted with that auger," said Zeb.

"I like lots of pegs to hang my stuff on," replied Enir carelessly.

"What are you doin', tradin' with them Flathead?"

"I'm figgering on doing a little trading," replied Enir, then asked, "What kind of Indians are those

170

camped over there? I didn't recognize their haircuts."

"I think that they're Dakotas," replied Zeb. "That's why they were a little skittish about goin' any farther west. Them Flathead of yours have a pretty bad reputation."

Enir, still anxious to keep the conversation away from his connection with the Flathead, said, "I suppose that I had better get started on building three packs with all this stuff. It might run into a pretty big job."

"What's the hurry?" asked Zeb. "You're goin' to stay a day or two, ain't ya?"

Enir hesitated. "I'd like to, Zeb," he replied, "but I have quite a bit of stuff in that old lodge."

"Yeah, I know what you mean," said Zeb. "Them pilferin' rascals." Enir said no more but started arranging the material he had purchased into three separate packs.

The Dakota squaws balked when they reached the head of the Waterton River, but all that Enir had to do was call Wo-dan to him, ruffle the hair upon his back, and look menacingly toward them. They quickly retrieved their packs and moved docilely forward. When they reached the stream below the waterfall, Enir paid them each an extra dollar, and without a word they departed hastily along their back trail. Enir stood for a moment watching them run, then said to himself, they weren't half as tired as they pretended to be.

Because the stream was still swollen from the melting snow in White Bosom Bare, Enir had to make many trips to transport all of his goods across it. He was forced to walk very carefully upon the slick boulders to keep from falling, but he finished at last without getting anything wet. He was very tired

171

because he had shouldered by far the heaviest pack, but the sun was still high, so he decided to leave everything but the two rifles and one case of ammunition and go on to the village. So, after hiding his supplies well beneath the branches of a spreading juniper, he moved on.

When he reached the village, he turned the two rifles over to I-lip-a-taw, and refusing to answer any questions, he escorted So-he and the children to their own lodge. "I have many things to show you," he told So-he as he relaxed upon his bunk. "But I am very tired and hungry. I will tell you about it after we eat." So-he smiled and began preparing his favorite dish, wapiti roast with windy weed sauce.

Enir spent two days resting from his long trek before he enlisted the aid of two strong squaws to transport his purchases to the village. Most of this time he spent holding Sa-ra, who, he was certain, was the most beautiful baby that had ever existed. He was enthralled by her alert look and gentle disposition. He noticed that she was vastly different from Tall-One when he was tiny. Tall-One had always been quick to squall loudly at things that displeased him, and his voice was very coarse. Sa-ra seldom cried, and when she did, her voice reminded him of the meowing of a cat. But when he looked at her, she was so perfect and beautiful that she reminded him of a delicate flower.

The remainder of the summer passed swiftly, or so it seemed to Enir. Because he had a late start in procuring meat to dry, he worked hard at it for a while. Since he had another mouth to feed, he thought he would need a lot more meat. So-he's mother came often to help with the two babies, and it was she who advised Enir to slow down.

"Find something else to do for a while," she told him. "Or the flies will carry away the children."

So Enir used his new auger to build a cradle for Whispering-West-Wind, and he also bored many holes in the walls for pegs to hang the numerous garments that So-he and her mother had made from the new cloth he had brought. He made one trip to the moraines but found no trace of Bat or Shadow, nor did either one of them visit the lodge during the entire summer. It may be, he thought, that they have left the valley for better hunting grounds, and the thought gave him deep comfort.

Wo-dan had become so proficient in the hunt that one day Enir prevailed upon So-he to leave the children with her mother and accompany him. When they had reached game territory, he handed So-he the bow and smilingly said, "Since this bow is named for you, you should be able to use it." So-he made no protest, and Enir received the surprise of his life when she killed her first deer with a single arrow. "I did not know that you could shoot so well," he said.

So-he smiled again and said, "Yes, my father taught me how to hunt, but when I grew up, he had me put the bow away."

"Do you mean that you have hunted with this bow?" So-he merely nodded. "You never told me that," said Enir.

"Nor did you ask me," replied So-he, smiling.

Chapter 17

Early the next spring, while the snow still lay in great patches beneath the juniper limbs, Enir received a summons to appear at the round lodge to sit in council. He went straight to the lodge of I-lip-a-taw and asked him why he was summoned to meet with the chiefs in council. I-lip-a-taw was evasive and asked in turn why he did not go and talk with Chief Wa-neb-i-te. Enir decided that he would just wait and find out about it when he went to the meeting.

When he entered the round lodge on the appointed day, Enir found only five people present. Chief Wa-neb-i-te, I-lip-a-taw, Na-bab-i-ti, and two strangers whom he recognized as Nez Perće subchiefs. No words were spoken, and he was motioned by Chief Wa-neb-i-te to take a seat beside I-lip-a-taw. Directly after he was seated, almost all of the braves in the village filed quietly in and formed a ring around the walls of the round lodge, leaving the six of them in the center.

When all were seated, Chief Wa-neb-i-te rose, and taking a pinch of ashes from the small fire around which the six of them sat, he distributed a tiny bit of it in all four directions, at the same time invoking the aid of the Great Spirit at the meeting. After this formality had been taken care of, he sat back down and began speaking in a very forceful voice.

"My friends," he began, "I do not have good news for you. The news that I have for you is very bad. The war that has been waged among the paleface is over. And it failed to do what in our prayers we asked for. It did not annihilate him or stop him from pushing farther into our country. Even now, the soldier-paleface are knocking at our door. I have just returned from a council presided over by our Chieftan, Al-a-go-ri-o. He has already entered into an agreement with the great chieftan of the Sioux, who in turn is in agreement with other chieftans to the south to consolidate our warriors and drive the paleface forever from our land."

Wa-neb-i-te paused and gazed fiercely about him. Presently he began again. "Although our warbows are the strongest in the land, they are not strong enough to compete with the thunderstick. As all of you know, our bravest and strongest warriors are often slain before they take a single scalp. The only way that we will ever defeat the thunderstick soldiers is for us, ourselves, to obtain thundersticks. The only place for us to obtain them is from the paleface. This we must do. But before doing so, we must teach ourselves the secrets of their use. It is for this reason that I have summoned you here. The Great Spirit has seen fit to send among us a mighty warrior from a distant land. This warrior has fought and won wars with the thunderstick. He will teach us. For those who do not know, this I will say: This warrior has slain the greatest of grizzlies while alone in the forest with only a bow for a weapon. He has slain one of our most noted warriors with his bare hands, even when this warrior held a knife in his. He has also defeated two of our braves with his bare hands, using only a single blow for each. When a man who had abducted the daughter of one of our chiefs eluded our entire group of trackers and escaped to the rim of the mountains, this warrior trailed him and slew him with a single arrow. This warrior has also tamed the greatest of timber wolves and taught him to guard his lodge. I will now give unto this warrior the power of a chief whose words you must obey." He then signaled for Enir to rise, then kneel upon his left knee. When Enir complied, Wa-neb-i-te laid his spear across his left shoulder and said in a very solemn voice, "Enir Halverson, I make you chief among my people. Henceforth, you will be known as 'Iron-hand,' chief of our thunderstick warriors. They will obey your command, go where you send them, and follow where you lead. Let Chief Iron-Hand rise and speak." And Wa-neb-i-te took his seat beside I-lip-a-taw.

As Enir rose from his kneeling position, he looked straight into the eyes of I-lip-a-taw, and where he had expected to see guilt, he saw a gleam of pride. Suddenly he remembered that he was supposed to speak. He let his eyes travel over the entire assembly, then he spoke in as forceful a voice as his excitement would permit him to muster. "My fellow Flathead warriors, it is with pleasure that I accept the position in which you have placed me. But before I teach you the use of the thunderstick, I must first teach you the care of it. Unlike the bow, it cannot be dropped into the water or allowed to become covered with dirt and sand. It must not be dropped upon the rocks, thrown upon the ground, or handled by children. There are many other things that I will teach you, but these things you must first remember." And, deciding that this speech would do for a starter, Enir sat back down.

After the meeting had been adjourned and while he walked beside I-lip-a-taw back to his lodge, Enir looked at him and said, "I fear that my task will be very difficult."

I-lip-a-taw smiled and said, "Do not worry so deeply, my son. The Flathead will be quick to learn. Now you will find that what I have told you is true. Only those who are quick to think and act live to be warriors."

"It is not that I doubt their intelligence," replied Enir, "it is the small things that are so important about the thunderstick."

"Do not worry," replied I-lip-a-taw. "The Indian's eyes are very sharp, and he will surprise you with his knowledge of the importance of small things."

Because they had only two thundersticks and a large group to teach, Enir decided to limit the course to only two days to see how they progressed. This course he divided into three parts. First was a study of the mechanism of the thunderstick. Second was a strictly supervised course in dry firing, and third, each warrior fired one shot for a record. The target used for this was a wooden image of a soldier-pale-face upon whose chest was placed a piece of doeskin about three inches square. After the warrior had fired, the doeskin was removed and given to him. It was considered as his record. Those who missed would await their turn and take the course again. Those who did not miss would stamp their mark upon the piece of doeskin and turn it in to Chief Wa-neb-i-te. At certain intervals, Enir was called in to choose from these records certain warriors to be sent to other villages to teach the use of the thunderstick. Thus was the educational system expanded.

It was several weeks after Enir had completed his duties as an instructor and while he was busily engaged in bringing in his annual supply of meat that he received another summons to the round lodge. He was informed that this was an important meeting and that he had received the notice two days early.

He was also informed by I-lip-a-taw that Chieftan Al-a-go-ri-o would be present. He told So-he of this and gave voice to his fear of being sent away upon some mission. To his surprise, So-he showed great pride in the position which he felt he had been shanghaied into taking. Later that evening, he heard her say to Tall-One, when he offered his usual resentment at being put to bed, "Is that any way for the son of a chief to act?"

When Enir entered the round lodge at the appointed hour, he wore the new beaded doeskin suit So-he had made for him, and his dark auburn hair looked well in the style of the Flathead. He immediately recognized the high Chieftan Al-a-go-ri-o but did not hasten to drop his eyes when the big chief stared into them. Several times, while they awaited the arrival of others from the villages to the south, he caught the piercing eyes of the great chief upon him. He watched every detail of the ceremony when, after they had all assembled, Al-a-go-ri-o rose to make the supplication to the Great Spirit. Then, in a low, slightly resonant voice, Al-a-go-ri-o began to speak.

"I am sure that you all know of our agreement with the other tribes. It is all that is left us. Well we know that an agreement with the forked-tongued paleface is worthless. Even the great white father, whom we have heard so much about, speaks with the tongue of a serpent. We must remind ourselves that we are fighting for our lives. To emphasize this point, I call your attention to the lowly rabbit. Never has a hunter heard the death cry of a rabbit, and seen that rabbit survive. We know that he always dies. Why? It is because he has never trained himself to fight. We are not rabbits. Neither shall we give the paleface the satisfaction of listening to our cry for mercy, which like the rabbit's would go unheeded. Our plea shall be the war cry and the boom of the thunderstick. I will now tell you why I have summoned you to this meeting. As you all know, we must have many thundersticks. You also know that the only place we can obtain them is from the paleface themselves. Now, my scouts have informed me that among the paleface there are many whose thirst for the yellow metal is far greater than their honor. Although it is very distasteful to deal with such people, it becomes extremely necessary. They have the thundersticks, we have the yellow metal. They are divided, we shall consolidate. I see in these conditions a great opportunity to strike, and strike we will. Wa-neb-i-te, the chief of this village, has informed me that one of his chiefs possesses great knowledge of the yellow metal. I-lip-a-taw, the chief of scouts, whom all know well, has informed me that this chief is sure there is a great supply of yellow metal in our sacred valley. I do not consider it within my power to order the desecration of White Bosom Bare without a popular vote. But before I call for such a vote, I would ask that each of you ask yourself this question: Why did the Great Spirit see fit to place the gold in our sacred valley? It is just possible that you will receive the same answer that I, myself, received. Now, since this vote will represent a personal message from the Great Spirit, I will ask that there be no open discussion upon this matter. Outside the door of this lodge, two bushes have been set up. One upon the right and one upon the left. After each one of you has communed with the Great Spirit, you shall rise and walk out of the lodge. As you pass by these bushes, you shall hang your medicine bag upon one. The one upon the right is for those who have received yes for their answer. The one upon the left is for those who have received no. Whichever bush contains the most medicine bags, that is the answer we shall take." And Chieftan Al-a-go-ri-o sat down and leaned his head into his palms.

After a few minutes spent in silent meditation, one by one the chiefs began to rise and walk slowly out the door. Enir followed behind I-lip-a-taw and hung his medicine bag upon the right-hand bush beside those of the chiefs who had preceded him. Only one medicine bag did he recognize. This was the one belonging to none other than Na-bab-i-ti, the messenger of the Great Spirit. Chief Wa-neb-i-te and Chieftan Al-a-go-ri-o were the last to emerge, in that order. They went through the formality of hanging their medicine bags upon the right-hand bush. Al-a-go-ri-o gave thanks to the Great Spirit in the sign language, then retrieved his medicine bag and reentered the lodge. One by one the other chiefs followed, each retrieving his medicine bag as he passed the bush.

When the circle had been reformed, exactly as it was before, Al-a-go-ri-o rose and resumed his speech. "Let us all thank the Great Spirit for his continued interest in our welfare," he said. Then he paused a moment while he appeared to be considering something and continued, "Chief Wa-neb-i-te will choose the ones to go upon this errand, and they shall be placed under the command of Chief Iron-Hand. Na-bab-i-ti will guide them up the stone ladder under whatever conditions he chooses, to accept this gift that the Great Spirit has seen fit to bestow upon us. Chief Iron-Hand will instruct you on what equipment will be necessary to take. One thing I must stress: Haste is vitally important. The soldier paleface is advancing toward us, and no time should be wasted. While the yellow metal is being recovered, our chief of scouts, Chief I-lip-a-taw, will select the ones who will go forth with Chief Iron-Hand to purchase the thundersticks. He shall also point out the places of danger to Chief Iron-Hand, and since he is familiar with all the trails to the south, he shall advise him on what trails to take. It will be the responsibility of Chief Iron-Hand to purchase only the thundersticks we can use and the thunderbolts that will fit them. Chief Wa-neb-i-te will make certain that only responsible and dependable men shall be used, and that only the wisest will act as his contacts."

Enir was not surprised when the meeting ended so abruptly. This was how it had been with all Indian business he had seen transacted. When a thing was over to them, it was over. There was never any handshaking, backslapping, or complimentary session afterward. This pleased him, for he had always frowned upon the duplicity and hypocrisy practiced so frequently among his own race, especially in their business transactions.

When, on the following morning, Enir went in search of tools to dig with, he was directed to the community root cellar. After diligent search, he found several discarded prospector's picks, half a dozen worn-out shovels, a sledge hammer, and two crooked crowbars. "Ye Gods," he whispered to himself. "How am I ever going to sink a shaft with this junk?" He went straightaway to I-lip-a-taw and told him the many things he would need. He stressed the importance of saws, axes, digging tools, and possibly blasting equipment. He also mentioned nails for building sluice boxes and several other smaller things.

I-lip-a-taw looked toward the distant peaks for a moment, then asked, "How do you know that you will need all of these things? I never see them upon the backs of those who search for the yellow metal. You go first and see. If, after you have found the yellow metal, you still find that these things are necessary, then we shall get them. I have a saw with handles, which you may take, also two very sharp axes. Take them with the other things we have and go and see." Then, tapping his forehead, he continued, "Use the things that you have here. It is possible that they might be enough."

They began their journey early the next morning. Four husky braves were chosen to accompany Enir and Na-bab-i-ti. Enir was so excited that the pangs of sorrow he felt at being separated from his family were dulled considerably. He was about to be enlightened as to the whereabouts of the mysterious stone ladder, and the very thought of it caused a thrill of excitement to possess him. He had assumed that the psychological effect of the ancient legend of White Bosom Bare would cause the braves to be nervous and hesitant, but when he glanced into their stoic faces, he saw only a gleam of anticipation in their sharp, dark eyes, a gleam which, he decided, might be a reflection from his own.

Straight to the waterfall Na-bab-i-ti led them, then across the stream and to the foot of the bluff on the eastern side. Here, with the spray from the falls enveloping them and with the foam from the boiling pool lapping about their knees, they traversed a narrow ledge, which, during the centuries, the lapping waters had worn into the stone wall. All the way to the great waterfall Na-bab-i-ti led them without hesitation, but when they reached the falls, he called a brief halt. The noise was too deafening for words, but by the sign language he informed them that to breathe deep was dangerous in the heavy mist and also cautioned them not to let the falling water hit them. Then, with a last warning to watch close and follow his actions, Na-bab-i-ti ducked around the edge of the roaring falls and into a dark, misty cavern. Turning sharp to his left, he waited for all to come close together, then walked carefully to the other side of the waterfall. Here they found a wide crack in the stone cliff, whose bottom was very steep. The old medicine man did not hesitate, however, but climbed steadily on for perhaps half an hour. By this time they were quite far above the roaring of the water, and Na-bab-i-ti called a brief halt.

Speaking in his deep-chested voice, Na-bab-i-ti gave some brief instructions. "For a long way the trail is narrow and steep. Be careful that you do not let a stone roll from beneath your feet or you will fall. The trail will soon become wider, but to fall anywhere is very dangerous."

As they moved slowly up the steep incline, Enir glanced up toward the top of the narrow gorge. He saw the bulging walls on either side of them and discovered that they were traveling the floor of a tremendous crack in the curved mountain. He also found that this floor had been formed by stones falling from the top of it and wedging themselves in it. This was the reason for such steep rises and dips. The trembling mountain it is sometimes called, he said to himself, and he silently prayed that it wouldn't tremble until they got out of there. So this is the stone ladder, he continued to muse, but this musing brought up the eventual question, which even this ladder did not answer. How did the animals get from the breeding ground to the valley? The answer he arrived at was very simple: They didn't.

Because the fault almost paralleled the curved mountain, it was very late when it gradually disappeared and they found themselves on top of the mountain, where the air was very chilly. Na-bab-i-ti stopped, and turning to Enir said, "Chief Iron-Hand, my task is finished. You will now take the lead." Enir looked at the lowering sun, then at the scanty timber along the top of the mountain. He also noted the tired faces of the braves and the sweat upon their brows and clothing.

"It is very cool now, and when the sun sets it will grow colder. Let us cross over the top of the curved mountain and find a place to camp for the night." He saw a strange look come into the eyes of Na-bab-i-ti, and he thought that he was going to speak, but after a few seconds he signaled assent and they moved on.

Enir had so much trouble trying to keep his eyes off the picturesque scene before him that it was difficult for him to choose a campsite. The whiteness of the snow, the shadows, which seemed to emphasize the curves of a bosom, and the bright-green flower-dotted meadow below seemed to stretch endlessly before his eyes. The slanting rays of the sun seemed to form a purple background on the distant mountains, which also added beauty to the scene. White Bosom Bare indeed, he said to himself.

About a mile below the crest of the curved mountain, they came to a small glade where the grass had been cropped rather close, and here he decided to spend the night. He ordered a campfire built in its center and a low brush wall built around its perimeter. When the sun set, the picture of White Bosom Bare faded quickly, and the twilight was very short. Not many minutes after darkness had settled, a distant wailing sound reached their ears, and Na-bab-i-ti looked at Enir quickly. Presently the same sound was heard in the opposite direction, and within minutes it seemed to rise all around them. The eyes of the entire group were turned toward Enir, but he only smiled reassuringly. "It is only the mating call of many porcupines," he said. "Their voices are echoing from the mountain behind us. I have heard it many times, but never before have I heard so many." This seemed to pacify the braves, but Na-bab-i-ti's eyes remained slightly wider than usual. "There is no danger," Enir said to him in an effort to allay his uneasiness.

"It is a warning," replied Na-bab-i-ti. "Great Spirit always speaks with voices of his lesser creatures."

Enir thought for a moment, then said, "It is only a warning for others. The Great Spirit has given us the yellow metal. Let us rest." Na-bab-i-ti thought for a moment, then nodded his scarred head in agreement.

"Chief Iron-Hand is very wise," he said, and began to arrange his blanket near the fire.

They broke camp early the next morning and made good time traveling down the slightly sloping floor of the wailing forest. Enir noticed the wide variety of vegetation, more especially the different types of trees, and understood why the porcupines were so numerous in the forest. He also noticed the many small spring-fed streams and the tracks of many rodents. Food should be no problem, he told himself as they continued.

They reached the western fork of the stream that flowed east along the northern border of the wailing forest about noon. They followed it until they came to a large beaver dam, but they did not immediately cross over. The reason they didn't was that near the opposite end of it stood a gigantic elk bull, whose antlers were indeed as large as the limbs of small trees. They all stood and gazed at him with amazement, but the old bull seemed to be unaware of their presence. However, when Enir signaled them to continue on down the stream, the old bull moved slowly along with them, staying just opposite them on the other side. "We will be safe so long as we stay among the trees," he whispered. "For those antlers will not permit him to run through the forest."

"He is blind," said one of the braves. "Look closely and you will see that his eyes are white." Enir advanced to the edge of the stream and looked closely.

"You are right," he agreed. "But he is no less dangerous. You will notice that his ears are guiding him. Let us remain on this side of the stream, for it is my intention to follow it anyway." After haunting them for perhaps a mile, the old bull turned and slowly made his way back toward the beaver dam. Enir experienced a twinge of pity for the old monster, for when he turned, the outline of his rib cage was plainly visible through his heavy hair. Enir felt that the old fellow was probably lonely and followed them more for company than for any other reason, as he had shown no apparent resentment of their presence.

They moved steadily eastward along the stream until they came to another beaver colony. They circled a small lake and found another beaver dam over which the stream flowed wide and shallow. They crossed over the stream onto the bare, spongy ground along the foot of the great treeless meadow, where they made much better progress. Enir stopped occasionally to hastily pan a sample of gravel as they moved eastward, but not once did he find any trace of color. This did not worry him, because he did not expect to. There was one thing that they all noticed, though, that did worry them. This was the occasional track of a grizzly bear. They were all aware that the presence of so many trout in the stream would attract the bears, and they advanced warily.

Late in the evening they came to a broad, firm spot where several large boulders were strewn about near the mouth of a draw, and Enir decided that it would be a good location for them to stop for the night. He ordered the braves to build a low, circular brush fence around a small mound, and in the center of it they built their campfire. While two of the braves were adding brush to the top of the low fence, Enir overheard one ask the other how he felt. The other answered, saying, "I feel like bear feel on other side of curved mountain."

While Na-bab-i-ti and the others were preparing a meal, Enir strolled down to a small pool that had formed where the water from an unused beaver dam lazily entered the stream bed. Something on the bottom of this clear pool caught his eye, and he stopped still and let his eyes become accustomed to the shimmering of the water. For perhaps a full minute he stood slightly stooped, then he raised his head and gazed out over the lush meadow. There was a pleased look on his face as he returned to the campsite, but he said nothing. What he had seen were the footprints of Bat and Shadow. He was sure that there was no mistake, for the story he had read there on the bottom of the shallow pool was complete. They had crowded a deer, perhaps a buck, into this small pool and no doubt killed it. He was sure that his bones could be found somewhere near, hidden by the tall grass. It was knowing that they were both alive and had made their home in this vast valley so well stocked with game, that caused his heart to sing with gladness. So there is another entrance into this valley, he said to himself. Faintly at first but gradually growing volume until it was almost continuous, the forest began to wail. However the wailing did not last long, ending as it began, slowly. Enir knew that during the spring and fall this wailing would be much louder and more consistent, for these are the chief mating seasons of the porcupine.

Shortly after the wailing had ceased, Enir noticed Na-bab-i-ti glancing frequently into the great meadow before them. Remembering the story about the sea of eyes, he, too, glanced out over the grassy meadow. He was not at all surprised when he located several pairs of eyes reflecting the light of the campfire. He gave no sign that he had noticed them, but continued to glance in their direction at intervals. As the darkness thickened, these eyes increased in number until there was indeed a wall of flashing eyes in the half circle of firelight. Enir wondered why Na-bab-i-ti had not identified them as curious bovines by their variations in height and size. But when he realized the state of fear which surely had possessed him, he understood.

Enir did not call attention to the reflection of the light from these eyes until he was sure that there would not be any noticeable increase in their number. He was aware that the Indians were waiting for him to do so, but he still waited. Presently he said in a muted whisper, "Be ready, and at my signal let us all give the Flathead war cry in a single voice." After another ten minutes had passed, he was convinced that no more curious eyes would join them, so he gave the signal. When the coarse sound of six male voices uttering the bloodcurdling war cry of the Flathead slammed into the silence of the valley, bedlam broke loose in the meadow around them. There were grunts, snorts, and clashing of bodies, followed by the sound of many hoofbeats as the sea of flashing eyes immediately disintegrated. No word was spoken as they listened to the sound of the retreating hoofbeats, which gradually died in the distance.

After a moment's wait, Enir rose unconcernedly and began to inspect their supply of firewood. After satisfying himself that there was plenty, he assigned the four braves to equal watches. Knowing well the Indian's knack of reading time by the stars, he left them to arrange the watches. His only instructions were to keep the fire blazing well throughout the entire night. Having delivered these curt instructions, he immediately prepared a place upon the spongy ground and spread his blanket. He knew that the Indians would interpret this action as a signal for all, except the one whose lot it was to stand the first watch, to retire. Na-bab-i-ti approached him and in as low a voice as his disfigurement would permit said, "Mebbyso in early morning beast come."

"Mebbyso," replied Enir, then, remembering that bragging was not frowned upon among the Indians as it was among the paleface, he added, "and mebbyso he has already left this valley and someone has slain him." He covertly watched the old medicine man's eyes grow round as he looked upon Sohe's bow, which Enir had placed close by his side as he stretched out on his blanket. It was the same expression he had seen in them when Na-bab-i-ti had first seen the body of the great grizzly he had killed.

Enir fell asleep with his hand upon his bow. He was not nearly so much at ease as he pretended, and when he was awakened an hour or so later by the distant cry of a timber wolf, he secretly prayed that it was Shadow and that he and Bat would be attracted to their fire, or at least be nearby, should a grizzly happen to wander by their campsite.

But the night proved uneventful, and by the time day had fully dawned, they had gathered their meager equipment and were ready to move on. Enir did not bother to check for color in the stream, but hastened on to the place where it converged with the stream flowing west. It was almost midday when they reached it, and they all stood fascinated by the great rising and falling ridge of water that was formed as both streams converged to form a single stream flowing south. Signaling them to wait, Enir hastily checked the westward-flowing stream for color. He was not surprised when he found none, and he called them all together for a short conference. Seeing plenty of dry driftwood close by, he suggested that they build a small campfire and prepare meat. Then, pointing to the rather steep shoulder on the eastern bank of the large stream that the two smaller ones had formed, he said, "While the meat is being prepared, I will climb to the top of this shoulder and see how much of the big stream I can see. The yellow metal is between here and the waterfall. You will allow your eyes to be very sharp when we travel down it. Look well among the gravel at its edge. We will start when I return."

As Enir toiled up the steep shoulder, he was greatly assisted by the many small trees that grew thickly in places along it. Often he needed to rest, and when he did, he was again awed by the beauty of the scene below him. The bank extended steeply upward from where the waters of the westward flowing stream lapped against it, and the green vegetation upon the sides of the shoulder cast its reflection upon the stream, causing the water to have a dark-green cast. This, with the beautiful picture it bordered, was indeed very impressive. But Enir did not tarry long to admire the beauty. He realized that he was getting closer and closer to the bonanza of White

Bosom Bare, and the age-old thrill, which he had only slightly tasted, was creeping upon him.

While he was resting from a short, steep climb, his ears detected a high-pitched vibrating sound. "The singing snow," he whispered, and he moved quickly out into an open place where the great snowfield was visible. He could feel his eardrums vibrating, and his eyeballs also seemed to be in motion. He was looking toward the two peaks when he saw what appeared to be many tiny ants moving in opposite directions. While he watched, he saw more of them who were not so far away, and he quickly recognized them as deer, antelope, and wapiti, or elk. These were also fleeing in opposite directions, and he became very curious. Why, he asked himself, would the animals flee from one another? He glanced far up on the great, glaring snowfield, and sure enough there was a dim shadow moving swiftly toward him. Enir's eyes grew very wide. Was the legend true after all? Was there really an unknown death-dealing monster in this quiet valley? While he looked, the swift-moving spectrum became plainer and larger. Suddenly it bounded from the snow and disintegrated, spreading widely out over the meadow, and just as suddenly the singing stopped. Enir continued to watch, and presently he saw several large boulders rush from the grass and plunge into the stream below him. Enir's pulse gradually became steady, and he managed a small smile. "Singing snow," he said, "caused by a small avalanche composed of ice, stone, and soil and traveling swiftly over the great slanting glacier, creating a sound so unique that it is possible to count on your fingers the number of human beings who have heard it. Singing snow, indeed." Enir was so excited with his discovery that he forgot why he had climbed the shoulder and was halfway back to his starting place before he thought of it. "Huh," he said, then thought. Oh, well, I'll soon see all of the stream anyway, he said to himself, and continued to move back down the steep incline. "Small wonder that the mystery has never been solved," he whispered. "Had I not been standing in a place where I could see all of it, it might have gone undiscovered for another hundred years."

As he climbed carefully down the steep shoulder, he began to think more deeply upon what he had seen. Maybe, he told himself, it would not be a good idea to blast this one remaining mystery concerning the sacred valley. He had already accounted for the wailing forest and the sea of flashing eyes, and had hinted strongly to Na-bab-i-ti of the nature of the beast that had attacked him. "I'll wait until I have talked with I-lip-a-taw," he mumbled to himself, but he continued to mull it over in his mind as he continued his descent. This superstition had existed among the Indians for many generations and he was afraid that so simple an explanation for it would render him very unpopular among the Indians. He recalled how quickly Na-bab-i-ti had defended the wailing forest and also that he had received no congratulatory glance from any of them when he had given the order that had dispersed the sea of flashing eyes. Maybe I had best go easy, he thought.

When Enir had forded the stream and approached the campfire, where a great stack of roasted water rats lay untouched beside it, he noticed that the Indians were gathered in a tight group and were eyeing him with wide, unblinking eyes. He stopped before them and said, "Come, my brothers, let us be about our business. The Great Spirit has sent us here to get the yellow metal that he has saved for us. He did not say that he would stop the snow from singing

192

while we did so." The tension among them quickly eased, and Enir continued, "Let us be not like children. The Great Spirit has chosen us because we are brave men. Has he not imparted to us much knowledge about his sacred valley? Let us be satisfied. Now let us eat and be about the task he has given us." This seemed to completely thaw their chilly attitude toward him, and as he wrung the water from his clothing and hung it up to dry while he ate, they moved briskly about to finish preparing the meal. After it was done, they were quick to do his bidding, and he saw them glance at one another meaningfully, so he was convinced that he had used the right approach.

When they were ready to go, Enir stood for a moment and gazed at the swift water, and then said, "The banks of the stream are very steep in places." Then, turning to one of the braves who appeared to be both stronger and slightly more intelligent than the others, he said, "You will go with me and search one of the banks while I search the other." Turning to Na-bab-i-ti, he said, "You and the others will see that the tools are taken care of, and will go on ahead. Be careful that the saw and axes are not dropped into the water or allowed to fall upon the rocks and become dulled. It may be necessary at times to move far back from the water, but if we need you, we shall call." He then motioned them forward down the swirling stream.

Enir made several tests as they moved slowly down the swift stream but found no trace of color. He watched his companion closely and on several occasions directed him to bring samples of gravel from certain sand bars, but when evening approached, they still had found nothing to encourage them. This did not necessarily discourage him, for he was certain that the gold was there, and he knew that if they should overlook it as they passed, they would find color somewhere below and could trace it back. The steep walls of the canyon made it difficult to judge the time of day, but by glancing upward he could see that the shadows of the surrounding trees were growing very long, and he began to watch closely for a place to camp. Presently they came to a large open space where the walls of the bluff were very wide apart and firewood was plentiful. Enir called in Na-bab-i-ti and the other three braves, and it was decided that they would camp here for the night. Enir could hear the sounds of rapids not far below them, and he told them to go ahead and prepare the camp while he dropped down to see how great the rapids were.

As Enir approached the sound of gurgling water, he found a low waterfall, and directly below it the stream widened out and traversed a small open valley. This valley was perhaps half a mile across and almost perfectly round. There were many large trees growing in it, and it was covered with tall bunchgrass. It was a very beautiful spot, and Enir wished that they had pushed on. As he walked across the valley, he flushed several grouse, and he knew that they were nesting here in this protected valley. At the lower end of this valley and at the foot of the rapids, Enir paused. A distant roaring sound reached his ears, and by the position of the crest of the curved mountain, he knew that it must be the great waterfall. He quickly produced his gold pan and began to test the gravelly sand. Sure enough he found an abundance of color. Hastening back to the low waterfall at the head of the valley, he waded out into the shallows below it and quickly dipped up a large pan of gravel. Turning his back to the fading sunlight, he allowed the sand to drain slowly back into the water. Suddenly his body ceased to shiver from the cold, and a flood of warmth passed over him. The sand was rich with raw gold. "I knew that if it was not here we were in big trouble," he whispered.

He then moved to the edge of the stream just at the foot of the low falls and dug deep into the gravel with both his hands. When he had filled his gold pan and stepped back, he noticed many flecks of gold around the roots of the hairs upon his forearms. His breath became short and his blood turned to the fire. "The bonanza of White Bosom Bare," he breathed. "Raw gold by the ton, and I, Enir Halverson, have found it." Suddenly he felt like shouting and dancing at the same time as he fingered the heavy contents in the bottom of his gold pan. He was feeling a thrill that only one in a thousand prospectors feels. He closed his eyes and breathed deeply. When he did, the stern face of I-lip-a-taw confronted him, followed by So-he's smile of love and Tall-One's adoring eyes. When the tiny arms of Whispering-West-Wind were extended toward him, he opened his eyes and staggered back, and sat down upon a large rock. "It is not mine," he said in a low whisper. Then, with the icy water pouring over his moccasins, he slowly wiped the sand from his forearms and suddenly began to feel the cold wind upon his naked body. He removed his moccasins and donned his buckskin garments, then sat back down while he wrung the water from his moccasins. Stripe told me one time that many prospectors lost their minds when they made their strikes, and I suppose that is what is happening to me, he told himself as he laced his moccasins. "Anyway, I'm glad that I understand this before it gets too far away," he said with a sad smile. Gold for thundersticks, he said to himself. Then a sad thought came to him. All of the gold in the world would not save the redman. His era is over, but the gold will aid them in their determination to die like men and not like rabbits.

As Enir made his way back to the campsite, his mind was not on the gold he had found, but upon the strange impact it had had upon his thoughts. I can't understand it, he told himself. I have plenty of gold, gold that I never intend to take from the place where it is hidden. What would So-he have thought had she seen me? And I-lip-a-taw? I must never again forget my friends who have gambled their resources upon my integrity. I am a Flathead Chief, and never must I forget to conduct myself as such. Thanks to the Great Spirit, there were no witnesses. I must be careful and not allow excitement to show upon my face, he reminded himself as he approached the campfire. He both knew and appreciated the sharpness of the Indian's eyes and also their knack of interpreting one's slightest actions.

So, as Enir entered the circle of firelight, he allowed a slight frown to appear upon his face. This was easy for him to do because he had forcefully wrenched his thoughts away from discovering the gold and placed them upon the difficult task of transporting it to the valley below. As usual, he felt the sharp eyes of the Indians upon him as he nonchalantly sat down by the fire and, reaching out, tore a leg from a roasting duck and began to eat. The others all followed suit, except Na-bab-i-ti, who approached Enir and said, "There are trout roasting beneath the coals." Enir quickly glanced at the new gold pan upon the coals beside the fire and saw that in it was some simmering windy weed sauce. He nodded his thanks to Na-bab-i-ti, threw the duck's leg into the fire and sat back to wait.

While Enir waited for the fish to roast, his mind dwelt upon many different things. The future of So-he and his children caused his frown to deepen. It was impossible for him to adopt the Indian's philosophy regarding the survival of the fittest. Parental love had been so dulled by this philosophy that an Indian child was practically on his own from birth. This appeared to him to be closely related to selfishness, laziness, and indifference. Yet he could not deny that it had produced a strong, self-sufficient race. At least they all had an equal chance, such as it was.

As he gazed into the embers of the fire, he remembered a remark he had made the day after arriving in this valley. As they stood on the banks of the small stream at the edge of the wailing forest, he had watched the large trout jumping for insects and had remarked that they were very delicious roasted and dipped in windy weed sauce. They had remembered it and were now surprising him with his favorite dish. Why? He thought that he knew the answer. Because he had been fortunate enough to be in a position to solve the mystery of the singing snow, he had shown no fear of it. The Indians, who had been less fortunate, had interpreted his nonchalant attitude as that of extreme bravery and were paying their respects to him for it. It caused him to harbor a feeling of guilt, but he decided that it might contribute to the success of this venture if he left it that way. For the hardships and difficulties that he foresaw in the task before them called for all the respect and cooperation he could get.

Enir fell asleep that night vainly struggling with the problem of developing, almost empty-handed, what promised to be the most fabulous gold strike in history. When he woke the next morning, Na-bab-i-ti was already supervising the getting together of their equipment, and Enir casually told them that the gold was only a short distance away, that he had found it the evening before while reconnoitering the rapids. "There is a small valley there," he continued, ignoring their surprised looks, "where many grouse are nesting. It is an excellent place for our camp." Then he gave the order to proceed.

When they reached the valley, Enir chose a well-drained spot, and there he directed the three braves who were with Na-bab-i-ti to start clearing for a permanent lodge. After they discussed the plans, he took the tall Indian who had been working with him, and with a pick and shovel they began to trace the source of the yellow metal. All that day, while Na-bab-i-ti and his braves labored on the lodge, Enir and his companion dug many exploratory trenches, and finally, at a place where the stream had once flowed, Enir found what he was looking for: an unbelievably large deposit of free gold. As he gazed down upon it, he felt again the fire in his blood, but he quickly quenched it by forcing his mind to center upon the other problems. "This solves only one of our problems," he said. "We must now find a way to move it to our valley."

Leaving the tall Indian to dig a trench that diverted part of the waters of the stream into a large basin where the gold could be panned clean, Enir went to assist in the erection of their lodge. It was while boring the holes in the lodge poles to bind them together that an idea came to him and caused him to forget the work he was doing. He sat down upon a nearby stump and gazed blankly toward the dimly roaring sound not very far to the south of them. Presently he snapped out of his reverie, and together they hurriedly bound the lodge poles into a large wooden tepee. As he stepped back to survey it, he could not help but wonder how such a neat job could be accomplished so quickly, especially by these children of nature who had never been taught the function of angles, the laws of stress, or even the art of measuring. But he did not ponder long, because other problems were crowding his mind.

As soon as the lodge was finished, Enir called a conference. He waited until the campfire had begun to burn brightly before he started to speak, because the sun had ducked behind the curved mountain and dusk was fast approaching. He noticed the anxious expression on all their faces as he at last rose. "My friends," he began, "we have reached the first milestone of our difficult task. We have found the yellow metal. Our next task will be far more difficult. We must move the yellow metal to the lodge of Chief Wa-neb-i-te. This will require the work of strong men. If there are any among you who are not willing to perform this duty, let him speak." He waited a full minute, but nothing but the clucking of a mother grouse, whose young had been frightened by the workers, disturbed the silence. "I expected no protest," he continued, "but I must be sure. Now I want one very brave man, who is willing to return alone and descend the stone ladder. He will carry my message to Chief Wa-neb-i-te. It is a message that we cannot say with smoke." Enir started to say more, but he was interrupted by Na-bab-i-ti.

"I will go," spoke the medicine man in his deep voice. "Here I can do little, but this I can do swiftly and well."

"It shall be as you say," said Enir. "Tomorrow, I will prepare my message."

Early the next morning, Enir chose a medium sized tree and directed two of the braves to fell it.

When this was done, he marked it off into blocks of approximately eighteen inches in length. He then directed the braves to saw these blocks very carefully with I-lip-a-taw's saw. He then took the one-inch wood auger and began to bore a hole directly in the center of the end of one of these blocks. When the hole was as deep as the auger would bore without danger of damaging it, he began to fit a small limb into the hole. While he was doing this, he instructed the tall brave who had been acting as his assistant while searching to begin boring a hole in the center of another block. "You must be very careful," he said, "that you do not bend or break the auger. Bore very slow. If you learn to do this well, I will assign to you this task and you will not dig."

The tall Indian looked at him silently for a few seconds, then replied, "I will do it carefully and well, but not because I mind to dig. It will be because we have no other auger, and because I understand what you are planning to do." Enir was taken slightly aback by this answer and his face showed it when he looked into the intelligent eyes of his tall companion. What a fool I have been, he said to himself. For surely I-lip-a-taw had chosen the best scouts for this important task, and I have been treating them like children.

To cover his embarrassment, he asked, "Do you think it will work?"

"It will work," replied the tall brave. "We may lose some of them, but they will find many."

"I fear," said Enir, "that if we load them too heavy, they will sink to the bottom and never reach the waterfall."

The tall brave looked at the block thoughtfully for a moment then said, "Leave big space of nothing between limb and gold. Maybe make it float."

"Yes, I intended to," replied Enir. "How big a place of nothing would you suggest?" The tall brave was again thoughtful. Presently he pointed to the pond he had formed where the gold was to be cleaned and said, "Try there first." Enir looked again at the tall brave and his estimation of his intelligence advanced another notch. So they found that each block would safely carry about 8 oz of gold.

So day after day, from dawn to dusk, small lodgepole blocks poured over the great waterfall. Every clear evening, the man in the valley who talked with smoke, sent up his tally. The loss was considered negligible. A few of the blocks struck sharp edged stones in their swift descent and had split open. Others had been crowded into some sluggish eddy above the falls and had been delayed until after nightfall. All of these were recovered at the rapids far below the waterfall by the squaws who were sent there by I-lip-a-taw as safeguards. So after ten days of careful checking, Enir found that not a single block was unaccounted for. The sharp-eyed Indians had even kept a count on the number which had split open against the rocks.

On the evening of the tenth day, after the first gold-filled block had leaped from the top of the waterfall, the scout who read the smoke, came to Enir with a strange message. "Message say, chief come down," said the scout.

Enir smiled at the scout's agitated look and said, "Yes, I have been expecting such a message." And the scout seemed relieved. Enir knew that he had been afraid he had misread the message.

So Enir left the tall brave in charge but specified that he was still to be the hole maker. "You will make any decisions that need to be made," said Enir. "But I do not trust anyone else's skill making the hole." He then departed for the stone ladder and the lodge of Wa-neb-i-te.

Enir secretly dreaded the task of descending the stone ladder. One day, he had asked Na-bab-i-ti some pointed questions about the steep places in the bottom of the fault, because he well knew that this trip was coming up, and even then he feared it. Na-bab-i-ti had told him always to descend backward on the steep places, and if he should slip, to lie flat upon his stomach and guide his direction with his hands. Enir felt just a little ashamed of his fear after he had arrived at the bottom of the steep climb without an incident, but as he passed beneath the falls, he thought of the heavy blocks of wood that were rushing past and he ducked very low.

Chapter 18

When Enir presented himself at the lodge of Wa-neb-i-te and was shown the many bags of yellow metal, he could scarcely believe his eyes. They were neatly stacked upon the floor of the round lodge, and Enir estimated that there were at least two hundred pounds of gold. Wa-neb-i-te's eyes shone with pleasure, and he said, "Chief Iron-Hand has done well. Is there anything that the braves whom you left in the sacred valley are in need of?"

"They are very tired," replied Enir. "If you could send them each a squaw, who will keep them from being lonesome, and also give them time to rest and hunt, they would be very grateful. For nowhere is the game more plentiful and nowhere do the roots, the berries, and the wild fruit grow so close together. But because the trees are getting farther away and the saw and axes no longer cut so well, the work grows more difficult each day."

"This I will do, Chief Iron-Hand. Also I will send I-lip-a-taw to sharpen the saw and axes. You will now go to your lodge and rest and hunt, for soon I must send you upon another mission. When things are ready, I shall summon you."

Enir enjoyed being reunited with his family. Sa-ra seemed to have grown during his brief absence, and he was sure that Tall-One's English had improved. So-he smiled continuously, and Wo-dan was anxious for the hunt.

When he told I-lip-a-taw, in privacy, what he had

learned concerning the wailing forest and the singing snows, I-lip-a-taw did not seem surprised. But when he gave him the details about the vast gold deposit, he became very excited. "It is as I have long thought," he said sadly. "Should we have allowed ourselves to have been governed as a people, abolished many tribal laws, and not have been so quick to welcome strangers on our shores, we would have been able to preserve our land. The great war chief is right, we must all stand together. But the great war chief was born too late. There is no way now that we can save our land. I have told no one about this, but I will tell you now, my son. I have traveled much farther into the land held by the paleface than anybody knows. I have seen much, and I know their strength and their selfish desires. However, it is like Al-a-go-ri-o has said. Naught remains but to fight or cry like the rabbit. He was also right when he said that our cry, like the rabbit's, would go unheard. Our country, which is filled with so much beauty and so many riches, is swiftly becoming like a worm-eaten apple. Our people will soon be driven hither and yon, forced to live in slavery and dejection. They will be forced to eat what the paleface throws them, and many will starve when food is plentiful everywhere. It is much better to die. This I believe, that the only ones who will survive are those who are weak, those who have no pride and those who are not yet old enough to know what is happening. Many years from now, the paleface will point to the descendents of these and say such are the redmen. This I also believe, my son: There were people here before the Indian came. Maybe our forefathers exterminated them even as the paleface will exterminate us. Likewise will the paleface someday be exterminated. It is my belief that the stay of the paleface will be the shortest of all. For in his own selfishness, he will destroy himself. But first he will destroy the beauty of this land."

Enir listened to the sonorous voice of I-lip-a-taw, and himself began to wonder if the paleface were as greedy and selfish as I-lip-a-taw had said. His thoughts were interrupted by I-lip-a-taw, who said, "Tomorrow I go with four squaws into the valley of White Bosom Bare. My squaw will remain to be with your family when you are again called away. Your task will be beset with many dangers, so think well, my son. May the Great Spirit continue to smile upon you. Goodbye." And I-lip-a-taw, the man whom Enir regarded as the wisest among the Indians, turned slowly away.

When Enir took Wo-dan upon the hunt, he found game in such abundance that much of the pleasure was taken from it. He attributed this to the absence of so many hunters from the forest. He went to the village and told all of the squaws whose husbands were away or unable to hunt that he would hang the deer in trees beside the trails and that those who needed meat could help themselves. This worked well for a time, but as Wo-dan became more efficient in trailing the wapiti to his hiding place and many of the huge carcasses hung from trees awaiting the arrival of the squaws, the women began to complain, and Enir was forced to slow down.

When Enir told So-he of finding the tracks of Bat and Shadow in the sacred valley, her eyes shone with delight. "Do you think that Wo-dan will ever go to be a wolf?" she asked.

"No," replied Enir. "But someday he may find a female wolf and bring her here. If he does, you must be very careful. I fear that she will not be even as friendly as Shadow. I fear that she will be very vi-

cious. You must never allow the children near her."
So-he looked thoughtfully out into the forest.

"Maybe he will find none," she said.

"He will find one, said Enir resignedly.

"Maybe I should stop Tall-One from riding his back," said So-he. "But I can never stop them from playing together. Wo-dan never tires of playing."

"I don't think that it will happen soon," said Enir. "Wo-dan is still quite young."

Sa-ra had now fully accepted Enir's presence and would hold out her tiny arms to him each time he entered the lodge. Each day she seemed to grow more beautiful, and her widely spaced eyes began to reflect an interest in everything unusual. She would hug Wo-dan's neck and point her tiny finger at the multicolored birds that frequented the open space before the lodge. Her grandmother told Enir that she would be almost exactly like So-he, but maybe not so shy. "So-he was always shy of strangers," said So-he's mother, "but Sa-ra trusts everybody."

One day while Enir sat upon a stump, busily whittling a toy for Sa-ra, he let his mind review the last speech that I-lip-a-taw had made to him. He heard again that sincere and sonorous voice and saw again the graceful signs which supplemented the beautiful Salish language. He held a deep respect for I-lip-a-taw's wisdom, but he could not fully agree that things would be as bad as the old bowmaker had predicted. Yet he was in full sympathy with the Indians. This land was rightfully theirs. He could see plainly that the paleface were the aggressors and that they had no respect whatever for the Indians' rights. For a man or a group of men to shoot down unarmed men, women, and children was to Enir nothing but cold-blooded murder, and he would steadfastly resist them in every way possible. It was while pursuing this train of thought that he saw Wo-dan signal the approach of something or someone, so he rose and looked up the trail. Presently a brave came round the bend, and Enir quickly recognized him as a messenger from Chief Wa-neb-i-te. A few words of greeting were exchanged, then the messenger delivered the summons from the chief. Enir instructed the man to tell Wa-neb-i-te that he would be there, then turned and slowly entered the lodge. Enir's heart was very heavy, for he knew that he would be long absent from his family. He hesitated to tell So-he, but knew that he must.

When Enir finally mustered the courage to tell So-he about the summons and had given voice to his fear of what he would be called upon to do, the leafy branch that she waved slowly above the faces of the sleeping children did not falter and a look of stoic resignation slowly took possession of her radiant face. "You shall wear your beaded suit and your feathered headpiece," she said in a low voice. "You shall speak, and the other chiefs will listen. For you, my Enir, are wiser than they. My father has told me that if there is anyone who can bring us victory over the paleface, it is you. I know that you will be gone long, and this my father told me to tell you before you went away: While you were in the sacred valley, I went with my father to the village near the great lake. There we visited this great man, Father De-Smit'. My father and he are friends. We gave him the names of our children, Enir and Sa-ra, and he put them into his large book where many other names are kept in the strange markings of the paleface. My father said that this should be done for their protection. I spoke with this man in the language of the French, and I believe that he is a very good and kind man. He also put my name and yours into the great book, which he called a record. But I did not give him the cane from the medicine bag you made for me, nor did I tell him or my father about it. So go, my Enir, and do the things that you are called upon to do. The Great Spirit has told me to have no fear and also that you shall return. Yet I cannot keep the sadness from my heart." Enir gently removed the branch from her hand and embraced her tenderly.

"You are very wise and beautiful, my So-he," he said huskily. "You will listen to the wisdom of your father and remember all of the things I have told you. You will also remember the promise of the Great Spirit. When my work is finished, I shall return."

Chapter 19

When Enir arrived at the round lodge that evening, there were seven scouts present. Four of these were strangers to him, but he recognized the other three. Two were from the group who had accompanied Chief Al-a-go-ri-o on his last visit, and the other one was none other than the tall brave he had put in charge when he left the sacred valley. They waited in silence until two more scouts arrived, then Chief Wa-neb-i-te rose and said, "Warriors, Chief Iron-Hand will be your leader." He pointed to the stack of neatly tied bags of raw gold and continued, "It was he who provided us with the yellow metal. It is he, also, who understands better its value to the paleface. You will obey his orders and keep nothing from him. He alone will be the judge of the people with whom we seek to deal." Then, pointing to the brave who sat farthest from Enir, he went on, "Beginning with you, you will all rise and tell us what information you have uncovered concerning the thundersticks, and also of the honorless paleface you have found who are willing to betray their friends to possess the yellow metal."

After each brave had reported, it was very plain to both Enir and Wa-neb-i-te that in order to obtain enough thundersticks to meet their needs, they would have to go very near to the land that was now occupied by the thunderstick soldiers. They looked at each other in silence. Enir was waiting for the order that would take him far away from his family and loved ones. Wa-neb-i-te was hoping that he would volunteer to go. Presently Enir turned to the group of braves and asked, "Do any of you know any paleface trappers upon the banks of our streams?"

"Yes," replied one of them. "We know many. But we know of none who can be trusted. They all drink firewater, and none of them has respect for the Indian. Most of their squaws hate them and stay only because the Indians will not allow them to return."

After a moment, another one said, "I know of one whose father was a trapper and whose mother was a Flathead, or a Nez Percé. He now lives far to the south and has many horses. The horses he has are of the very best. They are called after his name, which is Spotted-Horse. I, myself, do not know him well, but my friends say that he can be trusted. This I do know, that both the Indians and the soldier-paleface give him yellow metal in exchange for the spotted ponies.

Enir looked questioningly at Wa-neb-i-te and Wa-neb-i-te nodded saying, "It might be well for Chief Iron-Hand to check on this man and his horses."

So it was arranged that on the following day they would leave as a group and remain together until they reached the lodge of Spotted-Horse. To his embarrassment, Enir learned that henceforth all of his travels would be made on horseback. He confided to the tall brave who was with him in White Bosom Bare that he had never ridden anything but broken horses. The brave smiled and said, "This I suspected. But do not worry, you are quick and strong; I shall teach you." And teach him he did. For the first several days Enir was so sore that he could scarcely mount, but he was determined to master the art of bareback riding, and this determination, coupled with the expert knowledge of his instructor, soon enabled him to master the art. But as Chief Iron-Hand, he was not satisfied until he had forced himself to become an expert horseman, which did not occur, even though he concentrated much upon it, until they had reached the land of Spotted-Horse. By then, Chief Iron-Hand feared no horse and had even begun to practice tricks of his own devising. "I have learned three things," Enir whispered to himself. "To sleep with my ears open, to think with my mouth shut, and to see what I am looking at."

After looking over and studying closely the nature of Spotted-Horse's spread, Enir decided that it would be better if they did not all ride in together. So, choosing the tall brave to accompany him, he ordered the others to fall well back into the hills and make camp until they returned. On the way to the lodge of Spotted-Horse, Enir told his companion that they would first attempt to buy horses. "If these horses are as I have been told, we are in need of some. But we only want the best. Which ones we purchase, I will leave to your judgment." The tall brave merely nodded, but Enir was well aware that he recognized the importance of good fast horses in the business that they were entering into.

When Enir was ushered into the presence of the half-breed Spotted-Horse, he received quite a surprise. He was a small man, and he wore the cloth clothes of a paleface. He also wore the boots and the floppy headpiece of a paleface. But Enir noted that the sharp eyes, which regarded him steadily, were the eyes of an Indian. Also, the slightly hooked nose, beardless face, and square chin spoke plainly of his Indian ancestry. When he advanced to greet them, Enir was quick to note the long, sinewy arms, the slightly turned-in toes, and the bowed legs. Yes, he told himself, here is a man of great power and influence. I will do well to gain this man's confidence.

When Enir stated his business, he juggled a bag of yellow metal in his hands. The sharp eyes of the horse rancher moved quickly from the bag of gold to Enir's face and surprised the appraising stare in Enir's eyes. But with a wave of his hand, he dismissed the trade talk and called for the squaws to bring much food. He then motioned them to enter a large room that adjoined the main lodge, saying, "We will eat first. I see that you are of my mother's people and must have traveled far."

After he had seated them at a large stone table that was surrounded by stone benches, he stepped to an outside door, and Enir heard him speaking to someone he could not see. By listening closely and watching the signs given, Enir made out the following request: "Go quickly to the canyon of black stones. Bring the largest horses to the pole canyon. Throw to them the paleface hay, then wait for me."

After a bountiful meal of roast buffalo hump and strange roots, Spotted-Horse led them to a small box canyon, where about fifty spotted horses were feeding in front of a high row of staunch pole bars. Spotted-Horse merely waved his hand, then stood by while Enir and his companion climbed upon the barred entrance and began to study the herd. Enir saw at once that they were indeed fine horses, but he remained silent while the tall brave appraised the herd. He had never seen an Appaloosa before, and they all showed the marks of careful breeding. One stallion caught his eye. He was large and had a wide forehead, small ears, and soft, gentle eyes. After studying him, Enir decided that as a horse he was perfect.

After the tall brave had examined the herd to his

satisfaction, he signaled for Enir to bargain for ten of them. Enir was quick to catch the signal, but so were the sharp eyes of Spotted-Horse, and without waiting for Enir to speak, he motioned for them to follow him back to the lodge. There he produced a hand-made wooden balance. Then, from a certain pile of neatly arranged stones he chose ten and placed them upon one of the boxlike structures on one end of the balance. He motioned to the boxlike structure on the other end and said, "The yellow metal that it takes to lift the stones is my price." Enir placed the bag of gold upon the balance and it immediately sank. He motioned for Spotted-Horse to add another stone, but it took still another before the bag slowly rose. Thus did Chief Iron-Hand come into possession of twelve Appaloosa horses.

Enir spent the remainder of the day and part of the next morning talking with Spotted-Horse, while his companion and the braves employed by Spotted-Horse singled out the horses he had bought. Enir had made only one stipulation, which was for the tall brave to be sure that the stallion was in the group.

To Enir's delight, Spotted-Horse talked freely about the soldier-paleface and told him the position of army forts and encampments. He also told him which trails led to them and which ones led around them. He readily admitted that he sold horses to the thunderstick soldiers, but said also that he heartily disliked them. He said that they were arrogant and insulting. Enir found him to be in full agreement with I-lip-a-taw on the inevitable fate of the Indian, and Spotted-Horse said that he was hoarding the yellow metal against the time when he would be forced to live under the paleface rule. Enir was secretly elated to learn of Spotted-Horse's deep thirst for the yellow metal. He told him of how the paleface with their thundersticks had frightened away the deer and the wapiti, and that the bow was no longer ample for obtaining meat. He said that he had been sent out to acquire thundersticks for them to hunt with, but that the paleface would not sell them. The paleface wanted the Indian to starve. He dropped many strong hints that the Flathead would be willing to part with their yellow metal, provided that they could get thundersticks in return. He then subtly withdrew and turned the initiative over to Spotted-Horse.

Spotted-Horse first began to pry for a lead on where the yellow metal was coming from, but Enir remained evasive. Finally he asked Enir how much yellow metal he would give for each thunderstick. Enir replied that he did not want just any thunderstick, that he wanted only the ones that he could get thunderbolts to fit, and only those which would shoot far and straight like those of the soldier paleface. Finally the little half-breed admitted that there were men hidden on his ranch who might be able to obtain a few of these thundersticks. However, it would cost the price of one horse stone for each one of them. Enir winced visibly at the price and said that unless there were many thunderbolts to go with them, he would not be interested. Spotted-Horse asked him how many thunderbolts it would take to get him interested. Enir spread his fingers on both hands five times, and this time Spotted-Horse winced. He immediately began to argue for more gold, but Enir pretended to begin to back off. This worked beautifully, for Spotted Horse immediately became conciliatory and quickly agreed that he would do his best to obtain the thunderbolts. At last, Enir told him that if he could get a hundred thundersticks and the required number of thunderbolts to send up the smoke and he would send a brave with the yellow metal. Spotted-Horse was thoughtful and asked how long this brave would wait. Enir told him ten days. Spotted-Horse argued for twenty, and Enir finally told him that if he got them in ten days, he would throw in an extra stone's worth of yellow metal. That sealed the bargain, and Spotted-Horse, after instructing his men to give Chief Iron-Hand all the help he needed, mounted his own horse and told them goodbye.

Chapter 20

During the following years, the band of outlaws who rode spotted horses became very famous along the ragged, poorly established border that separated the east from the west. Chief Iron-Hand and his spotted stallion became the talk of the border from Montana to Texas. Often, entire villages were sacked and stripped of firearms. The strangest part of the story was that they were never known to take a scalp, commit murder, or rape. The only lives that they were known to take were those of the soldiers who were sent to capture them. Although they were accused of many murders and depredations, none was substantiated except those that accompanied the theft of firearms, pack mules, and explosives.

One of the tales that was told and sworn to by several ran as follows: Chief Iron-Hand and his band had just surrounded and taken control of an isolated mining town, when Iron-Hand appeared upon the street and was seen to snatch a small child from her mother's arms. The woman fainted, and when she regained consciousness, she lay in the shade of a tree where Chief Iron-Hand had carried her. By her side sat the chief himself, with her child in his arms. The child was playing with his feathered warbonnet. When the mother begged for the return of her child, the chief said, "Be not so selfish, woman. I have a baby girl whom I have not seen for over a year. She, too, is very beautiful. This child has no fear of me, so why should you? Is it not well known that I take only the lives of those who first try to take mine? The Indian, whose land you steal, has much more honor than the paleface who steals it. Would you, too, not fight to prevent your child from becoming a slave to those who look upon her as a wild beast? Think, woman, of the heartbreaks suffered by the Indian who sees his land stolen, his family murdered, and his children taken into slavery."

Then he thrust the child into her mother's arms, saying, "Take her, lady, and teach her hate and selfishness. Teach her to disregard the rights of others. Teach her to lie, steal, and play God. Tell her that the Indians who befriended your forefathers during the first long winters upon our shores are no better than the badger or the coyote. Teach her to hate us. Allow her to grow up with the understanding that the ones who wrote the book you read were speaking only of the paleface. Teach her that he who controls the weapons of thunder is greater than this God you pray to. Tell her that the Great Spirit of the red man is an imposter. We know that we cannot win, but there will be many among you who shall also lose. In the history that this child's children shall read, the Indian shall never be referred to as a coward, liar and thief. I go now. I may never again hold my child in my arms, but I believe that when she grows up, she will be much more proud of me than this child will be of you." This woman also said that Chief Iron-Hand spoke in perfect English and that his eyes were gray.

Chief Iron-Hand was known among the traitors and gun runners as a man who always kept his word. One old outlaw once said, "If Chief Iron-Hand says that he'll pay you, you can always depend on it. If he says that he'll kill you, you can pretty well depend on that, too." So Chief Iron-Hand became a legend throughout the border land. Some branded him as cruel, others as haughty, and all said that he was brave. But never was it even rumored that he was not honest in his dealings, or truthful in his statements. He was respected by his associates and cordially hated by the military.

His contacts reported that some dissension was still present among some of the tribes. But Enir thought that if he could manage to hold up the onslaught of the thunderstick soldier for a long enough time for the tribes to get fully organized, all petty disagreements could be smoothed out. So he distributed the rifles he had collected to whichever body of organized resistance was closest to his field of operation. Consequently, the Flathead, who were farthest to the north, seldom received any of the thundersticks. Chief Al-a-go-ri-o dispatched a message ordering him to release no more firearms to other tribes until the Flathead were sufficiently armed. When Enir received the message, his heart sank. Surely, he told himself, Chief Al-a-go-ri-o was intelligent enough to see the wisdom of his move. But after contemplating, and mentally placing himself in Al-a-go-ri-o's position, he could see the sense of his argument and began to feel differently. He was convinced that Al-a-go-ri-o held small hopes of winning a lasting peace. He was also equally convinced that the chief was determined his people should not die like the rabbit. "Anyway, he accepted all responsibility," he mumbled to himself, "and, after all, he is my chief."

After gathering a small pack train of rifles and ammunition, he led it northward. On the second day he was accosted by one of his former customers, a Ute chieftain whose name was Pe-ru-ta. Pe-ru-ta was the high chief of the Ute, and Enir held him in very high respect. However, when he told Pe-ru-ta that

218

the thundersticks had been ordered by his own chieftain, Al-a-go-ri-o, to be delivered to the Flathead, Per-ru-ta became very disturbed. "The lives of both my warriors and their families are in great danger," he argued. "I must have the thundersticks."

"I am very sorry, Chief Per-ru-ta," Enir replied, "but I cannot disobey the orders of my own chieftain."

"I, too, am very sorry," replied Per-ru-ta, "but I cannot allow our friendship to cause the death of my people. I will take thundersticks." When he said this, Enir's band suddenly brought their rifles to bear upon Per-ru-ta and his delegate.

"I do not surrender the thundersticks," said Enir. "Your warriors are many, but you shall not live to guide them. So tell me, Chief Per-ru-ta, which is more important to them? You or the thundersticks?"

The old chieftain was silent for several moments, then he said sadly, "You are a brave and loyal chief, Chief Iron-Hand. If you surrender to me the thundersticks, you will feel dishonored. On the other hand, if I should let the fear of death cause my people to die, I, too, would be dishonored." When he paused, Enir looked deep into his eyes and knew that he intended to make the sacrifice. Swiftly he began to search his mind for a way to break the stalemate.

"Why do we not let the Great Spirit decide on who shall have the thundersticks?" he asked. "Send one of your warriors to your village. Let him return with your mightiest fighter. He and I will fight without weapons. If he beats me, you shall have the thundersticks. If I beat him, you shall give me safe conduct across your land. Is that not fair, Chief Per-ru-ta?" Enir watched him closely.

After a moment's silence, he saw the old chief's face brighten, and he said, "It is fair." Then he turned and spoke to one of his warriors in the Ute tongue. Enir, who understood it well, heard him say, "Go swiftly to the village on the Pi-yi. Find Lo-tes-i-me and send him here quickly."

They camped that night beside a spring of clear, cool water. Enir doubled the guard because, although he did not doubt the integrity of Chief Pe-ru-ta, he was not sure of his warriors. Enir slept well that night, for he anticipated no difficulty in disposing of this Ute fighter the next day. In fact, he found himself pleasantly anticipating the interview, because he felt that the physical exercise would refresh his lagging spirit.

It was about mid-morning the next day when the bushes parted and into the circular open spot stepped the most gigantic and muscular animal Enir had ever seen. After a second look, he recognized this animal as a man and his ego shrank considerably, for no one had to tell him what this man's business here was. Enir let his eyes travel swiftly over this giant, for a giant he was. He stood almost seven feet and weighed in the neighborhood of four hundred pounds, and his head appeared to be resting upon his shoulders without the support of a neck. Enir also noted the ridges of bone that sprang from the base of his gigantic head and converged to form a large ridge across his brow. The giant's eyes were deep-set and narrow, and his thick lips and broad chin were set and determined. Enir let his eyes drop to his lower limbs and noted the tremendous muscles of his legs, then to his massive feet, which were bare and callous. He had already noted that the giant's arms reached almost to his knees and that his powerful hands were rough and thick.

Pe-ru-ta rose when the giant appeared, and as he

advanced to meet him, he cast a proud glance at Enir. "Hello, Lo-tes-i-me," he greeted him.

"I was told that you have a man here whom you wish of me to fight," replied the giant bluntly.

"Yes," replied Pe-ru-ta. "That is true, but first I must tell you of the rules by which I have agreed that you should fight. You shall use no weapons, not even a stone. If either of you fails to follow these rules, you forfeit the fight. You will fight with your hands alone, and you must stop when I tell you. This you must agree to do."

"I will agree," said the deep voice of Lo-tes-i-me. "But where is this man?"

Pe-ru-ta pointed to Enir and said, "It is none other than Chief Iron-Hand, the rider of the spotted stallion."

"No," cried Lo-tes-i-me. "Chief Iron-Hand is our friend."

"Yes," replied Pe-ru-ta. "He was our friend, but he has refused to give us the thundersticks to fight the soldier paleface. It is for this reason that you must fight him. If you win, we get the thundersticks. But, should he win, we do not. This we have agreed. Will you now fight?"

"I will fight," replied Lo-tes-i-me. "But why does Chief Iron-Hand refuse to give us the thundersticks?"

"He has been ordered by the Flathead chief, Al-a-go-ri-o, to bring them to him," replied Pe-ru-ta. "Why, I do not know. The soldier paleface is far from Al-a-go-ri-o's lodges, but they are almost before our own. We must have the thundersticks." Lo-tes-i-me was silent for a moment while his eyes stared at Enir.

"Why does Chief Iron-hand choose to obey Al-a-go-ri-o instead of Chief Pe-ru-ta?" he asked.

"Because Al-a-go-ri-o is my chieftain, and the thundersticks were bought with Al-a-go-ri-o's gold," replied Enir.

Lo-tes-i-me's large hands flexed nervously as he looked at Pe-ru-ta. Presently he said, "I will fight."

Enir turned to Pe-ru-ta and said, "I will go and prepare myself and speak with the Great Spirit." Then he turned and walked to where the horses were being guarded. There he quickly slipped off his clothing, leaving only a breech-cloth and his moccasins. He then opened the bag where the food was kept and greased his entire body with tallow. Finally he tied his hair up very tightly and approached the chosen arena.

The tiny level spot they had chosen for the contest was almost entirely surrounded by small trees and bushes. It was about sixty feet across at its narrowest place and rectangular in shape. The spectators had gathered at either end of this rectangle and left the center open for the duel. Enir saw that Lo-tes-i-me was waiting in the center, but he glanced quickly about for small indentions which might have been left when all the stones were removed. He wanted to be sure that he had good footing, because he intended to move faster than he had ever moved in his life. He knew that if he should slip, his life would be very short, for once in the grasp of this formidable giant, he would be crushed to death almost instantly.

When he stepped into the open and signalled that he was ready, Lo-tes-i-me spread his long arms and shuffled slowly toward him. He noticed that he slid his enormous feet over the grass without lifting them. This would keep him constantly upon solid footing and enable him to leap suddenly in either direction. Enir felt the skin tighten at the back of his neck, but the sensation suddenly passed when his eyes measured the great bloated paunch of the advancing Goliath. Just as the giant reached for him, he feinted to the right, then ducked quickly to the left and planted a blow in the giant's solar plexus with all of his power and weight behind it. Lo-tes-i-me's breath left him with a loud swish, and his great mouth fell open as he staggered back a step. Enir wasted no time but drove another powerful blow exactly in the same place. The great body of Lo-tes-i-me settled slowly upon its haunches as he struggled to regain his breath. Enir began hammering with both fists at the granitelike head, which was the only target left open to him. The blows that he struck were not ordinary blows, every one of them was powerful enough to upset any ordinary man. The skin broke upon the giant's forehead and face until his entire upper body was bathed with blood, yet he took it all without making a sound or allowing himself to be upset. Enir stepped back and brought his moccasin up under Lo-tes-i-mei's nose with all his might. The nose was loosened from its mooring and blood gushed out upon the grass, but the giant body still remained upright upon its haunches. Enir stepped back, panting from his exertion, and to his surprise, the great body of Lo-tes-i-me came slowly erect. His deep-set eyes gleamed wickedly from behind the pieces of torn and broken skin that dangled from his forehead. Once again the great feet began to slide forward over the grass, and once again Enir began to circle. He watched the blood pour from the mutilated face and bathe the great hairless chest. Enir decided that if he could keep him on the move long enough, the loss of so much blood would weaken him, but the great body seemed to be gaining strength and moving more freely. Enir watched closely, and presently he darted in and drove a tremendous punch to the giant's rib cage, just beneath the left arm. Although the sound of the blow reverberated like the sound of a war drum, Lo-tes-i-me did not stagger. After circling several more times, Enir drove another blow exactly in the same spot. This time the great body winced, but did not falter. I have weakened him in one spot, thought Enir, and as he circled once more, he saw that Lo-tes-i-me favored the left side as he turned. Enir again darted in to take advantage of his gain, but this time Lo-tes-i-me was ready. His giant arm seized Enir's waist and swept him into the bear hug from which Enir had been convinced there was no escape.

As the mighty arms began to tighten, Enir crammed his thumbs into the giant's eyes and pressed with all his might. Lo-tes-i-me shook his head fiercely, but the steady pull of those powerful arms did not slacken. Enir exerted all his strength against the pull, but the bloody torso still slowly approached him. Enir realized that he must act quickly, and the few seconds allowed him were about up, so he took a gamble. He braced his head against the giant's chin, relaxed, and struck upward with both elbows simultaneously. It worked. The steel arms slipped over his tallow-covered shoulders and once again he was free. He quickly renewed his attack by driving another punch into the giant's injured side. Again Lo-tes-i-me flinched but did not go down. Enir realized that he was too far spent to deliver a knockout punch. His only hope now was to stay free long enough to regain sufficient strength so that if he received an opportunity, he could drive another blow into Lo-tes-i-me's left side where he was sure a rib was broken. If he could hit it just right, he hoped that it would drive the broken rib through his heart. So he continued to circle. It was while doing this that he discovered that Lo-tes-i-me was blind. Blind but not beaten, Enir said to himself, and he had a sudden desire to quit and let Pe-ru-ta have the thundersticks. But he knew that if he did this, his status as a chief would be sacrificed and so would his reputation and influence among the Flathead. Mercy was a sign of weakness among all Indians, so Enir continued to circle. As Lo-tes-i-me turned, Enir saw that he was depending upon his ears alone to keep himself informed of Enir's position. So Enir took a long step to the right, then ducked quickly to the left and drove his fist into Lo-tes-i-me's injured side with all of the strength he had left. This time he felt the rib give way, and as his fist sank deep into Lo-tes-i-me's side, the great body fell inert in the center of the clearing.

Enir turned and looked straight into the eyes of Pe-ru-ta. He saw them open wide with surprise as he gazed at the fallen giant. Enir trembled with both anger and exertion as he confronted him.

"Are you satisfied now, Pe-ru-ta?" he asked. "How does it feel to know that you have sent a good man to his death? You are no better than the paleface who take what is not theirs. You knew well that the thundersticks belonged to the Flathead, yet you tried to take them for yourself."

Pe-ru-ta's face was calm and resigned as he faced Enir. Enir saw a deep sadness in his eyes as the Ute chief answered in a low voice, "Not for myself, Chief Iron-Hand. I would do nothing for what is left of my life. But for my sons and my grandsons, my friends and their wives and families. I love my people, even if the Flathead chief cares not that they die."

Enir stood for a moment looking into the care-worn face of the old Ute chieftain. Then he turned to his men and said, "Give him the thundersticks." Then, laying his hand upon Pe-ru-ta's withered shoulder, he said, "The Great Spirit has again spoken to me. The thundersticks are yours. We will return to the land of the paleface and get more." Pe-ru-ta's face brightened up as he quickly came to his feet.

"Chief Iron-Hand, you are a great chieftain. You win the thundersticks, then you give them to me as a present. Why?"

"Because I, too, love your people," replied Enir. "I did not win the thundersticks. They were mine already. I only proved to you that the power of the Great Spirit would keep you from taking them from me."

Pe-ru-ta looked long into Enir's eyes. "Chief Iron-Hand, you shall always be my friend. Never again will the Ute take the warpath against the Flathead. My country is yours; you can do nothing wrong while in it. My warriors will obey you and my squaws and children will bless you." Then he took from his medicine bag a bright multicolored feather. "Place this in your war bonnet so that all the Ute warriors may see it and be quick to lower their bows."

Enir looked at the symbolic trophy that he held in his hand, then out into the small glade where the ground was torn and the grass was drenched with blood. Never, he told himself, would he forget the battle he had fought there. As he looked, the giant form of Lo-tes-i-me stirred and groaned slightly, then the mighty man sat up. Enir turned quickly to Peru-ta. "Chief Pe-ru-ta," he said. "I ask that your warriors, before they take the thundersticks, assist Lo-tes-i-me to the village, where the medicine man may restore him to health." Pe-ru-ta quickly gave the order, and Enir said, "We shall leave the thundersticks in the clearing. Goodbye, Pe-ru-ta, and may the Great Spirit see fit to give you victory over the paleface." And Enir signaled for the pack horses to be brought forward and unloaded.

When this was finished, Enir called his men aside and spoke in a low voice. "This thought came to me while waiting for Lo-tes-i-me, but I had already made the agreement and knew I must wait. If we give the Ute the thundersticks, the soldier paleface at the big blockhouse will soon be called away to fight him. We will watch closely. When they all go, we will take blockhouse. Mebbyso we will get many more thundersticks then we give Pe-ru-ta. What are your thoughts?"

They were silent for a moment, then the tall brave who acted as Enir's second in command said, "Then the fight was for nothing."

"No," said Enir as he pointed to the feather that Pe-ru-ta had given him, "not for nothing. We can now move freely across the land of the Ute."

The Indians looked at each other for a moment, then one of them said, "Chief Iron-Hand is very wise."

"He is very brave also," said another.

When nothing more was said, Enir mounted his spotted stallion and led the way to a trail that went west, and his mind was very busy making plans to capture a well-manned fort, which he knew would be the most daring adventure he had thus far undertaken.

Chapter 21

The news had finally reached the head of the military that a large band of renegades, possibly aided by subversives, were operating along the rugged borders of the northwestern territories. Entire villages had been stripped of firearms and many settlements raided. Wagon trains had also been plundered, and waterholes fouled. But what worried him the most was that gun running had grown from a few isolated cases to a thriving business. Several gun runners, upon being apprehended, were found to be in possession of rather large amounts of raw gold. This, and the fact that armed resistance was becoming more and more frequent, caused quite a stir among campaign leaders, thereby causing many replacements and much head scratching.

Captain Ivan Scraggs, a well-known Indian scout, was sent from his post in the north midwest to a fort on the Platte River, which was the nearest stronghold to the latest development. When he reported to Colonel Kraig, the commander of the outpost, he was told that this rumor had not been exaggerated. He was immediately ordered to take charge of all scouting activity and to ferret out the source of these disturbances before they grew any worse.

Captain Scraggs immediately organized an expedition composed only of experienced Indian scouts and pushed into the mountain region to the source of the latest rumor. After interviewing some of the victims of these raids and upon being advised of the nature of them, he returned to the fort quite puzzled. When reporting to Colonel Kraig, he informed him that this band was both well organized and utterly unpredictable. They were kept well informed of all military movements and knew exactly where each weak point was located. He also told him that the band was both well equipped and extremely well mounted. They were led by a Chief Iron-Hand, who claimed to be of the northern Flathead tribe, but his band seemed to have been chosen at random from several strong tribes along the frontier. The gruff Colonel Kraig informed him that he already knew this, that what he wanted was not information, but results. He told the captain to use any method he saw fit and to requisition any assistance he needed, but to stop that band of agitators as soon as possible.

Captain Scraggs decided to employ some friendly Indians and to distribute them to the places where these disturbances might most plausibly occur in an effort to get a rough map or outline of the territory where this band was operating. The results he obtained were very disheartening. Two of these Indians were found staked on ant hills and the other two were found with arrows in their hearts. He tried several more schemes that had worked for him in the past, but, to his chagrin, all of them eventually failed. By this time he had begun to get desperate. For, despite the combined efforts of both the scouts and the troopers, this part of the frontier had gradually developed from a skirmish line into a battlefield. Tribes who had heretofore been considered docile had become vicious, well-armed savages, and the meager forces sent out from the post suffered defeat after defeat. The Ute had begun to offer quite a bit of armed resistance. The rumor came to Captain

Scraggs that Chief Iron-Hand had extended his operation into that area.

With these developments, Captain Scraggs decided to put his skill and knowledge of Indians to the supreme test. From what he had learned, prospectors and trappers were unmolested by the group, so he decided to disguise himself as a frontiersman and go alone into the field of operation in hopes of obtaining some useful knowledge upon which to base his offensive.

A small fort had been erected in an isolated valley far to the southwest, reasonably close to where this band was known to be operating. He decided to visit this fort unrecognized and see for himself just how this band operated. With this in mind, he let his beard and hair grow, purchased the necessary equipment and slowly pushed his way into the mountain wilderness.

This type of life was not at all new to Captain Ivan Scraggs. He had been an Indian scout for many years and knew well the people with whom he would be dealing. He was also familiar with the vocabulary of the frontiersmen, their philosophy of life, their dress, their equipment, and their habits. He knew the Indians well enough to know that his movements would be observed, and that the slightest deviation from the customary actions of a frontiersman would be noticed. So he forced himself to go slow, be always conscious of his actions, and do all things as naturally as possible.

When he arrived at this outpost, he was told that a large force of armed Ute had attacked a battalion of troopers who were on a reconnaissance detail and that they were threatened with annihilation. Every available man had been called to march to their rescue, leaving only five troopers and an elderly mess sergeant in charge of the fort, or what the natives and frontiersmen called a blockhouse. He immediately applied for shelter and protection, introducing himself as Ivan Scraggs, a prospector who had wandered a little too far from the beaten path and would like to remain a few days to recuperate. The old mess sergeant welcomed him, and they soon became quite well acquainted.

Early the next morning, Ivan was donning his clothes when he heard the mess sergeant in the tiny kitchen preparing coffee. He rose and went in to join him.

"Thought I'd give the bi's a little bresk," said the sergeant. "Lord knows they have got hit acomin'. We got a young Louie in command hayr, and he is a stickler fer regulations. Of course he's gotta be. If'n yew knew anythin' 'bout tha army, yew'd know why. Half tha trooper hayr air older 'n he is, and if'n he didn't keep 'em in hand, they'd have him ashinin' their shoes." Ivan remarked that it was a nice clean post.

"Hit shore is," agreed the sergeant. "Hit's scrubbed in an' out twice a week." While they were drinking their coffee, they heard a little disturbance in the barracks, and the old sergeant said, "They're probably playin' agin. They air all teed off 'cause they had to stay hayr. Crazy loons, they don't know when they're well off." Just at this instant, the door flew open and three tall Indians entered and in a businesslike manner proceeded to bind Ivan and the old sergeant hand and foot. No word was spoken and no resistance offered. They were too dumbfounded to speak, and they had no time for resistance. They were immediately carried out into the compound and unceremoniously dumped upon the ground beside the five troopers, who were also bound. There were

231

Indians all over the place, and Ivan saw that both the troopers and the sergeant were thoroughly frightened. The Indians withdrew a short way and talked briefly among themselves. Then four large bucks approached them and cut the thongs that held their feet. The Indians quickly ushered them out the gate and off into the forest a few hundred yards. There they bound each of their hands behind medium-sized trees and retied their feet. Then every one of them was efficiently gagged with a piece of foul-smelling rawhide, and the Indians quickly departed.

Ivan looked at the old sergeant, whose eyes bulged over the top of the gag until it seemed they would pop from his head. Ivan was not sure whether it was from fear or anger, because he knew that none of them had been hurt. The old sergeant began to emit grunts and tried to motion with his head. Ivan twisted around until he could look in the direction indicated. What he saw was a string of several pack horses being hurried through the forest, accompanied by a group of Indians riding spotted horses. Presently a crackling sound reached his ears, and he twisted his neck the other way and saw the whole fort ablaze. Then, drawing a deep breath, he relaxed his back against the tree behind him and said to himself, I have made contact all right.

The old sergeant was the first to dislodge his gag by rubbing the side of his face against the tree behind him. When it came loose, Ivan heard peal out upon the smoke-filled air a string of frontier oaths that completely described his own sentiments. There were a few words uttered by the sergeant that interested him greatly: Iron-Hand, spotted horses, gun thieves, and such. He became so eager to ask questions that he began to rub his own face against the rough bark of the tree behind him. It was a very tedious job. His neck cramped, his face bled, and his eyes and ears were filled with bits of dirt and bark. When he was just about ready to give up, the gag fell from his mouth, and he spit the ground bark from his throat and asked the question that was uppermost in his mind.

"Which one was Iron-Hand?"

The old sergeant looked at him and said, "Why, the biggest tun, that gray-eyed son-of-a-bitch. Didn't yew seen him alaffin' at us? Tha son-of-a-bitch, hal, he ain't no Injun, Injuns don't laff, he's a white son-of-a-slut."

"Have you ever seen him before?" asked Ivan.

"Naw, but I've heered of 'im. Tha lowdown dog-eattin' bastid."

"How do you know that one was him?" asked Ivan.

"Hal, I've talked ta peeple thet knows 'im" said the sergeant. "Hit was 'im all right, tha lowdown squaw-humpin' trater."

Ivan did a little thinking while the sergeant got his breath, and presently he asked, "How long do you suppose that we will have to stay here?"

The sergeant looked at him owlishly, then said, "Humph, yew kin leave any time yer reddy. Don't stay 'round on my account."

After they had strained at their bonds awhile the old sergeant seemed to quiet down a little. He looked over at Ivan and asked, "What 'n hal air yew adoin' in these parts nohow?"

"Right now I'm scratchin' my back," answered Ivan.

"I think that I'll try standin' up. Mebby then I can scratch me arse, thet's what's itchin'," said the sergeant.

"Tell me some more about this Chief Iron-Hand," said Ivan. "What all has he done?"

The old sergeant looked at him and asked, "What 'n hal makes yew so interested, air ye thinkin' 'bout joinin' 'im?"

"Naw," replied Ivan. "I'm thinking about catching him."

"Air yew outen yoor mind?" yelled the sergeant. "Why tha whole U.S. Army has been atryin' ta catch him fer a year er two. Jest what kind of a nut air yew anyway?"

Ivan was silent for a moment, then he said, "Well, somebody has to catch him."

The sergeant snorted in disgust. "Maybe atter yew sit here on yer arse fer a couple a days, yew can figger out jest how ter do it."

"Don't you think that the troopers will see the smoke and come to see about us?" asked Ivan.

"Hal," said the sergeant, "they air forty miles from hayr, and, besides, they got other things ta do right now."

For four long days and nights the hapless victims remained with their hands bound behind the small trees. Their shoulders ached at times, forcing them to work their way to a standing position to relieve the ache and their cramping leg muscles. They were very uncomfortable, but not in real physical pain. On one occasion a cold shower of rain added to their discomfort, but, aside from hunger and thirst, their pain was chiefly mental. They had all managed to dislodge their gags, but Ivan and the sergeant were the only ones who were close enough together to converse without having to raise their voices. This kept conversation to a minimum, which they considered to be to their advantage. They all knew that there were Indians all about, and this last flareup of hostil-

234

ities caused them to shudder each time they thought of what was likely to happen should they be found here in such a helpless condition.

One day, two middle-aged squaws happened by, and after observing the men from the cover of the forest, they came forward to investigate. They were standing near the sergeant and Ivan, staring with cold, unblinking eyes, when the sergeant began to plead with them to untie them.

"If yew untie us, we'll give yew much firewater," he said. But the two stoic females gave no sign of understanding him. Suddenly the sergeant moved crablike around the tree so that they could see that his hands were bound.

"Weee ooohh," said one of the squaws as she grabbed her nose with her thumb and fingers.

"Aaa-aawk," snorted the other as she, too, grabbed her nose, and together they ran.

"Hey, please come back and untie us," pleaded the sergeant. "Yew'd stink, too, if'n yew had been tied to a tree for nigh on to a week." The two squaws continued on toward the ashes of the fort.

"I wish that they would be at least bring us a drink of water," said Ivan.

"They ain't agoin' to," said the sergeant. "They air Injuns. They're worse than dawgs. A dawg would have at least licked our hands."

"I doubt that," said Ivan, "after that stink that you stirred up."

"By gad, I guess you think that yew smell like a bed of lilacs," snorted the sergeant.

Late that same evening a group of leg-weary troopers came into sight, and hearing yells, they passed on by the ruins of the fort and hastened to untie the men. When the sergeant started to tell them about their dreadful experience, one of the troopers quickly advised him to save his breath because he might have a lot of running to do. Quickly then, the trooper informed them that the lieutenant had been killed and that the other troopers were withdrawing behind a Ute onslaught. This group had returned to the fort to bring more ammunition in hopes of preventing a complete rout, but, the way things looked now, it was every man for himself.

So Ivan's adventure ended with his having to run about twenty miles after being tied to a tree for almost a hundred hours. It would be many days later that he would learn that the Ute had for some reason called off the attack without taking full advantage of the situation. Ivan did not tarry in that hostile vicinity, but circled wide and hastened back to the outpost on the Platte.

After weeks of dodging Ute war parties and circling through many miles of rugged terrain, Ivan at last made his report to Colonel Kraig. When he had finished, he immediately voiced his intention of discarding his filthy attire, visiting the post barber, and getting back into his uniform. The colonel looked at him with a slight twinkle in his eye and asked if he had noticed the changes that had taken place there during his two months' absence. Ivan quickly admitted that he had, then looked questioningly at the colonel.

"You see," began the colonel, "this is the end of the line now. That disturbance you spoke of has necessitated a complete survey of this hastily improvised camp or emergency station, and I want you to take over the task. You understand that this type of people will take much more freely to one of their own kind than they would to an officer, so I'd rather you made this survey before changing your identity. I am particularly interested in spotting undesirable characters such as whiskey merchants, gun runners, horse thieves, and such. There are also a lot of Indians here whom I'm sure are up to no good, so I would like your report as soon as possible. We do not anticipate the installation of marshal law, because we do not think the situation will exist long enough to warrant it. That will be all, Captain."

When Captain Scragg, alias Ivan the frontiersman, left on his assignment the next morning, he was far from pleased. To his way of thinking, the job had little to do with military action. Also, the novelty of working with this type of people had long since worn off. Besides, he did not know exactly what he was looking for. The three things that the colonel had mentioned were very abstruse. "I'm not a mind reader," he mumbled to himself, "nor am I a detective." A horse thief, a whiskey runner, or even a gun runner was certainly not going to confide in him or anybody else. But having no desire to lower himself in the colonel's estimation, he was determined to try his best to find something to report. As he prowled the outskirts of this big shanty town that had suddenly mushroomed here on the banks of the Platte, however, no clearcut ideas formed in his mind.

Ivan sat down upon a large flat boulder about two hundred yards above the writhing mass of livestock and humanity. He noticed that the colonel was right about there being a large number of Indians present among them. But a closer inspection showed that no certain tribe was in the majority and also that there were far more squaws and children than there were bucks, so he regarded them as no menace to the safety of the whites.

Suddenly he sat bolt upright and an intense gleam of interest appeared in his eyes. For in front of a large tepee was tethered a big spotted horse. Spotted horses were not uncommon in these parts, but this kind was. For this horse was exactly the type he had seen go charging by a tree under which he sat as the rider strove to overtake a certain pack train. Even under the circumstances, he remembered that if he could identify anyone in there, they could also identify him. He decided that he would just watch for a few minutes. Presently a nondescript Indian came out of the tepee, mounted the big horse, and rode away.

If that Indian is one of Iron-Hand's men, then there is a gunrunner around, he told himself convincingly. And it is also time that I do something. So, without confiding in the colonel, he returned to the fort and put twelve picked men into a disguise similar to his own. After he had instructed them thoroughly and stressed the importance of their remaining apart from each other, they were ready to invade this big ragtown. As per instructions, these men played poker, shot dice, and drank very lightly. Captain Scragg had ordered them to report the sighting of any exceptionally tall Indian buck or any large spotted horse or horses.

Captain Scragg was acting upon the theory that Iron-Hand, having more ammunition on hand than he did rifles, would sooner or later contact any gunrunner who might be hiding here, so he patiently waited. He well knew that if there was a gunrunner here, he wasn't going anywhere, but he wanted to get him located as soon as he could without exposing his plans.

One day one of his henchmen reported seeing two large, tall Indians, but none had reported anything about spotted horses.

"Where did you see the tall Indians?" he asked the man. The man replied that they were talking to the owner of a group of new wagons that were located near the large tepee. Captain Scragg was thoughtful for a moment while his fingers tugged at his soiled beard. After a short wait, he called a powwow in an old ragged tent he had bought for that purpose.

"Boys," he said, "I think that the man who owns the new wagons is a gunnie. However, we won't bother him just yet. I want to use him for bait. I want him kept under strict observation, however, and his every move reported. If any of you see any Indians of any type talking to him, report to me immediately. That is all." The powwow dispersed according to orders, one man at a time.

Chapter 22

After sacking and destroying the outpost, Enir led his band in a northeastern direction, keeping well behind the disturbance Pe-ru-ta's warriors were causing. He ventured as far east as he dared, because he sorely needed many more rifles to finish loading the pack train. He hoped to gain these at the few small towns in various mining areas along the eastern edge of the mountains.

It was in his fourth week of reconnoitering that he met a man with whom he had dealt before and whom he knew he could trust. It turned out that this man was searching for him and that he had a proposition to put up for his consideration. This fellow told him that he had planned a rendezvous with a gunrunner, but that the Army had stopped all traffic at an outpost on the lower Platte River. This gunrunner had several specially built wagons, and the guns were disassembled and were hidden in them. He stressed that the guns were in no danger of discovery and that the man had a legitimate business and was under no suspicion. But he feared he might be forced to winter there, and he needed the money that the guns would bring him. He also gave several other reasons why the runner was anxious to get rid of the guns.

Enir sent one of his scouts back with the man to check on his story. When the scout returned, he reported that the guns were really there. He also reported that this gunrunner had hatched a scheme to move the guns out in a piecemeal operation that sounded quite reasonable. He explained that there were a great many Indians mingling with the traders there and that the gunrunner's intention was to build small packs in which the small parts, including the broken-down stocks, would be placed and carried out by the squaws. The rifle barrels could be smuggled out in the pant legs of the bucks. All of this was to be done under the cover of darkness, but there should be someone nearby to meet them and relieve them of their loads so that they would all be present the next day just in case anyone got suspicious.

After thinking the plan over for a while, Enir decided that it might work. But he also decided that before committing himself, he would go and look the situation over. He wanted to meet this gunrunner, because if he had gone to all the trouble to build special wagons, he might develop into a useful source of supply. He called a powwow, and the plan was discussed in detail. Finally it was decided that they should split up, and a few of them would take the heavy ammunition on to a hideout that was well on the way to the Flathead country. The others would go with Enir to the place that the scout had already chosen as a good observation point.

Because they had loaded the pack horses quite heavily with the ammunition in order to conserve enough horses to move the guns, Enir gave them a full day on the trail before the rest of them moved toward the campsite. The scout who had been there instructed them all to mark the trail well, just in case it became necessary to use it as an escape route. When they reached the observation point that the scout had recommended, Enir was well pleased with it. From the brushy rim, the entire encampment was visible beside the broad stream. But the large, well-manned military installation that appeared to be very near it was visible, too. Enir glanced sharply at his men but saw no signs of perturbation in their faces, although he knew that they all realized they were treading on very thin ice.

Enir placed the scout who had led them here in command and told him emphatically that there would be no fires, cautioning them about the long eyes that the paleface officers carried on their saddles. He informed his tall lieutenant that he would accompany him into the camp and that they would arrive there in the early morning. He then posted the sentinels and gave terse orders on what action to take in case anything went wrong. He and his companion sorted out the clothing they would wear as a disguise and started on the long walk toward the disorderly campsite.

Enir encountered little difficulty in locating the new wagons and the man he was looking for because his scout had described him well, but it was almost mid-morning before he had a chance to make the contact. The gunrunner seemed surprised at Enir's perfect English, but he also seemed pleased. He indicated an open space near the new wagons and strolled toward it. Enir and his companion followed in a nonchalant manner.

When the man they were following ducked into the open space between the wagons, Enir glanced sharply about them. He quickly flashed the danger signal to his companion, but it was too late. A dozen armed men quickly surrounded them, and a dirty frontiersman with an untrimmed beard stepped forward and said, "The jig is up, Chief Iron-Hand, raise your hands carefully if you wish to live." Both Enir and his companion quickly complied, but the sound of a rifle shot rang out upon the morning air. The gunrunner, who had chosen to run for it, collapsed in the open spot with a bullet hole in his chest.

Enir glanced closely at the man who stood before him, then smiled and asked, "Who untied you?"

The man returned his smile and replied, "The retreating troopers," then asked, "Would you like to have a last word with your friend there, Chief Iron-Hand?"

Enir glanced at the dying gunrunner and replied, "I have no friends among the paleface."

When Enir and his companion, surrounded by the armed guard, moved toward the stockade, a thin plume of dust rose far up on the timbered crest of the mountain as a group of spotted horses moved swiftly through the rocky breaks. One of these horses was a great spotted stallion, but his scanty Indian saddle was empty and, securely lashed to the side of it, was So-he's bow and the headdress of a Flathead chief.

When Enir and his companion were ushered into the presence of Colonel Kraig, the colonel was surprised at the personality radiated by the tall, auburn-haired Chief Iron-Hand. He had listened to the many tales that had been circulated concerning this man's cleverness, fearlessness, and chivalry, but had pegged most of these tales as coverups for the failure of of his men to outwit him. Now he was not so sure that he had done him justice. The steady, intelligent eyes, the proud carriage, and the muscular physique of the man aroused his curiosity. As the colonel studied this tall young man, he suddenly became aware that the sharp, unwavering eyes of Chief Iron-Hand were likewise studying him. "So you are the renegade gunrunner who rides a spotted stallion?" asked the colonel rather gruffly to hide a strange sense of embarrassment.

"No, sir," replied Enir. "I am Chief Iron-Hand of

243

the Flathead tribe, in charge of reconnaissance and forage. I am not a renegade, and I claim the immunity of a prisoner of war." The colonel looked at Enir for a full minute before he spoke again.

"Do you realize that the rifles you placed into the hands of those savages have cost us hundreds of lives?"

"Oh, certainly sir," replied Enir. "You will also agree that they have saved the lives of many of these savages, as you prefer to call my people."

"They cannot win," replied the colonel. "I am sure that you are intelligent enough to know that, so why do you persist in keeping them stirred up? You are to blame for all of this useless slaughter, not us."

Enir looked at the colonel for a moment, then said, "I believe that it was one of your own statesmen who once said: 'Is life so dear or peace so sweet as to be purchased at the price of chains and slavery?' Yes, we know that we cannot win. But the longer we fight, the less of us there will be to suffer the humiliation of slavery and dejection."

The colonel pushed his chair back a space, and surprise showed upon his face. "Say, just who are you anyway?" he asked. "Are you some foreign mercenary? You are not an Indian. Where did you receive your education?"

"I received my education at Liverpool, England," replied Enir, "and I am a Flathead chief. I am also married to the daughter of a Flathead chief, and I have two children." The colonel, who was definitely taken aback by this outburst, was silent as he drummed his fingers upon the top of the crude desk.

"Which chief are you the son-in-law of? I happen to know a few of them."

"Chief I-lip-a-taw," replied Enir. "He is in command of the scouts."

"I-lip-a-taw, I-lip-a-taw," repeated the colonel, then his face suddenly brightened. "I knew an Indian by that name once," he said. "What does this chief do?"

"He is an expert bowmaker," replied Enir, "but he does other things equally well."

"Such as scouting?" asked the colonel. Enir did not reply, and the colonel's brow slowly darkened. "I see," he said slowly. "All of those trips that he made for bow wood were also for another purpose." After a moment he asked, "Where is this chief now?"

"I do not know," replied Enir sadly. "I have not seen him or my family for more than a year."

The colonel's eyes held a faraway expression as he silently drummed his fingers upon the desk. Presently he called to the guard, and when the soldier entered, he said to him, "Take him away and treat him in the regular manner, but guard him closely. You will also see that both he and his companion are isolated, but there will be no irregular treatment." So Chief Iron-Hand was led from the presence of Colonel Kraig, commander of the outpost on the Platte River.

Chapter 23

Shortly after the steel door had clanged shut behind Enir at the jail in which he and his companion were confined, an orderly left the colonel's office rather hurriedly. The errand upon which he had been dispatched was to seek an Indian runner whose name was Skippy. Skippy was a southern Indian of a little-known tribe who was considered the best runner on the frontier. He spoke the language and dialects of almost every tribe in the northwest and was often used by the Army scouts to infiltrate the enemy-held territory. He was also used by the colonel to get word to redoubts and, on several occasions, to arrange a powwow with warrior chiefs.

Skippy was small, but he was very lithe and swift. He knew the country well and seemed to have the knack of foreseeing the movements of certain bands. However, Skippy did have one fault that sometimes irked the colonel. He steadfastly refused to conform to military regulations. He preferred to play a lone hand and demanded pay according to the task he was called upon to do. The colonel tolerated him because he could perform duties that no white man could.

When Skippy was brought to the colonel's office, the orderly was dismissed, and the colonel sat and regarded Skippy for a moment in silence. Presently he asked, "Could you go far into the north to the land of the Flathead?" Skippy did not immediately answer but sat looking at the colonel in silence. "There is a

Flathead chief to whom I must get a message," said the colonel by way of explanation.

After a few more moments of silence Skippy replied, "Flathead bad. Ute also very bad. To reach the land of the Flathead would be very dangerous." The colonel waited, because he had known that this would be his answer, but he also knew the Indian. Presently Skippy asked, "How much?"

The colonel held up one of the two bags of gold that had been taken from Enir and his companion and said, "If you find this Flathead chief and give him the words that I send by you, I will give you this. But if you do not, but do find a warrior of the Flathead tribe who will deliver this message for you, I will give you half." Skippy was thoughtful for a moment, then he rose.

"No," he said simply.

"But it is very important," said the colonel, "and I have no one else to send."

"Then go yourself," replied Skippy as he started to the door. The colonel's face became very red, but he controlled his anger.

"Wait," he called. "How much?" Skippy returned rather reluctantly. He was well aware of the danger of such a mission, and he had no doubts about what would happen to him if he should try and fail. He was also aware that he dare not refuse the colonel without first convincing him that the trip was too hazardous. Many thoughts flashed through his mind as he slowly returned to the colonel's desk.

After standing in silence for a moment, he said, "Gold will open many mouths. It will also buy much firewater, which will cause some to speak words that without it they would not speak. The Flathead are sharp, and they have many scouts. No one can come into their country without their knowing that he is there. This I will tell you, and this I will do. I will take with me the bag of yellow metal. With it, I will go to the land of the Flathead. There I will buy firewater until I find someone who will carry your message to this chief. Then, if I live to return, you give me another bag of yellow metal. Skippy has spoken."

The colonel rolled the bag of gold back and forth for a few seconds, then said, "If you will swear by the Great Spirit and the laughing waters, I will agree."

Skippy breathed deeply and said, "I will swear."

"Good," said the colonel. "Return when your shadow is long; I shall teach you the message." Skippy departed, but the colonel noticed that there was no look of pleasure upon his face.

Left alone at his desk, Colonel Kraig's mind drifted back over some of his former visits with the old bowmaker. The thought that he had let the chief of scouts of a tribe that had suddenly developed into one of the most dangerous of his opposition slyly dupe him into revealing information that would be of great value to them set his blood on fire. He remembered that the old Indian had implied he was not really a member of any tribe, that he made and sold bows because it was an easy living and it gave him the freedom to roam about at will. He had used the English language so freely that the colonel had never really considered him an enemy at all. Therefore he had allowed himself freedom of expression on many subjects concerning the future of this great country. "Damn that lanky old buzzard," said Colonel Kraig to the silent office. "I don't even remember all I've told him." However, he distinctly remembered some of it, and it caused his blood to boil furiously.

After the colonel's nerves had quieted down a bit, he slowly began to compose a message. This, he realized, he had to do with care. It had to be simple enough for Skippy to memorize, yet detailed enough to get results. He composed and discarded several messages before he decided on one. He read the simple words aloud to himself, there in the privacy of his office:

"Chief Iron-Hand is in prison. He is being held by a man who is known to be a friend of yours, Colonel Kraig. He is at the outpost on the Platte River. He is wearing paleface clothes and is accused of being a gunrunner. If he is found guilty, he will be shot. He sends you this message hoping that you will come and prove that he is a Flathead. If this is proved, he will be considered a prisoner of war and his life will be spared."

"That ought to do it," the colonel whispered. He recalled again his former visits with the old bowmaker. As they had no written language, once the colonel got his hands on I-lip-a-taw, there was no way for the Indians to take advantage of the plans he had disclosed unwittingly. He knew that if I-lip-a-taw was not present to point out the vantage points, the information would be valueless. He glanced again at the message saying to himself, "I hope the old rascal thinks enough of his son-in-law to bail him out."

Chapter 24

When the lookout, whom Enir had posted well down on the side of the ridge, observed the happenings at the encampment, he hastened back to where the others waited and breathlessly told of what he had witnessed. The scout whom Enir had left in command, as he had been directed, wasted no time in giving the order for a rapid retreat. But it was a sad group of warriors that fled across the rugged terrain to the northwest. There was not a single one of them who would not gladly have gone to Enir's rescue had he not ordered them to do otherwise. But for many moons they had obeyed his orders, and none of them questioned them now.

It took three days of hard riding for them to reach the place where the pack train waited, but they did not tarry when they did so. The scout whom Enir had left in command quickly divided the packs, and they turned their faces toward the north and began the long trek back to the land of the Flathead. There the scout had orders to make a full report to Chief Waneb-i-te and to abide by his decision.

It had been a very dry and warm summer in the southern mountains where they had been operating, consequently, the group did not notice for some time that the same condition existed in their own country. But when they began to arrive at well-known water holes and found their bottoms dry and cracked, they began to look askance at one another. Game was also scarce where always before it had been plentiful, and they began to feel more ill at ease than ever. "It is very strange," said their leader. "Things have changed more in two summers than they have in my entire lifetime." They all felt the same apprehension, but none of them remarked upon his comment.

Just before they reached the place where they intended to camp, they saw a dark cloud approaching from the northwest. They saw great flashes of lightning and could hear the distant rumble of thunder. "It has been very dry," said their leader. "But I think that the rain will soon be returning. Since it is still very far, I will suggest that we do not stop but push on until darkness." This they all agreed upon because there was little shelter at the camping post that they had intended to use. Before darkness came, the dark storm cloud had approached very near and the great thunderbolts caused the ground to tremble beneath the feet of their mounts. At the first protected place, the scout ordered a halt and instructed them to cover well the packs of ammunition. "The drought will be broken soon," said their leader. "See that our thundersticks and thunderbolts are upon high ground."

True to their leader's prediction, the storm struck just at darkness. The driving rain was accompanied by one of the worst electrical storms any of them had ever witnessed. The rain, the blinding flashes of lightning, and the tremendous thunderbolts made sleep impossible, so they all huddled beneath the few buffalo robes they had and conversed in awed whispers. At the height of the storm, they all noticed that the ground beneath their feet began to tremble, and far to the north they heard a dull roaring sound.

"It is a mighty wind," said their leader. "I fear that the entire valley might be blown away." No one answered him, but they huddled closer together, and each of them mentally implored the Great Spirit to extend his mercy to them. Finally the great roaring ceased and the rain slackened. Some of them slipped from the shelter and checked the horses, but a few moments later a cold wind sprang up and drove them once more into the protection of their robes. "I do not understand," said their leader. "How can winter come in mid-summer?"

"I fear that the Great Spirit is angry and will take the lives of all of us," said another. They continued to huddle together beneath their scanty shelter, until, within an hour, the cold wind began to lessen and the storm retreated across the mountain range.

When day finally dawned, they crept from their shelters and began to converse in awed voices. "I know of nothing to do but load our packs and continue," said the leader. "The Great Spirit has spared our lives, and there is surely some reason for it. Let us ride out like warriors and search for this reason." By the time they had adjusted their packs, the temperature had risen considerably. "I think," said the leader, "we will find that a mighty hailstorm has dropped much ice in our valley." Many heads nodded in acceptance of this explanation. "We will take the short trail down the mountain," continued the leader. "Our horses will have to move more slowly, but by doing so we can reach the village by tonight."

As they circled the peak on their right, they reached a position where they could look out upon their own valley. Their leader halted, and raising his hand to shade his eyes from the early morning sun, said, "Look." He pointed to where he had expected to see the familiar scene of White Bosom Bare. As the others crowded their horses up beside him, low groans and gasps of disbelief rose from every throat. Always before, from this position, the beautiful scene of White Bosom Bare had stood out like a bright cameo, which had acted as a stimulant to the weary traveler who was returning home. Now all that they saw were two slender and badly torn peaks of raw earth and broken stone. The vast meadow below them, which had always looked very bright and verdant in the sunlight, was now a great tract of raw and badly scarred wasteland. It looked like it had been scarred by the paleface's plow. Another thing that deeply disturbed them was that in many places snow was visible upon the top of the curved mountain. Also, there were patches of snow upon its steep southern side.

As they viewed the drastic picture before them in silence, their leader raised his hand and said in a trembling whisper, "The Great Spirit was angered because we desecrated the sacred valley for the yellow metal. Now he has destroyed it." When nobody else spoke, he continued, "Let us hurry to the village and see what Chief Wa-neb-i-te has to say."

In their haste, they cut to the right of the village where Chieftain Al-a-go-ri-o resided and rushed on to their own village. When they reached the stream that the trail followed, they were surprised to see that it was so low that only a narrow, swift channel of muddy water remained. "It carries only the muddy water of the rain," said one of them. Their leader said nothing, but motioned them across it and on toward their village. They moved very slowly now because the horses were very tired. But the tough Appaloosas trudged wearily on, and they reached their village between midnight and dawn. They saw what looked like most of the population of the village gathered beside a huge fire near the banks of the muddy stream. The leader halted them, then gave the cry of the nighthawk.

Presently it was answered, and they rode wearily in. The tired horses shifted their ears toward the strange sound of lamenting squaws. Nobody greeted them as they rode slowly past, and when they reached the open space near the center of the village, their leader halted them. After a moment he dismounted and signaled for them to unload the horses, while he, himself, walked away toward the lodge of Wa-neb-i-te.

From the subdued voices of those who came to assist them, they learned of the fate of I-lip-a-taw and all of the others who had gone into White Bosom Bare. Someone said that Wa-neb-i-te had told them that the dry summer had weakened the grip of the glacier around the base of the two peaks and that the great thunderstorm had jarred it loose, thus devastating the sacred valley and burying the wailing forest in snow and ice. They said that it had also dammed the stream above the waterfall and that a great lake was forming in the valley of White Bosom Bare. Regardless of this explanation, each and every one of them gave voice to the belief that no matter how it was done, it was the anger of the Great Spirit over the desecration of the sacred valley that had caused it.

Chief Wa-neb-i-te showed great grief over Enir's capture and ordered that the great spotted stallion and three of the spotted mares be given to So-he and her mother. The scout who had led the returning braves volunteered to take the horses to the lodge of I-lip-a-taw's squaw. The low moans of grief and weeping of children ceased when he rapped sharply upon the door of the lodge. Presently, the door was opened, and the tear-stained face of So-he confronted him. The scout looked down at the toes of his moccasins for a few seconds, then he resolutely raised his head and informed her of the fate of her husband. Instead of again yielding to grief as he had expected, So-he's face paled slightly and her eyes became fiercely penetrating as they looked steadily into his.

"Where were you when my husband was captured?" she asked. "Were you and the others running away? Why were you not all captured?"

The scout was so taken aback that for a moment he could only stare at her. "We were obeying the commands that he gave us," he replied when he had recovered from his shock. "I was acting as the lookout," he continued. "My orders were: If he was captured, to flee with the pack train, elude the soldier-paleface, and bring the thundersticks to this village. These orders we obeyed."

So-he's face became calm, and she said in a low voice, "Forgive me." And once more her tears began to flow.

"I have brought to you these four ponies and two bags of yellow metal by order of Chief Wa-neb-i-te," the scout continued. "I have also brought you Chief Iron-Hand's bow and headdress. The bow is yours already, but the headpiece you must also keep. If one is chosen to replace Chief Iron-Hand, let him earn his own headpiece." And the scout placed into her hands the rawhide lead ropes of the horses and quickly departed.

As So-he stood in the doorway of the lodge and watched the scout depart, she had the sensation of the world disintegrating about her, and her head began to grow dizzy. Suddenly a small face was shoved into the doorway beside her, and a rather coarse childish voice said, "What are they?" Before she could recover her wits enough to answer, she was jostled from the other side, and immediately all four horses suddenly threw up their heads and lunged backward. So-he was jerked from the door of the lodge, and she stood helplessly watching the four spotted animals gallop away. While she watched, a huge cold nose was shoved into her hand, then a warm tongue caressed her wrist. "Go away Wo-dan," she said wearily, and the great dog looked at her questioningly. She watched one of the Indian men go quiet the horses, and presently he led them to the large tree beside which sat I-lip-a-taw's workbench. There he tied them, and after glancing strangely at Wo-dan, he returned to the group of men with whom he had been talking. "Come, Wo-dan," said So-he, and she re-entered the lodge.

"What are they?" Tall-One asked again as he followed her into the lodge.

"They are horses," replied So-he.

"You mean like the one my daddy rides?" asked Tall-One.

"Yes," replied So-he. Just then So-he's mother came from the lean-to, and So-he asked, "Did you hear what the brave said?"

"Yes, I heard," replied her mother. "And it is well that I learned about horses long ago. They will be very useful to us now."

The next few days were very busy ones for So-he and her mother. Tall-One and Whispering-West-Wind were taught the use of the horses, how to ride upon their backs behind So-he and her mother, how to approach them, and the danger of being stomped or kicked. So-he's mother taught her how to fashion hobbles made of soft rawhide ropes, how to put a slip-knot upon a stake so the horses could graze around it, how to gain the confidence of the horses by always being gentle, and many other things. So-he, being both muscular and active, learned to ride very swiftly, and Tall-One immediately fell in love with the horses and also learned well the art of riding. The greatest task was getting the horses to accept the presence of the great wolf-dog Wo-dan. So-he's mother finally solved the problem by taking a slender rawhide rope and tethering Wo-dan near the horses, but making him understand that he was to leave them alone. Wo-dan learned swiftly, but the horses took a while before they accepted the wolf-dog.

After a few days of patient training, they took their first ride. So-he carried Whispering-West-Wind in her arms, and Tall-One rode behind his grandmother. Wo-dan felt left out at first, but So-he, noticing this, persistently taught him that he was always to precede them. Being trained to answer and to interpret signals, Wo-dan was quick to understand, and it gave him the feeling of importance that So-he had hoped for. Also, they would pause frequently and let the children play with him, so, eventually, the daily ride was looked forward to by the great wolf-dog. This pleased So-he, because she was depending heavily upon Wo-dan for the success of the adventure she had secretly been planning in her mind.

Because So-he asked so many questions and showed such an intense interest in riding, her mother became very curious. Finally, one day, she asked, "Why do you spend so much time with the horses, and why do you always ride the large stallion?" So-he replied that it was because she was determined to learn to ride well. "Why?" asked her mother.

"Because," replied So-he, "I am going to the fort where Enir is imprisoned."

"No, no, you cannot do that!" her mother exclaimed. "The paleface will enslave you. They will force you to sleep with them and will starve and beat you until you are broken and old long before your time."

"That I must risk," replied So-he stubbornly. "If I can be near Enir, I will be happy."

"You do not understand the paleface," insisted her mother. "They are an arrogant people. They are also a cruel people. They have no respect for the Indian, more especially a squaw. They will send other men to you for gold, which they themselves will keep. You will be forced to stay in a lodge that stinks, wash their dirty clothes, do much dirty work, and if you refuse, they will beat you."

"I do not believe that," replied So-he. "Enir is a paleface. I am sure that among the paleface are many who are like him, gentle and considerate. It is these I will speak to, and maybe I can convince them that my Enir is not a bad person who should be left to rot in a prison."

"You still do not understand," argued her mother. "There are no such paleface at this place. All there are are the soldier-paleface who have been taught that the Indian is only a beast. They are taught that only dead Indians are good Indians. Your father, who was among them many times, told me this. He told me that only those who have a desire to kill are admitted among the soldier-paleface. They all drink the firewater, and the most cruel and heartless are considered heroes. Think long upon these things before you let your heart tell you things that are not true. I-lip-a-taw was wise; he knew much about the soldier-paleface. He would not have told me these things if they were not true."

So-he became very thoughtful as she listened to her mother speak. She began to remember a few things that she had overheard while her father and mother were talking, but at the time her childish mind had disregarded them. Now some of it was recalled to her memory, and she became very thoughtful.

Chapter 25

Chief Wa-neb-i-te selected four of his most trusted scouts and went with them to inspect, as best they could, the conditions that existed above the great waterfall in the center of the curved mountain. They found that the enormous landslide had effectively blocked the stream above the falls and that not even a trickle of water entered the former stream bed. They could also see a great wall of ice and snow, which at many places extended high above the top of the curved mountain. Along the open space at the foot of this mountain were other great patches of snow and ice that had not yet melted. They saw where many slides from the top of the mountain had broken trees and scattered debris along its base. They saw no game or spoor of game; it appeared that the north end of the valley had been completely deserted.

Upon returning to the village, Chief Wa-neb-i-te immediately called a general assembly. When the male population had all gathered at the open space near the center of the village, Wa-neb-i-te rose and began to speak.

"My friends," he began, "the things that I must tell you are very bad, and it grieves my heart that they are so. We must make haste to gather everything that we have and prepare to leave the valley. The rains still continue in the mountains above, and the valley of White Bosom Bare is becoming a great lake which has no outlet. I fear that soon the curved mountain will give way to the pressure of the water and this entire valley may be destroyed. Even if it should not, this valley will no longer be a suitable place in which to live. The ground will become dry, the swamps will dry up, and the wapiti, the moose, and the deer will hasten to other feeding grounds. So I must command you all to go to your lodges and begin to make ready to move south, to the valley of the great lake. I have already sent a messenger to our chieftain, Al-a-go-ri-o, and when he reports that things have been made ready for us, we shall be prepared to depart. Now I order all the chiefs to meet with me at the round lodge immediately. The rest of you are dismissed."

Inside the round lodge, the meeting of the sub-chiefs was short and businesslike. Chief Wa-neb-i-te stood before them and said, "I wish to thank all of you for the support that you have given me during the years that I have been your chieftain. But our business here is finished. We no longer need to guard the sacred valley, as it no longer exists. You shall continue to carry out my orders until we reach the valley of the great lake. At that time, we will all become like other braves. I will no longer be the chieftain of a village, for I shall have no village. So I also must become only a brave. On the trail, our people shall need our advice, but when our journey ends, we must remember that our authority ends also. This, my friends, is all that I wished to tell you. You are now dismissed."

So the evacuation of the once-beautiful valley began. The yellow metal that remained was loaded upon the pack animals brought in by Enir's band and carried to the lodge of the big Chief Al-a-go-ri-o. The warbows, hunting bows, hides, thundersticks, and other things that were considered community property were made ready to be placed upon the travois that were hastily being built. The entire village became a beehive of activity. The excitement of this activity temporarily crowded aside the grief and sorrow, as they all plunged into the task.

After the men had come for the warbows, bowmaking tools, and other things that were considered community property, there was plenty of room in I-lip-a-taw's lodge. So-he's mother suggested that they do their packing in privacy. When So-he produced Enir's headpiece, her mother looked at it closely. She then explained what the multicolored feather given to him by Pe-ru-ta stood for. There were six other feathers in the headpiece, and each of them was symbolic. The slaying of the bear, the barehanded slaying of Ba-ep-o-lic, the finding of the yellow metal in White Bosom Bare, the transporting of the metal to the valley via the waterfall, the slaying of Stout-Boy, and the one sent to him by Al-a-go-ri-o for his success in obtaining the thundersticks. The one presented to him by Chief Pe-ru-ta was to be worn either above or below the others so that it could be seen easily and quickly recognized.

So-he sat buried in thought as she studied the headpiece. "Could I wear this headpiece into the land of the Ute and be also honored?" she asked her mother. Her mother looked at her strangely and replied, "Only if you could convince Pe-ru-ta that you were Enir's squaw. You see, unless the Ute warriors recognized you, you would be taken before Chief Pe-ru-ta. If this were not so, many warriors would wear feathers of their own making."

"Then to me this feather means nothing?" asked So-he.

"Yes, it means something," replied her mother. "I am sure that you would have no trouble proving to

Chief Pe-ru-ta that you are Enir's squaw. The questions he would ask should be easily answered." So-he laid aside the headpiece and was thoughtful the remainder of the day.

That evening, after the children were asleep and the garrulous voices of the squaws who were packing had ceased, So-he turned to her mother and said, "Let us go into the land of the Ute. I understand that it is near to the place where Enir is imprisoned. There we will seek this chieftain who is Enir's friend, and maybe he will help us with our plans."

"What plans?" asked her mother.

"Plans to free my husband," replied So-he. "The others for whom he risked his life may desert him in his time of great need, but I shall not. If you refuse to go with me, then I shall go alone. Somewhere I shall find those who have courage enough to do for him what he has done for them. If the story told me by the scout who witnessed Enir's battle with the giant is true, then maybe this Ute chieftain will remember that Enir gave him the thundersticks after he had won them, and maybe he will not be afraid to help him now."

"It is not that the Flathead are afraid," said her mother defensively. "It is because it is useless to go against the soldier-paleface who have many thundersticks. There is no point in their giving their lives for nothing."

"If my father were alive, he would think of something," said So-he. "All my life he taught me, when a task seems difficult, to think deeply upon it. By doing so, oftentimes the most difficult-appearing task will become easy. This and many other things he taught me while I helped him with his work. My husband has also told me that careful thinking will accomplish many things, even things that at first appear impossible. Do you believe that if it were I who was in prison, Enir would stand by and do nothing? I am going, Mother. If you wish to go with me, I shall be glad. But if you do not, then I shall go alone."

Her mother stared aghast at the fierce expression upon the face of her gentle daughter, So-he. "But you are no warrior," she said. "You are just a girl."

"Did I not go with Wo-dan into the forest and bring in much meat while Enir was away? Did we not eat well instead of starving upon roots and berries? Can I not shoot better than half the braves in the village? Enir once told me that in the country from which he came, there were women teachers. He said that women could think as well as men. Now I shall prove him right."

"But what about the children?" asked her mother.

"Wo-dan will watch over them while I am away, and we both will watch over them while on the trail. If the Ute are friendly to me, they shall also be to the children. From the news that I have gathered, Pe-ru-ta is a great chieftain, and this I believe."

For many moments So-he's mother sat and regarded her closely. Surely this was not the same gentle little girl whom she had taught to sew, make pemmican, make soft diapers, and blend beads? But when her thoughts traveled back to her first meeting with I-lip-a-taw, their pattern slowly changed. Once again she saw the wounded braves, the bloody battleground of tribal wars. Once again she heard the young maidens sing the praises of the tall warrior whom she later wed. As these thoughts emerged from her buried past, she began to realize that So-he was also the daughter of I-lip-a-taw. It was then that she asked herself what I-lip-a-taw's council would be if he could speak now. Would it be to leave her husband to his fate, or would it be to let her try? Even if she should fail, she would be in a better position to explain to her children in later life just what had happened. If she did nothing, what would Tall-One think of her when he grew up? I must not misjudge her wisdom, she told herself. Did she not choose Enir for her husband before she even knew his name? Finally she turned to So-he and said, "Let us think more upon this before we make a decision."

So-he answered very slowly, "I fear that if we wait longer he might be taken far away to some other prison where we could never find him. My heart tells me to go now, without delay. This I intend to do."

"Then I shall go with you," said her mother, surprised at the feeling of relief that followed her decision.

"Then I see no reason to wait longer," said So-he. "Let us make our packs tonight and leave in the darkness before dawn, so none shall try to stop us. You select the food and clothing, I shall get the horses and build the packs."

Chapter 26

While Skippy, the runner, sat in the uncomfortable chair across the desk from the stern-faced colonel, he fidgeted nervously. Many times he repeated the message that the colonel had given him, until, at last, the colonel said that it was enough. "Just remember," said the colonel, "that you do not know the man who gave you this message. That you know only that he is a friend of I-lip-a-taw's and that he has paid you well to deliver it. You shall also be able to describe Chief Iron-Hand well. Are there any questions?"

"Yes," replied Skippy, after a moment's pause. "I would look at him once more."

"I anticipated this," replied the colonel, "so I left the door of the guardhouse unlocked. You may do so now if you wish." Skippy rose and slipped out of the colonel's office like a shadow.

When Skippy entered the guardhouse, he stopped several steps away from the barred cell in which the two large Indians stood. He felt just a little conspicuous in the presence of the two Flathead who towered so high above him. He had never been so close to a Flathead warrior before, and the tales he had heard of their great strength and bravery caused a feeling of awe to possess him. While he stood with the two pairs of sharp eyes boring into him, he almost forgot what his business there was.

"I need help," he said in a voice that was barely above a whisper. Neither of them spoke, but he knew that they had heard him, so he waited. Presently Chief Iron-Hand answered him.

"Help for what?" he asked.

"I have been instructed to carry a message to one of your chiefs, Chief I-lip-a-taw. I have never been to the land of the Flathead, and I would like to know how to reach it."

After another moment's silence, Chief Iron-Hand asked, "What is this message?"

Skippy repeated the message just as the colonel had instructed him, all the while letting his eyes take in every detail of the large chief's person. When he had finished, Chief Iron-Hand asked, "Who sends this message?"

"The colonel himself," replied Skippy.

"Why does he send it?" asked Chief Iron-Hand.

"I do not know, but I do know that this chief is a friend of his and that he has visited him many times on his quest for bow wood."

After another pause, Chief Iron-Hand asked, "Does the colonel think that I have lied to him?" Skippy made no reply, but gave the sign that maybe it was true.

After a longer pause, Chief Iron-Hand said, "This I will tell you. To reach the land of the Flathead, you must travel far to the northwest until you come to the forked mountain, which is in the range beyond the Tetons. After you pass it, you will turn north while the forked mountain is on your right. Go north until you reach a small river, which is the river of the sun. Follow it until you come to a larger river which flows south. Follow up this river into the land of the Flathead."

"Then I must pass through the land of the Ute?" asked Skippy.

"The Ute are our enemy," said Chief Iron-Hand.

"If you tell them that you also are our enemy, they will let you go in peace." Skippy thanked him in the sign language and retreated silently out the door.

After a few moments Enir yawned and asked his companion what he thought of their visitor. "I think that maybe he is on his way to the Happy Hunting Ground," replied the scout, then after a moment he asked, "Do you really think that he bears a message?"

"I do," replied Enir. "It was rehearsed too well to have been made up."

"What do you mean?" asked the scout.

"Did you notice that even as he spoke, he was also getting a picture of me in his mind?" The scout was silent. "This is what I think," said Enir. "I-lip-a-taw has visited the colonel many times, this the colonel told me with his eyes while we were being interviewed. I think that the colonel knew not that I-lip-a-taw was a scout, and that he told him things that he should not. Now he wishes to get I-lip-a-taw into prison also."

The scout was silent for several moments, then he asked, "If you think this is true, why did you give him the proper directions?"

"Humph," replied Enir. "I gave him nothing that he did not already have. No one is so simple that they know not where the land of the Flathead is. He got what he came to get."

"And what was that?" asked the scout.

"A good description of me, the better to convince I-lip-a-taw that I am here," replied Enir.

"I think that he will never pass through the land of the Ute," said the scout.

"I am not so sure," replied Enir. "He is much like the fox or the coyote. But I have no fear for I-lip-a-taw. His eyes are very sharp, and so is his mind. He will quickly see the treachery in the story. But what I do fear is that he will try to promote an attack upon this fort. That would be disastrous. We can never win a battle with the paleface by giving them more advantage than they have already." After this outburst, both men were silent for several moments.

"I wonder what I-lip-a-taw knows that worries the colonel?" asked the scout.

"I have no idea," replied Enir. "But whatever it is, you can rest assured that Chief Al-a-go-ri-o knows it, too. I-lip-a-taw is too shrewd to hold back important information."

So day after day the two captives prowled the narrow confines of their prison and worried. Not so much about their own fate, but that they would be used to bait a trap that would result in the useless death of many of their comrades.

Enir had already examined the heavy iron bars that were set perpendicularly and about five or six inches apart. Their ends were tightly fitted into large hand-hewn beams that formed a rectangle in one corner of the guardhouse. He had also watched the jailer very closely and had noted that he took no chances when he served them their food. There was a shower stall and a commode in one corner of the jail, and rough slabs of wood hanging from the wall by two short chains formed their bunks. It was easy enough to see that escape was out of the question, and judging from the attitude of the colonel, so was release.

Chapter 27

When So-he, her two children, and her mother rode silently away from the village, it was so dark that So-he could not see the trail, but the big stallion solved this problem for her. He immediately took the lead and also set the pace, which in the darkness seemed quite fast. When they were safely away, she confided to her mother that the big horse seemed to have taken over. "Let him," replied her mother. "His knowledge of trail riding far exceeds ours, and I am sure he is traveling at the speed Enir has taught him."

It was mid-afternoon before they reached the fork in the trail that So-he was watching for. It was a dim trail known as the high trail, which branched off to the southwest. The trail they were riding continued on southeast to the main Flathead village. This she knew because she had traveled it with her father, but all she knew of the high trail came from the many stories she had listened to concerning it. She knew that somewhere in the direction it led was a great forked mountain, which supposedly marked the northern boundary of the land of the Ute.

When they reached this fork in the trail, So-he stopped the stallion and said to her mother, "Let us follow the high trail. It will lead us to the land of the Ute much sooner than any other trail, and no one will follow to try to stop us."

"I have been told that the high trail is very dangerous," replied her mother. "I fear that it will be a bad trail for horses."

"But these are Enir's horses," replied So-he. "They are used to dangerous trails." Then, without waiting for further argument, she turned the stallion onto the high trail and took a firmer grip upon Whispering-West-Wind, who had fallen asleep in her arms.

For several days they followed the high trail. Water was plentiful, but game was scarce. Grouse, trade rats, and wild berries were all the food they found to supplement the dried meat they carried, but it was sufficient. Grass for the horses was their greatest worry, because in the steep, rugged terrain it was very scarce. But the sturdy Appaloosa horses were good at foraging, and occasionally they found a small meadow where they would tarry until the horses were well fed. Wo-dan became very gaunt from his scanty diet, and So-he was surprised to see how much he resembled Shadow. He was anxious for the hunt, and although So-he kept her bow in readiness, they found no spoor of deer along the trail. So-he could not keep from worrying about Wo-dan becoming so much like Shadow, the great wolf. She often wondered what his reaction would be should he meet with a female wolf, but then she recalled his great love for the children. He would patiently stand until Tall-One had helped Whispering West-Wind upon his back so he could take her for a ride. Surely he would not desert them, she told herself, but nevertheless she worried. The great wolf-dog played too important a part in their lives for her not to. Without him she could not expect to obtain meat. Also, without his protection the cougar would invade their camp and frighten the horses away. She had never realized how much she depended upon the great dog until these thoughts began to enter her mind.

At last, after they had almost given up hope of

ever emerging from this vast and rugged region of broken rocks and hanging crags, they glimpsed, far to the southeast, a massive mountain whose peak was enshrouded by heavy clouds. "Look," said So-he as she drew the stallion to a halt. Her mother did not immediately speak, but shading her eyes from the mid-morning sun, she gazed long at the dark blue mass of elevated land. Presently the top of the cloud thinned, and there above it was the cloved peak that had given the mountain its name. So-he, who was also watching, sighed wearily. "I did not think that it was so far away," she said. But her mother, whose thoughts were more practical, gazed out over the great basin before them and saw the eagles playing, a great wedge of geese disappear into the tree tops, and the many spots of lush grass, in some of which buffalo cows were resting with their calves.

"It is time for us to find a place to rest and regain our strength," she said as she directed So-he's attention to the sleeping buffalo.

After circling many small swamps where even the wily beaver took no alarm at their presence, they came to a beautiful stream where the water was so clear that the trout could be seen resting upon its gravelly bottom. "This is a good place for us to camp," said her mother.

"But, Mother," protested So-he, "it must not be so very far to the villages of the Ute. We must not forget the reason we came."

"I know," replied her mother. "But let us not go into their presence looking like renegades. The horses are tired, the children dirty, and our own clothes need to be washed and mended. Let us bathe many times and apply the moosetail to our hair."

So for several days they lingered there beside the clear stream. The children were delighted as they swam in the cool, invigorating water. So-he took Wo-dan and hunted in the forest, keeping well away from the snorting buffalo. Wo-dan worked very effectively, for he, too, was anxious for a change of diet.

While her mother washed and repaired their clothes, So-he polished their scanty trappings with tallow and soapstone. She also plaited Sa-ra's dark flaxen hair, and with a hardwood ember she singed the dark hair of Tall-One. All the time this was going on, many strips of venison hung drying over the broad campfire. Her mother also removed So-he's beaded buckskin dress from the pack and hung it so the wind would straighten out the wrinkles.

So-he looked at it and said, "Mother, we are not going to a feast."

"But we are going to meet the great chieftain Pe-ru-ta," replied her mother. "You must remember that you are the squaw of Chief Iron-Hand, whom, it is said, the Ute hold in high honor. You must do nothing that will subtract from this honor."

"But Mother!" exclaimed So-he. "Chief Pe-ru-ta is a very old man."

"Humph," replied her mother. "He is still a man. No man is so old that he no longer appreciates a beautiful woman. You shall wear it. You must also learn to smile again, for the lines in your face have become very deep."

"But how can I smile with Enir in some dark prison?" she asked.

"I do not expect you to go around smiling all of the time," her mother replied. "But you must learn to smile when it is expected of you."

During the several days that it took them to circle the great mountain, So-he learned much from the large spotted stallion. By watching his ears, she learned to tell when buffalo were present in the vicinity. She even learned to distinguish whether it was a herd or a lone buffalo bull. If a lone bull was loitering on their trail, the big horse would always circle, but if it was only a few cows or even a group of mixed buffalo, the stallion would snort and shake his head. This would send the herd running in every direction. She also watched Wo-dan when the timber was thin enough. He would often cause a large disturbance in a herd, especially if there were calves present. Also, if a large herd of buffalo was directly before them, the stallion would come to a complete stop and shake his proud head.

After they had turned south and were leaving the great mountain behind them, the buffalo became fewer and the trees much smaller. Their way here seemed to follow a gravelly ridge that extended as far south as their eyes could see. On their left was the dark, distant wall of smoky mountains, while on their right was a vast ocean of purple sagebrush. Often, far out in the sagebrush, she could see the black humps of many buffalo, but along the broad ridge she saw only deer and antelope.

On the second day after they had reached this ridge, So-he suddenly pulled the big stallion to a stop. For there in the gravelly sand were the tracks of several horses. Her mother came forward to study the tracks and informed her that the horses were being ridden but that the tracks were many days old. So-he called Wo-dan to her and gave him the sign that she used when she wished him to circle very wide. She then settled back to watch him as they proceeded on along the ridge. If there were Ute hunters in the vicinity, she knew that Wo-dan would detect them, and she did not want to be surprised. Her mother produced their headpieces, which they donned before they continued on toward the south.

Although her mother had insisted that they were a long way from any regular hunting ground, she kept a close watch on the great wolf-dog as he circled before them.

Chapter 28

When Skippy left the outpost on the Platte River, he did so in much the same manner that a coyote would depart from a raided henhouse. He ducked into the sagebrush and slunk away, stopping often to check his back trail. There were several reasons for this furtive action. First, Skippy was a loner. He disliked company on the trail, more especially when he was upon a secret mission. Second, Skippy had many enemies, both in the Indian population and in the white. He was regarded by them as a quisling and an informer whom nobody could trust. But his chief reason was not because he was not respected among them, but because of the bag of yellow metal he carried. He was well aware that so long as he was in possession of it, his life was in danger. Even a soldier-paleface would not hesitate to take his life for half the gold that was contained in the plump bag he carried. Although he was convinced that no one besides himself and the colonel knew he was in possession of it, he well knew the suspicious nature of the people with whom he was associated. He was fully aware that to them, the morning paper was written on the surface of the sand dunes and also broadcast by the many voices of birds and the wail of the hungry coyote. To the alert, sharp-eyed trapper, who could tell by the tracks of a wolf whether it was male or female, and if it were female, whether or not she was carrying whelps, his normal light-footed trail would now stand out in bold headlines, advertising the extra weight that he carried. So for these reasons Skippy hid his trail well.

When he reached the cover of the timbered foothills, he paused, and from a place of concealment he studied his back trail closely. Then, with a look of relief upon his otherwise stoical countenance, he quickly disappeared into the jumble of rocks and bushes as he hurriedly placed distance between himself and his starting point.

Skippy traveled very carefully when he reached the land of the warlike Ute. He had paid no attention to the advice given him about the Flathead chief, Iron-Hand. He knew that if the Ute captured him, his only hope was to buy his freedom with a glib story of stealing the gold from the paleface. However, the thought of losing the gold was distasteful enough to cause him to exert the utmost the skill for which he was noted.

Skippy had had many narrow escapes, and there were times when it had appeared that his discovery was certain, but his adroitness in the art of camouflage, plus his ability to move very swiftly, had eventually brought him through. As he stood near the foot of the forked mountain, he felt an exhilarating thrill of victory. But when he gazed into the far north toward the land of the Flathead, the feeling suddenly left him. By keeping close count, he realized that it had taken him almost twenty days to cross the land of the Ute. Now, he realized, it would be almost impossible for him to go to the land of the Flathead and return before the vicious winter gripped this mountainous country. His only hope was to find some warrior or group of warriors who were going in that direction and could take the message for him. He did not know how far it was from where he stood to the edge of the Flathead country, but he reasoned

277

that it should not be far. So, with this thought in mind, Skippy moved toward the forked mountain with all the speed he could maintain.

When he reached the edge of a large basin, which was bordered on the east by a broad open space, he climbed to the top of a pinnacle of stone to map his route. While doing this, he detected some movement among the stunted trees far to the northwest, so he remained still and waited. Presently he made out four horses moving directly toward him. He glanced quickly about and discovered what appeared to be a dim trail, which passed very close to where he lay. This knowledge did not worry Skippy; he was confident that he could hide in the rocks and shrubs until they had passed. But his curiosity was deeply aroused. Were they Ute or Flathead? he asked himself as he quickly sought a place where he would be less exposed. He found an ideal spot, where he could observe the trail by peeping between two upthrusts of stone that were very close together. Here he could look upon the trail and still be concealed from the sharpest of eyes. So he made himself comfortable and waited.

For perhaps a quarter of an hour the horsemen were hidden from him as they traversed a wide swag, and when they came into view fairly near to him, his breath caught in his throat and his heart began to pound. He quickly changed his position and studied the trail behind them very closely. For miles along the sparsely timbered ridge, nothing moved. Skippy sat slowly down upon a stone. "Two Flathead squaws and two small children, all alone with four good-looking horses," he breathed to himself. After waiting a minute or so longer, he again peered through the crack in the rocks. This time his eyes opened a bit wider and his head became a little dizzy.

The girl in the lead was very young and beautiful, and she was riding the most magnificent spotted stallion he had ever seen, even though he had spent his entire life among horses. He saw that this girl held a small child in front of her and that the horse appeared to be very docile. Also, he noted there was no thunderstick visible, nor was there a bow held in readiness. He tore his eyes away from the girl and studied the other rider. He saw a good-looking middle-aged squaw, who had a small boy riding behind her, holding the lead ropes of two beautiful pack animals. When his eyes turned again to the girl, he noted that she was not concentrating upon the trail before her, but that her eyes seemed to be roving about the countryside to her right, as if she were looking for something. They must be looking for their men, thought Skippy, and a sly grin appeared upon his pinched face, because he well knew that there was no one for many miles in the direction in which she was looking. Their men have probably been captured by the Ute, he said to himself, and all the while his mind was actively planning how he could gain possession of both the squaws and the horses. The plan was not long in presenting itself for but a few steps away was a heavy clump of juniper bushes that grew very close to the trail. He could hide in them and at the proper moment could dart from them, and with a tremendous burst of speed he could dislodge the girl and be in possession of the entire setup before they realized what was happening. So Skippy ducked behind the edge of the ridge and moved swiftly to the bunch of juniper shrubs where he settled down to wait.

He flexed the muscles of his legs and trained his ears to catch the muffled tread of the horses, because he knew that he did not have very long to wait. His head was slightly lowered, and his ear was listening for the tread of the lead horse, when his downcast eyes saw a shadow flicker just a few feet to his right. He rolled his eyes toward it, and suddenly his tomahawk was in his hand and his heart in his throat, for he found himself staring into the unblinking eyes of the largest timber wolf he had ever seen in his entire life. The beast stood almost four feet at the shoulder, and its long, narrow eyes were boring into his in a manner that caused his blood to turn as cold as icewater. The great mouth was slightly open, revealing fangs that were inches long and as sharp as needles. Skippy instinctively realized his disadvantage and automatically backed into the open.

Never before had he experienced the fear that now gripped him. The small tomahawk that he held in his hand would be useless against such a beast, for Skippy well knew its speed and ferocity. His only hope was to shout for help from the two squaws, but when he opened his mouth to shout, a slender arm shot suddenly over his shoulder, and he felt the stinging edge of a sharp knife as it cut through the outer layer of skin on his throat. Skippy stood very still as the tomahawk was snatched from his trembling fingers and his knife lifted deftly from its scabbard. Suddenly the knife at his throat flicked like the tongue of a serpent, and he heard his bowstring snap and felt his bow slide to the ground just as the knife again rested its sharp edge against his throat. The great wolf remained crouched before him during this swift action, its narrow green eyes never wavering from Skippy's frightened stare. Suddenly the knife darted from his throat, and he immediately felt its sharp point pierce the skin between his shoulders. "Down, Wo-dan," he heard a feminine voice say when the great beast moved a menacing step forward. The beast halted, but a hair-raising growl rumbled deep in his chest. Skippy shrank back slightly, but the knife held firm and he felt the blood trickle down his back. Skippy's knees were trembling when he heard the holder of the knife order the other squaw to bring a piece of stout rope. Soon his hands were jerked behind his back and bound securely. When the big wolf backed slowly out of the juniper and started to circle him, Skippy felt compelled to turn with him. He saw that the other squaw now stood beside two wide-eyed children, but the holder of the knife had turned with him. He felt the trembling point of the knife again touch his back, and a voice asked very softly but sternly, "Who are you?" Skippy started to turn, but the knife moved forward enough to stop him quite quickly.

"I am only a messenger on my way to the land of the Flathead," he said weakly.

"What message do you bear?" asked the voice.

"I bear a message to a chief named I-lip-a-taw, who is a chief of scouts," replied Skippy. A long moment of silence followed, during which So-he and her mother glanced guardedly at each other.

"We are of the Flathead," said So-he. "What is this message?"

"It is from a friend of Chief Iron-Hand, and it is for Chief I-lip-a-taw's ears alone," said Skippy, but he made the mistake of letting his evasiveness show in his darting eyes.

"Do you know I-lip-a-taw?" asked So-he.

"Yes, he is a friend of mine," replied Skippy.

"When have you last seen him?" she asked. Skippy thought swiftly, but not swiftly enough to prevent the flashing shadow of the knife in his eyes.

"On his last trip for bow wood," he replied.

"And when was this?" asked So-he in a careless manner.

"It was early this spring, just after the snow had left the ground," guessed Skippy. Suddenly he was whirled around, and the knife was again at his throat. This time the voice of the girl was both fierce and strong.

"You will talk swiftly and straight," it said. "If you lie, you will go quickly to the Happy Hunting Ground without your head." With the knife biting through the skin along his throat, Skippy made a full confession. The only thing that saved his life was the fact that he described Chief Iron-Hand well. The knife was reluctantly removed, and a slender, strong hand searched beneath his tunic and retrieved the bag of yellow metal which was hidden there. Presently he was assisted upon the back of one of the pack animals and given these brief instructions: "If you try to escape, I shall send Wo-dan after you . . . alone." So-he exhibited the bow, which she had lifted from her riding saddle. "Do you see the small tree beside the trail?" Just as Skippy looked in the direction she indicated, the bow twanged and an arrow zipped by him and imbedded itself deeply in a tree no larger than his ankle and many steps away. "If you speak without being spoken to or should you make a sound of any kind, I will kill you," she said very low and impressively.

So-he and the others then mounted, and they rode steadily until the sun approached the western horizon. Skippy could hear them talking guardedly, but he was not familiar enough with the Salish language to understand. They camped that night near a small stream. Skippy was calmly tied to a tree, and Wo-dan was placed quite near to guard him. Skippy not only made no effort to escape, but each movement he made was with the utmost care.

They rose early the next morning and rode hard. The news about Enir caused So-he to become very anxious. She knew that Skippy was not lying when he told of how he had entered the prison and talked with him. It was about noon when So-he noticed the strange actions of Wo-dan. She immediately signaled him to return to her, then tied him with a long, slender rawhide rope and handed it to Tall-One, saying, "Keep him close to your side, for I think the Ute are approaching." They had been riding in this manner for perhaps an hour when a dozen or so Ute warriors unconcernedly joined them and silently escorted them to a small lake where many other braves waited. No words were spoken. They rode into this Ute campground, and the warriors who escorted them took charge of their mounts. Skippy was shoved roughly to the ground and again tied to a tree. All of the Ute came close to Wo-dan, whom Tall-One kept beside him. Whispering-West-Wind alighted from her grandmother's arms and went straight to a tall Ute warrior and held up her hands to be lifted. The warrior picked her up, and the other braves laughed loudly. Whispering-West-Wind pointed her tiny finger at the fire and spoke the Flathead word for hungry. The tall brave smiled and carried her to the fire, where a half of buffalo was roasting. He selected a generous slice that seemed quite cooked and began to tear off slender shreds to feed her. After she had eaten, she took the piece of meat from the brave's hand and walked over and gave it to Wo-dan. Wo-dan gulped it, and again loud laughter arose from the Ute warriors. They were all served a generous helping of the delicious meat, but no one said anything to them.

After they had finished eating, the leader of the group approached So-he's mother and asked her who they were and whence they came. Her mother was thoughtful for a moment, then she pointed to So-he. The chief smiled and then directed the same question to So-he. So-he told him that she was the wife of Chief Iron-Hand and then told of her father's death and of their present mission. The chief did not show any surprise at her answer and looked again at the big spotted stallion. Presently he turned to So-he and asked who their captive was. So-he told of his accosting them upon the trail and of his admission of attempting to lead I-lip-a-taw into a trap. The chief rose and went over to examine Skippy's bonds closely. He then gave him a good sound kick and returned to the fire.

Early the next morning, the chief assigned two warriors to escort So-he and her party to a large village to the south. Before he finished, he motioned them aside and gave them many orders that So-he could not hear. The two warriors returned, and each of them looked at So-he with admiration and respect. The others departed before So-he's mother had finished arranging their packs. So-he watched them put Skippy upon the back of a poor old mare and lead her away. She was never to learn his fate, nor did she worry. She had long since decided that Skippy was exactly what he was: a traitor, a liar, and a quisling who had no place among honest men.

They entered the main village of the Ute long before sunset, but all day they had noticed smoke signals both in front and behind them, so they were quite sure that their arrival was expected. They also suspected that their presence in the vicinity had been known for several days.

So-he was quite surprised when they suddenly arrived at the hidden valley in which the large village was located. She was pleased with the semi-permanent lodges, which resembled those of the Flathead, but her greatest surprise came when without pause she was ushered into the presence of the famous chieftain of the Ute, Pe-ru-ta himself. At first she was quite nervous, but the friendly old chieftain quickly put her at ease and immediately gave her a position of honor, a place by his side around a large sunken arena where the entire population of the village was gathering.

While they were awaiting the arrival of those who were delayed, Pe-ru-ta turned to her and said, "I wish you to meet a friend of Chief Iron-Hand." He turned to a brave who stood near and gave him some instructions in a low voice. The brave quickly departed and returned almost immediately, accompanied by one of the most remarkable men So-he had ever seen. He was of great height, and his chest and forearms were gigantic. She saw that his feet were bare and so large that they were almost unrecognizable as human feet. His legs resembled the trunks of trees, but his stomach seemed to be drawn from fasting. This mighty giant brushed aside his escort and quickly approached So-he. Dropping to one knee, he reached out a hand that was as large as a bear's paw and grabbed both of her hands in it. So-he was startled, but the giant's grip was gentle.

"Lo-tes-i-me greets the beautiful squaw of his friend Chief Iron-Hand. May the Great Spirit see fit to assist you in your plans to free him. If she needs me to help her, she needs only to speak." So-he looked into the eyes of the giant and noticed that they were both bruised and red. Although they still showed the marks of battle, those eyes were very sharp, and they quickly detected the shock in the eyes of So-he. "Yes, I am he who was beaten by Chief Iron-Hand in a fair fight, and I am not ashamed. Chief Iron-Hand is the only man who has ever beaten Lo-tes-i-me, and no man has ever beaten Chief Iron-Hand." So-he was quite taken aback, because she knew the details of Enir's fight with this great giant.

"I thank you, Lo-tes-i-me," she said as she attempted to grip the huge fist which held her hands. "I know little of your fighting games, but I assure you that my husband is not proud."

Lo-tes-i-me rose and said, "The scars are nothing. My wounds are now healed, and I can join the battle to free the great friend of all the people, Chief Iron-Hand." He then turned and strode away with a gracefulness that seemed impossible for one of such tremendous bulk.

After the crowd had gathered, they were entertained by some acrobatic stunts performed by several braves. Then some trick riding, spear throwing, and other feats, but the sun was getting low, and Pe-ru-ta cut the entertainment short. He then ordered So-he, her mother, and the two children into the arena. Wo-dan accompanied them and held his head very high as he surveyed the throng of Indians who sat on various benches of stones along the west side of the large bowl. Pe-ru-ta introduced them, Ute-style, to all the important members of his settlement. He then ordered the spotted stallion brought forward, and So-he mounted him and put him through his various paces as she cantered the length of the arena amid loud cheers and shouts of approval from ordinarily stoic spectators. In this manner was So-he introduced into the Ute society.

Chapter 29

When the party honoring the wife and the family of Chief Iron-Hand was over, and long after everyone else had retired, Chief Pe-ru-ta sat upon a crude bench before his lodge and dug into the ground with his scratch stick. Many small holes he dug and refilled before he finally rose and strolled away into the starlit night. After a while, he halted before a certain lodge and rapped firmly upon the outside of the buffalo-hide door. Presently a squaw opened it a tiny bit and peered sharply into his face. Upon recognizing him, the squaw threw open the door and called urgently for her husband. When her husband appeared, Chief Pe-ru-ta motioned him outside, and they strolled away toward the large corral where the hunting horses were kept. For a long while they spoke, then this man, quickly singling out a trim, speedy-looking pony and mounting him, rode swiftly away.

The next morning, after So-he and her family had spent a very restful night, she rose, and putting a slender rope about Wo-dan's neck, led him toward the wide stream that flowed past the village. To her delight she was joined there by Chief Pe-ru-ta, who politely inquired about her comfort. They chatted for a while about many things, but chiefly about Wo-dan's ancestors. After a while, Pe-ru-ta informed her that he was working on a plan to free Chief Iron-Hand and that it would be necessary for her to wait here in the village for a few days until he could test this plan. He also said that if it was successful, her husband would meet her here before many days. So-he was delighted, but the chieftain requested that she speak to no one about it until the plan was tried. He also asked and received permission to use her four horses. So-he was so excited that she took Wo-dan for a long walk, because she dared not return to the presence of her mother until she had regained her composure.

All that day, many smoke signals were seen in the surrounding hills, but to all except a very few Ute chiefs, the signals were meaningless. Late the next evening a very tired pony carrying a wiry old Ute warrior arrived in the village. This old warrior received no welcome from the occupants of the village; in fact, some of the squaws even spit toward him as he rode slowly past. Chief Pe-ru-ta merely glanced at him as he rode to the corrals and dismounted, but an hour later, when this same old warrior appeared at the back entrance of Pe-ru-ta's lodge, he received a warm welcome and plenty of food and drink.

Chief Pe-ru-ta's questions to the old Indian were very few and pointed.

"Does the white chieftain still desire many buffalo skins?" he asked. The old Indian nodded. "Did you promise to get them?" Again the Indian nodded in the affirmative. "When?" asked Pe-ru-ta.

The old Indian spoke: "As the smoke requested, in seven days at sundown."

Pe-ru-ta smiled and nodded. After a moment he asked, "How did you get away?"

"Ta-ha-ra is doing good job being me," replied the old Indian.

Pe-ru-ta was silent for several moments, and it was obvious that he was reviewing something in his mind. Presently he spoke. "I will have four horses at the hidden corral after sunset on the seventh day. They will be horses that none can catch. Lo-tes-i-me will be ready."

When the old Indian rose to depart, he faced Pe-ru-ta, and his eyes looked like twin rifle barrels as he spoke. "It will be very dangerous. You should tell Lo-tes-i-me to use much care and avoid noise."

"I shall tell him," replied Pe-ru-ta. And the old Indian, who acted as Pe-ru-ta's spy at the fort, departed upon a fresh mount.

For the next several days, ponies laden with dry buffalo hides slowly gathered at an appointed place. There their burdens were transferred to the backs of much larger horses. The bulky loads were arranged and adjusted, then removed and laid aside, each at a separate place. Upon the back of the largest horse was placed a special pack. Many times it was torn down and rebuilt until it finally met the approval of the brave who was in charge of the pack train.

On the morning of the day the pack train was due to arrive at the fort, the first snowstorm struck the mountains at the head of the Platte River. All through the day it continued, and toward evening it began to lay upon the cooled earth. The brave in charge of the train smiled. Pe-ru-ta is a very wise chieftain, he said silently to himself as the strong horses forged through the shallow drifts. They reached the gate of the stockade between sunset and dark. The tired horses were led inside, where they were placed in the care of a certain old Indian whose job was to do the menial tasks about the stables. He was also used occasionally to make deals with Indian hunters and trappers, but always in the company of soldiers who could speak the Ute language. Unfortunately, none of the soldiers could read the dim smoke signals, even if they had known where to look for them.

After the sergeant had watched the drivers of the pack train depart to the large encampment beside the river, he returned and examined the horses. He glanced at the packs that the old Indian had placed into empty stables and ordered him to feed the horses some hay. Then, brushing the snow from his coat, he retired into the warmth of the barracks.

The old Indian leisurely fed the hungry stock, then strolled back to the stables, where he seated himself upon a pack of buffalo hides and patiently waited until all the sounds inside the barracks had ceased and the guards had been posted. Then, without making the slightest sound, he unrolled the largest of the packs and watched the huge figure of a man slowly rise from among the scattered hides and painfully begin to flex his great muscles. The old Indian sat back down and waited until the large man signaled to him that he was ready. He then rose and silently led the way behind the row of stables, being very careful to avoid stepping in the places where the warm compost had failed to melt the new snow. They eventually emerged from the shadows near the back of a strong log building that had no windows or back door. As swift and silent as the flight of a nighthawk, the old one darted into the shadows of this building. A moment later the large man followed, and the two stood silent and unmoving for several minutes. Presently, from not so very far away in the forest, there came the grunting call of an inquisitive timber wolf. Several seconds later this call was answered from a few miles away. Neither of the Indians moved until these calls developed into the age-old communication of two distant wolf packs.

When this happened, the old Indian pointed to a

stack of short lodge poles and moved ghostlike to one end of them. The large man did likewise, and silently and swiftly a firm stack of poles began to rise in the shadows at the rear of the building. When it had reached a certain height, the old Indian motioned for the big man to mount it. After he had done so and tested it for staunchness, they both stood still until the wolf calls had intensified.

Inch by inch the back end of the roof began to rise above the logs upon which it rested. First one side then the other moved a tiny bit, and each time a leaning lodge pole on either side grew a bit straighter. The slight swaying of the roof was carefully timed to the noisy baying of the wolves, and no loud cracking sound was detected by either worker. Presently the large man reached up and began to tug patiently at the short log that formed the vertex of the gable. When it yielded, he passed it down to the older man, and after a few minutes the second log followed and was also laid gently upon the ground. The large Indian then forced his body through the opening and waited in the darkness until the other followed. The old man led the way carefully along the row of barred cells and presently stopped. At the whisper of movement inside, he gave the low call of the cricket. He then took the hands of the large man and placed them upon two perpendicular iron bars. When another two hands from inside the dark cell were placed upon his, he gently pushed them away.

Very reluctantly, the strong iron bars began to yield to the terrific pressure of Lo-tes-i-me's gigantic arms. Suddenly they gave way like the soft sigh of a breath of wind, and an oval-shaped opening appeared between the bars. The two eager occupants of the cell quickly forced their bodies through it, and the old man led them silently out through the open gable, then to the stockade fence, where the three of them were boosted over, leaving the old one alone in the stockade.

The old Ute stood still in the shadows and listened to the baying of the wolves. Presently the cry came that he was waiting for, and he smiled. With the gratifying knowledge that the escape had been successful, he carefully made his way to the stables, where he discarded the soldier shoes that he kept hidden for such purposes, and after redonning his moccasins, he walked leisurely to the tiny hut assigned to him and calmly retired.

Upon hearing the commotion very early the next morning, the old Indian came sleepily from his hut and made his way to the scene of the excitement. He found a group of soldiers ganged around a tremendous footprint made by a bare foot in the soft snow. Pushing his wrinkled face through the ring of soldiers, he looked silently at the track for a moment, then said in a surprised voice, "Big-foot."

"By all that is holy," shouted the sergeant in an excited voice. Then, turning to the group of soldiers, he said, "Fall back, don't anybody go near those footprints. I want the old man to see this." He then immediately raced away toward the officers' quarters.

After he had departed, the soldiers looked at each other in disbelief. They broke up into small groups, and the old Indian listened stoically to the many stories he heard them tell. "By Ned, I always thought he was a myth, but I wouldn't be surprised now to learn that there was a Paul Bunyan," said one of them.

"Me neither," said another. "I'm not even agonna argue anymore that there ain't no Santa Claus."

Chapter 30

When Enir mounted the great spotted stallion, he experienced another thrill on top of those he had already experienced during this memorable night. First was the thrill of being rescued after he had abandoned all hope. Second was the realization that Lo-tes-i-me had fully recovered from their terrific battle. Third, when he had been told that his family awaited him at the Ute village, he could barely resist a shout. Now, sitting astride the only horse that had ever come into his life, he became certain that the Great Spirit had taken a hand in his affairs.

It was not until they had traveled far into the land of the Ute that Lo-tes-i-me mentioned the death of So-he's father. This news staggered Enir, but when he pressed for details, he found that Lo-tes-i-me did not know them. Despite all of his other good fortune, this news was very depressing. For he had come to love the old bowmaker like a father, and he also knew how his death must have affected So-he. When he finally drew from the big Indian the news of So-he, their children, and her mother's hectic trip to the Ute nation; of her plea to Chief Pe-ru-ta for help; and of the way that she had handled things, he began to realize that despite her gentle nature, So-he had inherited some of the wisdom of I-lip-a-taw. He could think of no other plan that would have freed him, especially another that could have been executed so easily and so simply. Pe-ru-ta, he decided, was also very wise.

Late one afternoon as they approached the Ute village, Lo-tes-i-me informed him that the news of their success had preceded them, but he was not surprised. He had seen the smoke, but, being unable to read the signal, he had refrained from mentioning it. When they had stopped to eat at noon that day, Enir had borrowed Lo-tes-i-me's knife and had spent some time shaving and rolling his hair. When they had forded the river and were approaching the village, he let the big stallion take the lead, which was fitting to one of his rank. When the group at the corrals came forward to greet them, he had eyes only for So-he and his two children, who also were allowed to precede the other greeters. But when he sprang from the back of the stallion and started forward, he found his way blocked by a great snarling timber wolf who was the very image of his old friend Shadow. "Wodan!" shouted Enir, and the snarling stopped. The next instant, he felt two gigantic paws placed upon his naked stomach, and a yelp of pleasure issued from that great mouth. "Why he remembers me!" shouted Enir as he brushed him away and reached for his two children and So-he. His arms encircled them, and he became unable to speak for a few seconds.

"Where are your clothes?" asked So-he.

"We threw them into the fire," he shouted as he slapped the naked rear of his tall companion, who had halted beside them. Then, with his other arm around the shoulders of the tall scout, he said, "We did not want to mix their lice with our own."

When Chief Iron-Hand, his wife, children, and mother-in-law, and the tall scout had bade farewell to Chief Pe-ru-ta and their other Ute friends, they departed northward toward the land of the Flathead. Both of the children rode with their grandmother,

Whispering-West-Wind in front of her and Tall-One behind her. "We will carry them later," said So-he. "But for a while I have so many things to tell you, I do not wish to be bothered."

"But I can carry them," protested Enir.

"No," replied So-he, "I wish you to be free to listen." Enir smiled, but the smile did not linger for he knew of what So-he wished to speak.

After So-he had told him the details of I-lip-a-taw's death and had given him the names of those who were with him, he felt a deep sadness in his heart. When she told him of Wa-neb-i-te's report of the danger that threatened their valley, a look of deep concern appeared upon his face. He turned and looked back at the two children, who were squealing with delight as they broke twigs from the trees they were passing and tossed them into the air for Wo-dan to catch.

For a while he rode in silence, and when he spoke his voice held a deep sadness. "We will take the high trail straight to our valley," he said. "I wish to see our lodge once more, but we shall tarry only long enough to get some things that we shall need and clothing for ourselves and the children. From there we will go and recover Dead Man's Cache. Then we will travel far to the northwest, where, I have been told, there are many villages beside the big waters. They are villages of my own people, but your mother is half French, which makes our children more paleface than Indian. The freedom of the Indian will soon end, and the greedy paleface will rape this beautiful land, even as your father predicted. I think that if I-lip-a-taw could speak to us now, he would say that it was our duty to prepare our children to lead the life of the paleface. Therefore we will educate them and prepare them to live in a paleface world. We shall teach them to play paleface games and to read the books of the paleface. We shall also teach them the paleface law and the paleface custom, but we shall tell them the truth about our people. Of the things that they are taught in the paleface school we shall say nothing, lest they become warped in their thinking and fail to receive the knowledge they will need. With the money in Dead Man's Cache, I will buy much land, and upon it I shall build a lodge the likes of which you have never seen. There, we shall raise cattle and spotted horses, and we shall find a gentle mate for Wo-dan."

"What are cattle?" asked So-he.

"Cattle," replied Enir, "are like buffalo who, like the Indians, have lost their freedom, and the paleface drives them wherever he wishes them to go. When he is hungry, he eats one; when he gets too many, he sells some of them to another paleface."

"I do not think that I would want to raise cattle," replied So-he, and Enir smiled as he rode silently on.

Enir was not surprised at So-he's disinterest in his plans, but he knew that she would feel differently once they were settled. He remembered his own childhood back in the crowded and narrow streets of Liverpool. He smiled as he thought of how much more freedom Sa-ra and Enir, Jr. would have on the ranch that he planned. Then his thoughts drifted to Wo-dan. Could he be taught to distinguish cattle from wild game? Suddenly he smiled. This great intelligent dog would accept the cattle as easily as he had the horses. He will also accept a gentle mate and civilization just as readily, Enir went on to say to himself, provided he never finds out that he is not a dog.

MURDER ON LOCATION

GEORGE KENNEDY

Internationally renowned actor George Kennedy
finds himself playing both star and sleuth
in his own novel when murder stalks the set
in Mexico for the filming of a
major motion picture.
Whether the motive is sabotage
or personal vendetta, nothing is certain
except that everyone's a suspect—
even stars Dean Martin, Glenn Ford,
Raquel Welch, Yul Brynner and
Genevieve Bujold.   83857-5/$2.95

AN AVON PAPERBACK

Available wherever paperbacks are sold or directly from the publisher. Include $1.00 per
copy for postage and handling: allow 6-8 weeks for delivery. Avon Books. Dept BP. Box
767. Rte 2. Dresden. TN 38225.

Murder on Loc 6-83